"Please be careful. Ride safe."

He looked at her then fully, for the first time since she'd found him. "Nobody's told me that since my ma."

"You'd best do it." Lydia swallowed past a lump in her throat, but her voice broke anyway. "You won't be much use to me if you're shot full of holes."

In the dim light, with his hat pulled low and his jaw shadowed with stubble, he looked deadly, dangerous. The very real possibility that he could be hurt or worse tied her stomach in knots.

He palmed off his hat and hung it on the saddle horn, then reached for her.

One big iron-hard arm curled around her waist and he pulled her right into the unrelenting power of his body. Before she could blink, he kissed her.

Taken by surprise, she froze for a moment.

"Kiss me back," he rasped against her lips in a voice that had her legs going to water.

* * *

Whirlwind Secrets
Harlequin® Historical #979—February 2010

Author Note

Russ and Matt Baldwin have been part of the Whirlwind, Texas, series from the beginning. The brothers initially began in my mind only as ladies' men, but as I wrote book after book set in this small Texas town, these two cowboys began to take on depth. They had stories to be told, as well.

I knew one thing about Russ for certain——he'd been engaged to a woman who used him to conceal a tawdry affair she was having. That experience taught him to look twice at people. With him, what you see is what you get, and he won't be conned again.

Enter Lydia Kent, partner with Russ in Whirlwind's newest hotel and involved up to her gorgeous kneecaps in a dangerous clandestine endeavor. Smart and beautiful, Lydia's skittish behavior triggers the suspicion that's now ingrained in him. His curvy sweet-talkin' business partner is caught up in something more tangled than bad barbed wire and Russ intends to find out what. But when he exposes her secrets, he learns that the only thing more dangerous than her lies is the truth. I hope you enjoy their story.

Happy reading,

Debra

To all the cowboys with tough hides and soft hearts.

Special thanks to Maggie Price for answering every frantic call for help with calm and some darn good ideas.

Whirlwind Secrets

DEBRA COWAN

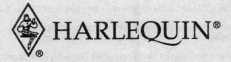

HARLEQUIN®

TORONTO • NEW YORK • LONDON
AMSTERDAM • PARIS • SYDNEY • HAMBURG
STOCKHOLM • ATHENS • TOKYO • MILAN • MADRID
PRAGUE • WARSAW • BUDAPEST • AUCKLAND

Recycling programs
for this product may
not exist in your area.

ISBN-13: 978-0-373-29579-1

WHIRLWIND SECRETS

Printed in U.S.A.

Chapter One

West Texas, 1885

She'd sued a man for failing to marry her.

Russ Baldwin knew that was how Lydia Kent, the new partner he had yet to meet, had gotten the money to invest in his hotel. Well, half his.

What kind of woman took a man to court for breach of promise because he'd ended their engagement? Russ wondered as he dragged his tired carcass up the wooden steps from the hotel's boiler room. He walked past the kitchen, the grand staircase and across the lobby to the big steel grate in the floor. The Fontaine was almost ready for business.

Too bad he would be selling his interest in it shortly. His gaze took in the polished oak floor that matched the large registration desk positioned to greet people when they walked through the double doors. Pewter wall sconces above the tufted sofas on either side of the desk would burn continuously once Russ turned on the gas lighting. The high ceilings and the staircase opposite the registration desk were accen-

tuated with oak molding, as was his office in the corner
behind him.

Today was the first time he'd lit up the boiler for the hotel's
steam heat and it hadn't worked. After an hour downstairs,
Russ thought he'd finally figured out the problem—a dirt
clod in one of the pipes.

The massive front doors were open and he watched the sun
sink into the prairie's horizon. It hovered for a moment in a
red-gold arc over the steeple of the church-cum-schoolhouse
that claimed the opposite end of Main Street. The sounds of
clopping hooves, rattling wagon wheels, and voices drifted in
as the people of Whirlwind closed up shop and went home.
Cooling October air swirled into the lobby, stirring up puffs
of dust. The scent of charring wood, the dirty bite of coal clung
to Russ as he knelt and stretched out a hand over the grate.

Hot moist air hit his palm and he chuckled. The dang thing
worked! It actually worked! Just like the steam heat down at
The Menger Hotel in San Antonio, where he had first seen the
system. He knew business would have to build slowly and
though this little town west of Abilene was growing quickly,
The Fontaine needed to cater mostly to customers of modest
means. But there were a few rooms for big spenders. He and
Miz Lydia Kent had agreed via telegram, as they had with everything else, that they would experiment with a few of the
same amenities featured at The Menger. So, a newfangled
heating system had been installed and gas lighting put in the
lobby. There was also indoor plumbing with four guest rooms
boasting adjoining baths.

Those luxuries would be the draw of The Fontaine. Russ
wanted a mechanical elevator, too, but there was no money
for that right now. He'd been fascinated with the one he'd seen
in San Antonio, riding it up and down the floors so many

times the manager had asked him to stop. He might be able to talk Miz Kent into it later, even though he would no longer be part owner.

He took a rag out of the back pocket of his denims and wiped his grimy hands. Still kneeling over the grate, he listened to the bubbling hiss of the heat. The light tap of shoes had him glancing over his shoulder. At the sight of luscious curves and porcelain skin, he got to his feet.

She was taller than most of the women in town, her head almost reaching his shoulder. Dressed in a black tweed traveling suit with a black flat-crowned hat perched atop dark upswept hair, she had Russ's full attention.

She wasn't from around here. Russ knew *every* woman within a three-county range and this little lovely wasn't from Taylor, Callahan or Nolan County.

He had a hard time deciding if he favored her lush breasts or gently flared hips. Or—hell—her face. Raven-black eyes set off skin that gleamed like pearls. From the delicate winged eyebrows to the pert nose and the plump bowed lips, her features were perfectly proportioned. Her heart-shaped face was flawless, her cheekbones high but not sharp, her chin round. Her carefully arranged hair bared an elegant neck. Even her ears were pretty.

"Evenin', ma'am."

She smiled, revealing a deep dimple beside her mouth. Russ felt as if someone yanked his world to a stop and started it spinning in the other direction.

Her gaze skipped eagerly around the lobby.

Before he could tell her they weren't open for business yet, she stepped closer in a swirl of lavender scent and pressed a coin into his hand.

"My trunks are outside. Could you bring them in, please?"

Her voice was low and husky, like whiskey laced with honey. "Thank you."

"Sorry, ma'am." If he hadn't already known she was a stranger to these parts, that smoky drawl would've told him. Deep South. Georgia? Alabama? He glanced down at the fifty-cent piece in his hand. "We're not open."

"Oh, I know. I'm the owner."

So, this was Lydia Kent. A man could fall right into those black-velvet eyes. Dismissing the initial pull he'd felt toward her, he reached up to stroke his mustache before remembering he'd recently shaved it off. "The owner, huh?"

"Yes."

"So am I."

Surprise flashed across her refined features. "You're Mr. Baldwin?"

"Russ, please." Returning her money, he forced himself to stop looking at her mouth.

She shifted, her cheeks coloring as she held out her gloved hand. "Lydia Kent," she said briskly.

He shook her hand, stunned when the brief touch traveled through him like the snap of a whip. Judging by the way her eyes went wide, he wasn't the only one affected.

Moving slightly away, she slipped free of his hold. "Um, how's your father?"

"His leg's on the mend," Russ said, feeling a now-familiar twist of guilt over the part he'd played in the accident. "And yours?"

"Very well, thank you."

"I didn't expect you for another week."

She seemed to stiffen. "Is that a problem?"

"No, ma'am. You just surprised me is all." Wearing grime and coal dust and sweat wasn't the way he liked to greet a woman, even if she was his business partner. His gaze trailed over full breasts and a tiny waist.

Her voice turned cool, polite. "Everything I needed done in Mississippi was finished early so I decided to come on out."

She didn't meet his eyes and Russ suddenly felt a low-thrumming tension in her. Maybe she was nervous due to being in an unfamiliar place. Or maybe she was wound up like this all the time.

Her gaze dropped to the grate at his feet. "Is that the steam heat?"

He nodded. Tugging off a black kid glove, she moved past him and knelt, stretching out her hand as he had. A smile spread across her beautiful face. "It works!"

"I had to fiddle with it a bit."

"And the gaslights?" She rose, giving her skirts a shake. Red dust floated to the floor.

"They're working, too. Just haven't turned them on yet for tonight." He started for the sconce on the wall behind her. "But I can."

"That's all right. I'd like to bring in my trunks first."

"Oh, you can't stay here." Which suited Russ just fine. He'd felt this kind of mind-addling attraction before and that had been a disaster. He had no intention of giving in to it again. "The hotel isn't finished."

"Well, foot." Disappointment settled over her features. And fatigue, Russ realized by the shadows under her eyes.

Glancing around the large room, she tugged on her right earlobe. "How long do you think it'll be before I can move in?"

"At least a week."

"A week! I guess I *am* early," she murmured.

"The window glass for the third floor hasn't come in yet. Neither has the furniture for your rooms."

She sighed, turning slightly to look out the open doorway flooded with fiery gold light.

"There's another hotel here in town where you can stay," Russ said. "Once you've settled in, I'll show you around The Fontaine."

Despite the eagerness on her face, she hesitated. She checked the small gold watch pinned to her bodice over her heart. "I think tomorrow might be a better time to look around. I'm awfully tired."

"Is morning all right or would you rather meet later?"

She looked startled. "Oh. You don't need to be here."

"I thought it would be good for us to go through the place together, make sure we're both pleased with things, see what else needs to be done."

"All right."

She didn't protest, didn't even blink, but Russ sensed she didn't want him there when she toured the hotel. Hmm, why not? He gestured for her to precede him out the door.

"I wish you'd sent word you were coming early. I planned to fetch you from Abilene. You wouldn't have had to worry about your luggage or getting to Whirlwind."

"I didn't mind."

Because it went against his nature to let a woman fend for herself on travel arrangements and such, his words came out sharper than he intended. "I do."

Her gaze snapped to his, fire sparking in those black eyes. "What?"

"It's not a good idea for a woman to go about alone in these parts."

"Why ever not? Since our fathers are in frequent contact, Mr. Baldwin, I think I would've been warned if the area was unsafe. Besides," she huffed, "I didn't want to impose."

Russ managed to keep from raising an eyebrow. His first impressions about people—especially women—were usually dead-on and Miz Kent seemed like an imposin' kind of woman to him. Still, he didn't need to get off on the wrong foot with her.

He gentled his voice. "The outlaw problem we've had the last couple of years is pretty much taken care of, but you never know who might come upon you with less than honorable intentions. It's best not to travel alone."

"I'm not alone. My maid, Naomi, is with me." Lydia gestured toward the open hotel doors then patted the skirt of her tweed traveling suit. "And I have my derringer."

"I guess you know how to use that?"

"Wouldn't do much good to carry it otherwise, would it?" she asked sweetly. "Would you be so kind as to point me toward the other hotel?"

"The Whirlwind. It's just down there." He indicated the two-story frame building at the opposite end of Main Street, diagonal to The Fontaine. "I'll take you over then fetch your luggage while you're getting settled."

"Thank you." Her voice was calm and pleasant; still Russ felt a jitteriness in her.

Felt a little in himself, too. "Did you have a lot of business to wrap up in Mississippi?"

"A fair amount."

There was nothing wrong with her showing up early, but Russ had never known a woman who did. He couldn't duck the sense that there was a story there. And there it would probably stay. Men always complained that women were unable to keep secrets, but hard experience had taught him some women could hide anything and lie straight to your face while doing it.

Stuffing the rag into the back pocket of his denims, he followed Lydia outside and slowed at the sight of a woman standing next to a loaded buckboard. Slight with creamy chocolate skin, she was every bit as beautiful as Lydia. Her black hair was swept up tightly, but instead of looking severe, the hairstyle only drew attention to her luminous brown eyes and stunning bone structure.

Lydia Kent was beautiful. This woman was breathtaking, regal. Despite the fact that her refined features were pinched with uncertainty until Lydia hurried to her.

Russ stopped in front of the pair. "Ma'am."

Though she didn't meet his eyes, she said quietly, "Hello."

They sure knew how to grow 'em in Mississippi. He smiled, trying to relieve her obvious unease. "I'm Russ Baldwin. You can call me Russ."

Lydia shifted closer to her. "This is Naomi Jones."

"My pleasure, Miz Jones." He shook her hand.

"Pleased to meet you." Her shy smile came and went quickly.

His gaze took in the trunks piled precariously high in the back of the wagon. "Let me escort you ladies to The Whirlwind."

Russ offered an arm to each woman, and after Lydia nodded reassuringly, Naomi accepted it. He didn't miss her slight wince at the movement or her stiff posture. Most likely sore due to bouncing in the wagon from Abilene to here.

A look passed between the two women. A look Russ judged as reassuring and desperate at the same time. It made him wonder again why his business partner had arrived so early and without word.

It could have been because of some business with that lawsuit of hers. Whatever it was, Russ decided he didn't want to know. After working night and day for the last month on the hotel, he deserved a reward and had intended to make a trip to Abilene for a little mattress thrashin' with Willow or Sally.

But thanks to Lydia Kent's unexpected and early arrival, he wouldn't be seeing any fun on a mattress today.

Oh, foot, Lydia thought the next morning as she approached her business partner. Russ Baldwin was just as sinful-looking as she remembered. And seeing him again set off a flutter of awareness in her stomach. She didn't know why. He certainly wasn't the first handsome man she'd ever seen. But when she met him on The Fontaine's wide front porch and he lightly placed his hand in the small of her back to guide her inside, there was no denying that his touch caused the same startling response she'd felt when he'd shaken her hand. Unnerving. Vexing, really.

Upon meeting him last night, she'd been surprised at his massive size. And today, dressed as he was in a light gray shirt that emphasized shoulders as wide as a wagon brace and dark trousers that clung almost indecently to powerful thighs, she was reminded all over again.

"Miz Jones decided not to come?" His voice rumbled above her head.

Tamping down the ridiculous giddiness inside her, Lydia smiled politely. "She had some things she needed to do this morning."

Mainly rest. Because of Naomi's bruised ribs, their abrupt departure from Mississippi had been even harder on her than it had been on Lydia. It hadn't helped that they'd looked over their shoulder the entire way. Naomi, especially, was a mass of nerves and Lydia had insisted she recuperate today. Naomi was so much more than a maid. She had paid a high price for her friendship to Lydia and Lydia's sister, Isabel.

Lydia touched the gold watch pinned to her bodice. The

timepiece and a pair of diamond earrings were all she had left of her sister now. She felt close to Isabel when she wore them.

Inside the hotel, Russ swept off his Stetson to reveal dark hair that was thick and damp. He was clean-shaven, and something about his strong jaw made her want to slide her fingers down his face and test its smoothness for herself. She had never experienced such a strong attraction to a man, not even her former fiancé, mealymouthed Wade Vance. Which made her decide she was delirious from travel and worry.

"You've seen the lobby." Russ swept his arm in a wide arc, encompassing the registration desk flanked by moss-green tufted sofas before turning toward the corner behind them. "That's my office."

Lydia followed him to an open door, already deciding that the dull gold-and-burgundy rug in front of the registration desk would have to go.

She paused beside Russ and looked inside a good-size room. Her eyes widened and it took effort to keep the surprise from her voice. "Oh, it's very…nice."

From the look of things, the man intended to live here. In addition to a giant mahogany bed and shaving stand across the room, there was a wide bureau of matching wood. To the right of the doorway, there was a large desk with a leather chair sitting behind it and a pair of the same dark brown leather on the opposite side. This wouldn't do at all.

"Are you planning to stay at the hotel?" The question squeaked out before she could stop it.

He arched a dark brow. "Can't tell if you're hoping I will or hoping I won't. Is there a reason I shouldn't?"

"Just curious." She managed to keep her voice light as she gazed around the furnished space, but tension began to knot inside her. "Since I'm the on-site manager and I'm here now,

I thought you wouldn't bother with the hotel any longer. I assumed I'd step in and you could get back to your ranch."

"I plan to stay until the hotel's open."

Lydia fought back exasperation. She could find a way to handle this. "If you're worried I won't be able to manage things, let me assure you I can."

"It isn't that, Miz Kent. I just like to finish what I start."

Even women? Lydia blinked. Where had that thought come from? Mentally chastising herself, she turned and followed him across the lobby to the wide staircase that boasted the same iron scrollwork as the outdoor balcony.

"There are a couple of things I'd like to wrap up." He slowed, keeping pace with her as they mounted the polished oak steps. "Windows for the third floor are one thing. I've been trying to get them delivered and installed for a month now. The company keeps putting me off."

"Who is it?" Reaching inside the pocket of her navy serge skirt, she took out her small journal and stub of a pencil to write down his answer.

She paused on the staircase to jot down the company's name and make a note about the window glass and the possibility of hanging a painting or two along the length of the wall that led upstairs. She looked up to find Russ Baldwin watching her intently and for a moment, she couldn't look away.

He had the bluest eyes she'd ever seen. Not sky-blue, but the darker, more intense blue of a blue jay's underwing. Fringed by thick, dark lashes, they were piercing.

She pulled her gaze from his and continued with him to the second floor landing. He led her to one of several whitewalled rooms furnished with a bed, a table, chair, washbasin and kerosene lamp. "I wish we could've put the gas lighting in every room."

"After a couple years of profit, that'll be possible."

She approached the solidly made bed and pressed the mattress. Firm but not hard. "Very nice."

"We used the Spanish moss you ordered for stuffing." He gestured for her to follow him across the hall to another open doorway. Pointing at the large tub and washstand with piped-in water, he said, "The plainer rooms on this end of the hall will share this bath. The four larger rooms at the other end have their own, like your rooms on the third floor."

"That will be a tremendous draw to customers."

"I think so, too."

As he showed her the rooms with adjoining baths, Lydia jotted notes and discussed hired help with him, asking him to recommend some people. There was no denying she needed Russ Baldwin for some things, but once everything was settled, she would convince him he didn't need to be here.

When they reached the doorway of her rooms on the third floor, a breeze gusted through the empty window frames, ruffling the pages in her journal. She held on to her flat-crowned hat as she looked around. The space she planned to use as an office was large, with a separate sitting area in the corner. A wall divided this spacious room from the two bedrooms and adjoining bath.

Walking to the far window, she looked out over the bustling town, scanning up the right side of Main Street, past the blacksmith's shop, the jail. Greetings were called and doors opened as people readied themselves for another day of business. "How long do you think it will take to finish out the guest rooms on this floor?"

"Once the carpenter gets here, maybe a week. Two at the most. He's due sometime in the next couple of weeks."

She could feel his gaze hot on her backside and she didn't

like it. Managing to keep the irritation from her voice, she turned and moved toward him. "You've done an excellent job with everything."

"Thank you. Ready to see the rest of the first floor?"

"Yes, I'm looking forward to it." As much satisfaction as she'd gotten from seeing the guest rooms, what she really cared about was the kitchen area.

Once downstairs, Lydia glanced at the small but elegantly dark-paneled dining area as she followed her partner into a spacious kitchen. Sunlight flooded the room through a wide window on the far side. On the back wall was a fireplace big enough for two hanging kettles and four of the three-legged pots called spiders. The stove was of a size to accommodate cooking several dishes at the same time. Pine floors gleamed with the sheen of newness as did the ample number of cabinets and work counters. "This is wonderful, exactly as I pictured."

She hoped the rest was, as well.

Russ grinned, causing a tug in her belly as he led her across the floor to the room she was most anxious to see.

"Here's the pantry, built to your specifications." Opening the door, he chuckled. "This thing is as big as one of our modestly priced rooms."

The dim space was wide and deep with smoothly planed shelving along the top for storage as well as bins and drawers below. A lantern hung beside the door frame. To Lydia's left, the smell of smoke and an open door revealing a short set of stairs identified the boiler room. At the back of the pantry, down another flight of stairs, was the separate room she'd requested for vegetables and other food storage.

She walked forward and opened the door, moving inside to the top of the stairs. A cool heavy darkness immediately engulfed her. Her gladness that the boiler noise wouldn't overwhelm anyone quickly edged into a sharp awareness of Russ Baldwin standing behind her.

Pulse skittering, she shifted, intending to turn and ask if he'd get a lantern, but he must've thought she was moving farther into the room because he took a step forward. She ran smack into his chest—hard, hot, deep. His big callused hand came up to lightly cup her elbow, steadying her.

"Whoa," he murmured.

She felt his breath drift against her temple. And along with the fresh pine scent of new wood, she caught a hint of leather and soap and clean male. She felt that dratted flutter in her stomach again.

Before she could move, he stepped back and said in a quiet even voice, "Let me get the lantern."

Nodding, Lydia sucked in a deep breath and tried to still her racing pulse. A few seconds later, a circle of yellow light spread around her and she saw Russ's strong features in the smoky cast of the lantern, his eyes dark and unfathomable.

They ventured downstairs into the darkness. Through the play of shadows, her gaze took in the still-vacant space. Perfect. She schooled her features so as not to show her relief that the room was exactly as they needed. "This will suit quite well."

"Glad you're pleased."

The quiet rasp of his voice reminded her that they were entirely alone, of how near he was. How near he would be in the future by living in the hotel.

Gripping her pencil tight, she turned for the door. "Shall we?"

Russ lifted the lantern, showing the path out. Lydia moved quickly back into the pantry, blinking her eyes to adjust to the light streaming into the kitchen. That window, which looked out onto the blacksmith's shop, would have to be covered.

As she stepped into the kitchen, she was torn between satisfaction and unease. This place was perfect, but Russ Baldwin was trouble brewing. As long as he lived here, the operation was at risk. She had to keep him out of her way.

Chapter Two

Russ Baldwin couldn't live at The Fontaine. Lydia had things to do that were none of his concern. Things that were a matter of life and death.

He might deny thinking she couldn't handle hotel affairs, but what other reason could he have for staying? She'd been careful to spell out in the contract that she was the on-site manager, and he'd agreed. So she would start managing. And she would begin with the horrid rug in the lobby.

After a delicious lunch at The Whirlwind Hotel, Lydia made her way across the street to Haskell's General Store, which sat between the newspaper office and an attorney-at-law. She stepped inside the mercantile, charmed by a wood-burning stove and two chairs in the center of the room. Haskell's was well stocked, with everything from brooms to boots and shovels to soap.

Crisp fall air drifted through the open door, mixing the scent of prairie grass with that of fruit and perfume. At the corner of a big wood-and-glass cashier's counter was a well-used copy of a Montgomery Ward & Company catalog.

A slight dark-haired man about Lydia's height stepped out

of a back room and met her gaze across the counter. "May I help you, ma'am? Charlie Haskell, at your service."

"Mr. Haskell, a pleasure." She moved closer and extended her hand. "I'm Lydia Kent."

"Ah, you're the other owner of The Fontaine." He gave her a firm handshake.

She smiled. "Yes."

"How are you liking Whirlwind so far?"

"Quite a lot, thank you."

"Your hotel looks as if it's coming right along. Shouldn't be long now before you're open for business, I'm guessin'."

"You're right."

"Oh, you're Russ's partner!" a feminine voice exclaimed behind Lydia.

Did everyone in town know everyone else's business? Lydia turned to find a striking brunette with green eyes and a smart red-checked day dress with a black-trimmed collar and sleeves.

The woman smiled, extending her hand. "I'm Josie Holt. My husband is the sheriff of Whirlwind. How nice to meet you."

Lydia shook the woman's hand and introduced herself. "I admire your dress, Mrs. Holt. You must tell me where you got it."

Mr. Haskell chuckled.

"Please call me Josie." Her eyes twinkled. "Charlie's laughing because I got the dress from me. I made it."

"Josie's our seamstress," the man supplied.

"You're very talented." Lydia eyed the garment even more critically. The woman's stitching could rival that of any of the professionals Lydia had used for her trousseau. The trousseau she refused to put aside and waste simply because of that lying polecat Wade. "Do you do alterations, as well?"

"Yes. My shop is in the back and I'm there most days." Josie indicated a curtained doorway at the rear of the store. "Come chat whenever you have time. You don't have to buy anything."

If the rest of Mrs. Holt's work was this good, Lydia couldn't imagine *not* buying something.

"I'd best get busy," the other woman said. "I apologize for interrupting your conversation with Charlie. When I heard you were Russ's partner, I couldn't help myself."

"I'm glad to meet you, too."

With a smile, the brunette squeezed the store owner's arm as she walked past him and toward the space she'd pointed out earlier.

Charlie beamed at Lydia. "Now, what may I do for you, Miss Kent?"

"I need to order a rug for the hotel lobby."

He walked around the counter and motioned her to the corner that held the catalog. "I thought Russ already did that."

"Yes, I'm afraid he did," she said drily, her gaze skimming over the pocket watches and spectacles in the glass counter.

The merchant barked out a laugh as he lifted the book and thumbed quickly to the section showing rugs. "Miss Josie tried to tell him not to choose that one."

Lydia smiled as another customer entered the store and Charlie slid the book over to her, excusing himself. When the customer left after a few minutes, Lydia asked if there were any fabric samples.

Mr. Haskell stepped into the back room and returned with a handful of swatches. She finally chose one of black, green and burgundy that she thought would complement the green of the sofas. She placed the samples on the counter while he wrote out the order.

Charlie glanced up from his pad. "This will require a deposit."

"All right." Lydia jotted the date, item and cost in her journal, glancing up when the man laid down the pencil and pushed the paper aside. "What do I owe you?"

He named a figure. "But I don't need the money until Russ signs the order."

"Russ?" She shook her head. "I can sign it. I'm not even sure where Mr. Baldwin is."

He hesitated.

"Mr. Haskell, is there a problem?"

He cleared his throat. "Russ has the hotel account set up so that you both have to sign for any orders."

For an instant, she thought she misunderstood him. "Beg pardon?"

The merchant looked uncomfortable. "You can't order anything for the hotel on your own."

"I don't understand." What did Russ Baldwin think he was doing? It was no fault of the shopkeeper's, so Lydia fought to keep the irritation from her voice. "I'll need to find him."

"He's in town. I saw him earlier."

"Thank you." She turned to leave.

"Here." Charlie tore the invoice from the pad and gave it to her. "You can have him sign the order when you see him. No need for you to have to traipse back and forth."

"Thank you, Mr. Haskell. I'll be right back."

Lydia made her way outside and started down the street toward The Fontaine. The closer she got, the more aggravated she became. She hadn't had to ask permission to spend money on anything since she'd ordered the sewing machine for Isabel's twelfth birthday. Their father had always given them an allowance and Lydia bought what she wanted. Except for the sewing machine.

Lydia's older sister had been terrible with money, had never been able to keep it longer than a week. What she excelled at was sewing. She'd wanted a new machine, but her allowance had been cut off because of her overspending. So Lydia had gone to their father, begging him to let her purchase the machine for Isabel and he had agreed.

The exact opposite of her sister in those two areas, Lydia was a mediocre seamstress and good with money. She certainly didn't need some overbearing cowboy to approve her every purchase for *her* hotel!

She stepped onto the smooth sandstone of The Fontaine's porch, then from the corner of her eye, saw Russ coming out of the blacksmith's shop to her left. Changing direction, she marched toward him.

"Miz Kent, nice to see you again." He touched two fingers to the brim of his gray felt cowboy hat in greeting. The sleeves of his light blue shirt were rolled up to reveal thick, hair-dusted forearms. Worn, close-fitting denims drew her attention to his brawny thighs.

When she realized she was staring, she yanked her gaze away and stopped in front of him. Once again, she was startled at the deep blue of his eyes. And the daunting width of his shoulders. Gracious, he was big.

The scent of clean male skin and spicy soap drifted to her as she plunged in, "Mr. Haskell informs me that I must have your permission to order things for the hotel."

"Not permission." Russ pushed his hat back and eased against the wooden wall of the shop, propping one booted foot behind him. "Just my signature. Both our signatures."

"Why?" Did Russ Baldwin think her untrustworthy? Did he know about Lydia's lawsuit against Wade and hold it against her? He wouldn't be the first although *she* had done nothing wrong.

"We're equal partners, Lydia."

Her pulse hitched at his quiet use of her Christian name.

"It's not about permission. I set up the account with Charlie that way so we'd both know what had been ordered, how much we were spending. We both have equal say."

"I should've had my say before you ordered that awful— that rug," she muttered.

In the bright morning light, she couldn't tell, but thought she saw amusement in his blue eyes. "You're wanting a different one?"

"Yes."

He shrugged. "All right. I own that you probably know a lot more about decoratin' stuff than I do."

"So, you'll sign the order?"

He nodded and she gave him the pencil and paper Charlie had sent with her. She watched as Russ flattened the page against the wall of the blacksmith's shop, her attention straying to the flex of muscle in his forearms while he signed his name. "Charlie'll probably need a deposit. He did last time."

"I can take care of that."

His mouth went tight as if he might argue, but he didn't. "All right."

Lydia started to leave, then hesitated. "We could get more done and open for business sooner if we didn't have to wait on each other. Then you can move back home and turn your attention to your family's ranch or whatever other business you have. And I'll deal with running the hotel, which is why I'm here."

"I reckon that's true."

When he offered nothing further, Lydia realized he didn't intend to change the arrangement. She had to get him out of here and to do that, she needed to prove she was capable of handling things on her own. What could she do to convince him?

The glass.

Getting the windows Russ had been unable to obtain would go a long way toward showing him that he'd be leaving the hotel in her very capable hands.

"For instance, the windows you ordered. Maybe I could speak to the merchant who sold them to us."

"He isn't holding us up because he wants to. He can't get the shipment, either."

"Oh." Lydia nodded and turned to go, but she wasn't giving up yet.

His deep voice stopped her. "I meant to tell you that both our signatures were required on hotel orders. It plumb slipped my mind."

He sounded sincere, Lydia thought. "It's all right. I know now."

"I'll be around here if you need anything else."

Good. You'll be easy to find when I show up with those windows. "Naomi and I are going to Abilene. We plan to leave shortly and return tomorrow."

"What do you need over there?"

"I'd like to look at mirrors, perhaps some dressing screens for the few rooms still lacking them. Is there anything you need?"

"Don't think so." Russ cocked his head. "You're not gonna try for that glass, are you?"

Yes, I am. "You said the shipment hadn't arrived."

"Right."

"Then you'd consider that a wasted effort, wouldn't you?"

"Yes." Speculation darkened his eyes and a grin tugged at his lips. "You dodgin' my question?"

"Good day, Mr. Baldwin." She smiled as she walked away.

He might not think she could get the glass and maybe she couldn't, but she planned to try. She would love to see his face if she managed to come back with those windows.

And late the next afternoon, his expression was everything she'd hoped for when she rolled the wagon to a stop between The Fontaine and the blacksmith shop where Russ once again stood outside.

The merchandise was protected with blankets. Lydia braked the wagon and he was there to help her down. By the time he gave Naomi a hand and turned back to Lydia, she had the top layer of blankets pulled back.

The look of incredulity on his handsome face had a laugh bubbling out of her.

"What the devil!" He came to stand beside her, his jaw slack. "How did you get this?"

"Well, it's not our specific order, but it will work. The supplier pointed me in the direction of a man with an unfinished house. The owner said his wife changed her mind about several things and he was willing to sell the glass. I gave him a penny more per square inch than what he paid and two nights free at The Fontaine after we open."

"You gave him... You got the glass and you offered the man a free room." Russ looked amazed. And slightly annoyed.

"Yes," Lydia answered. "If you're unhappy about my giving him a free room, I did it for advertising purposes. He can start spreading the word."

"That was smart. Real smart." Russ braced his hands on his hips, the movement pulling his shirt taut across his rock-hard arms and shoulders. "You planned all along to try and get that glass."

"I wouldn't say 'planned.' I didn't know what I was dealing with until I got there."

"I'll be." He rubbed his chin, still looking a little dazed.

She smiled over at Naomi, who stood quietly beside the shaded wagon, laughter in her eyes. Maybe now Russ would admit Lydia could manage fine on her own. He eyed her shrewdly. There was genuine admiration in his face.

Why couldn't he see the wisdom of leaving the hotel management to her? "Now we're that much closer to opening the hotel and I should be able to move in within the week. If we divided the labor between us, we'd get things done a lot quicker."

"I reckon." He stared at her for a long minute. "I think we should leave things the way they are for now."

Foot! Fighting to keep her face blank, she pursed her lips as though considering his words. "Very well. It's highly impractical, though."

"Maybe so." He reached into the pocket of his trousers and pulled out a piece of paper.

He took her hand and pressed a folded note into her palm. He released her, the brush of his fingers against hers sending a jolt of heat up her arm. She looked down. Another telegram.

"Tony, the telegraph operator, said you've been keeping him busy, what with getting one of these a day."

Lydia went still inside. What difference did it make to Russ how many wires she received?

"If they're about the hotel, we could go through them right now."

This one probably contained news from Daddy or Mama about her wounded brother-in-law's condition. The others contained information Russ shouldn't see. Crumpling the paper in her hand, she strove to sound casual. "Oh, they're probably not about the hotel."

"Hmm."

His gaze on her was sharp. Penetrating. He started into the blacksmith's shop. "If you need me for anything, just holler."

She *didn't* need him. That was what she'd been trying to get him to realize. "Thank you," she said drily.

"Anythin' to help." He grinned and tipped his hat to her.

Her hand tightened on the telegrams. They were just one more reminder that she needed to be very careful around Russ Baldwin.

It was obvious the man wasn't going to leave the hotel, at least not for a while. If she couldn't keep him out of her way, then she had to stay out of his. There was too much at stake.

She just beat all. A week later, Russ still couldn't get over Lydia managing to obtain the window glass. The woman might smell like soft sweet flowers, but she was pure-dee grit. If she had shown as much stubbornness about her former fiance as she had about that glass, it was no wonder she'd won the lawsuit. Still, as much as Russ admired her resourcefulness, he was also aggravated that he hadn't thought of doing what she'd done.

She'd moved into the hotel a couple of days earlier, but he'd seen her only in passing. They'd both been working hard, planning to open for business as soon as the second floor rooms were completed. As of yet, they hadn't scheduled the Grand Opening. Lydia and Naomi had made up all the beds, finalized the menu and cured the pots, kettles and other cooking implements. After putting in the third floor windows and moving furniture into the guest rooms, Russ had worked with the steam heat and the gaslight systems until he felt he could fix almost any problem they might have.

Just because he knew what Lydia was doing didn't mean he was any less curious about her. She'd received another

telegram the evening before. When Tony Santos had delivered
one for Russ, he'd also told him about Lydia's. That made
three since she'd returned from Abilene the previous week.
Who the hell got that many telegrams and why?

There was nothing wrong with it, but like most things
about her, the detail stuck in Russ's mind. Made him wonder
about her. She had been in his thoughts first thing as he rolled
out of bed and pulled on his trousers.

Standing in front of his washstand mirror, his eyes
narrowed as he thought back to a time in his life when another
woman had fooled him. Of course, he wasn't engaged to
Lydia as he had been to Amy Young.

Eight years had passed, but he still remembered the savage
bite of betrayal when he'd found out his ex-fiancée had only
agreed to their engagement so she could hide an affair with
another man. Oh, she'd liked Russ well enough, but it wasn't
him she'd wanted at all.

Since then, he'd learned to heed little doubts that crept up,
pay attention to any questionable behavior. Like Lydia Kent's
numerous telegrams. He wouldn't say he was exactly suspicious, but he was damn sure paying attention.

Swirling his shave brush around the wet cake of soap,
Russ lathered his face. He took one stroke down his jaw
with the straightedge, then paused at a loud clatter outside
his office. When he heard nothing further, he lifted his razor
again. Sudden yelling inside the hotel nearly made him
slice his cheek.

Noise like that could only mean trouble. He dropped his
straightedge and rushed to the desk, toweling the lather from
his face as he went. Grabbing his Colt, he jerked open the door
and stepped out, gaze scanning the foyer.

The first watery light of day coming through the windows

illuminated the man and woman on the other side of the room where the dining area gave way to the lobby. The woman's back was to Russ, but he could see the man's bearded face. And the gun he had leveled on the lady!

Not wanting to spook the man, Russ edged across the floor, his revolver pointed down against his thigh. From the corner of his eye, he caught movement. A quick glance showed Lydia and Naomi halfway down the stairs; he held up a hand for them to stay there.

"Hey, mister, what's going on here?" Russ kept his voice low and calm. "Why don't you put the gun down?"

"No!"

"No need for a weapon in the hotel." He drew close enough that he could see rage burning in the man's eyes.

The stranger wore a three-piece suit, rumpled but nicely made. The woman wore a tattered, shapeless dress, her hair hidden by a dark kerchief. She was huddled into herself, visibly shaking.

Russ tried again. "Let's talk about this."

The man ignored him, cajoling softly, "Minnie, I'm sorry. It'll never happen again."

The woman shook her head, half turning toward Russ.

"Please come home." The stranger moved a step closer to her. "I'm sorry. I really am."

If it hadn't been for the marks on the woman's temple and cheek, Russ would count this as a spat, but those bruises told a different story. He wasn't walking away. Inching closer, intent on putting himself between the pair, he said, "That gun is no way to talk."

"This is between me and my wife," the man snarled, still not lowering the gun. His gaze stayed on her. "You're coming home with me."

He jabbed the weapon in her direction and she flinched.

Russ leveled his Colt at the man and thumbed down the hammer. "Lay down your weapon. I'll plug you if I have to."

"Leave us be. This is a family matter." The man glared at Russ. The woman lunged for the staircase.

"You're not leaving me!" he roared.

Before Russ could blink, the man pulled the trigger. A loud crack split the air. Someone screamed. The woman fell, landing on her side. In the next instant, the stranger swung his gun in Lydia's direction.

In one motion, Russ aimed for the man's shoulder and fired, but at the last second, the man wheeled toward Russ. The bullet hit him square in the chest. He cried out and stumbled back. Another round exploded from his weapon as he hit the floor, then he lay motionless.

The acrid smell of gun smoke tinged the air. Russ hurried over and kicked the gun away, kneeling to check for a pulse. Nothing. He checked the woman, finding the same. Blood spread across her back, sticking her dress to her.

What the hell had just happened?

"Everybody okay?" Operating on adrenaline, Russ stood and turned, his gaze dropping to the bottom step where Lydia now sat. Looking dazed, she had a hand clamped to her right upper arm. Blood covered her fingers and soaked the sleeve of her dark green wrapper.

She was hit! Russ rushed over and laid his revolver on the floor, going to his haunches in front of her. "Let me see."

Her eyes were huge with shock. "I think it's just a graze," she said breathlessly.

There was too much blood for a graze, he thought. "Where are you hit? Shoulder?"

"Upper arm." Her voice shook.

He reached for her, but she wouldn't move her hand. "Lydia, I need to look at it."

"It hurts." She was pale, trembling.

"I'll go easy." He sent an imploring look to Naomi.

The black woman eased down beside Lydia on the step and put an arm around her waist. "It's okay. Let Mr. Baldwin look."

Slowly the brunette lowered her hand. Blood plastered the velvet to her skin.

When he touched her, she gave a low moan that grabbed Russ right in the gut. He pulled back. The same sick feeling that had twisted his stomach when he'd heard about Pa's accident hit Russ again. He pushed the memory away.

"Can you get out of your wrapper? If not, I can cut off the sleeve."

"I can do it." Lydia fumbled with the sash at her waist and the fabric parted to reveal a white, high-necked nightgown with delicate buttons running down the front.

Naomi slipped the wrapper sleeve down her friend's un-injured arm.

Russ studied the ashen-faced woman in front of him. Her full breasts rose and fell rapidly against the soft fabric of her gown. The scent of body-warmed lavender drifted around him. Her dark eyes were sharp with pain, the single braid of her sleep-mussed hair lying over her left shoulder. "Let's get you in my office."

"Oh, no!" She looked appalled. "I'm in my nightclothes."

As if it were all right to be wearing them in the lobby where anyone could see. Russ bit back a smile. "Lydia, your wrapper needs to come off so I can look at your arm. You don't want me to do that out here, do you?"

"N-no." Her skin was waxy and blood still seeped steadily from the wound.

Naomi moved to help her up.

"I've got her." Russ shifted to the side and scooped Lydia up in his arms, gathering the dressing gown around her.

"Oh!" She clutched at his forearm as if to keep her balance. "I can walk."

"This will be faster."

"Really, I can walk," she insisted in a weak voice.

"Glad to hear it." But he didn't put her down.

Naomi hurried behind them like a mother hen.

Lydia didn't argue further as she found herself sinking into the warmth of Russ's body. Cradled against his bare hairy chest, she rested her head on his shoulder. Pain seared her arm and she could feel the hot trickle of blood. Struggling not to cry, she forced herself to focus on something else. Her gaze caught on the sculpted corner of Russ's jaw.

Only half his face was shaved. He must've been interrupted by the disturbance. There was a dab of shaving soap just below his ear and Lydia breathed in the spicy scent. "I'm bleeding on you."

"I'll wash." He looked down, concern in his blue eyes as he stepped into the office which also served as his living quarters.

He walked across the room and laid her on his huge, sleep-rumpled bed. She made a sound of protest, starting to sit up.

He put a hand on her shoulder. "Stay down. You look like you could pass out any second."

She obeyed. He sat on the edge of the mattress, his shoulders blocking most of the light. Lydia felt dwarfed. The sheet and quilt were shoved to the foot of the bed and she could smell him here, too.

Agony drove into her flesh like needles and she felt a tear trickle down her cheek. "I don't think it's very deep."

"Hard to tell," he said.

Naomi came to stand next to her and Russ drew back, allowing the black woman to lean over and ease off the other wrapper sleeve. When she finished, she moved the garment out of the way on the opposite side of the bed. The nightgown's sleeve was blood-soaked, clinging to Lydia's slender arm.

"You're still bleeding a lot." Russ turned and grabbed his razor from the washstand behind him. "I need to cut off your sleeve."

"No! This gown is part of my trouss—is new."

"It's that or get you out of it." At her blank look, he said meaningfully, "All the way out of it."

When she realized her choice was lose a sleeve or be naked, she nodded. "All right."

She'd barely agreed when he made a clean slice at the top of her shoulder seam and ripped the sleeve in half down to her wrist. The crimson-stained halves dropped away from her arm, revealing dark streaks of blood. Russ closed his straightedge, setting it aside as he bent over her.

The gaslight wasn't strong enough for Lydia to judge the extent of the wound, but Naomi lit the kerosene lamp beside Russ's bed and held it up.

"Thanks," he murmured.

The amber light fell over a shallow line of flesh furrowed out of Lydia's arm. The wound slashed about four inches diagonally from her upper arm to her shoulder. As careful as Russ was in his examination, she winced.

"I don't know if you need stitches." He was so close his breath feathered her chin. "I'm sending someone for our nurse."

"Naomi can take care of me. She doctored everyone back home."

As if he didn't hear her, he turned to the other woman. "The water in the basin should still be warm. Would you grab the clean toweling off my washstand and wet it?"

Lydia chafed while her friend did as he asked, then returned with the cloth. Russ's head bent as he carefully placed the damp fabric over the wound. Lydia found herself staring at the nape of his corded neck, the supple sun-bronzed skin of his wide shoulders and back. His hands were big just like the rest of him, but his touch was soft as a feather.

The warmth from his torso and the hand on her flesh sent out heat like a furnace. She told herself to focus on him rather than the agony in her body.

Suddenly there was a pounding on the hotel's front doors. The sound was muffled, but audible. As was the strong male voice that called out, "Russ? What's going on?"

"That's Ef." He glanced at Naomi. "Would you hold this steady? I'll be right back."

Naomi took over and he stepped out of his office. After a moment, Lydia heard the low murmur of masculine voices. First Russ's, then one she didn't recognize. The words *shot* and *blood* were all she could understand.

Keeping an eye on the door, she whispered to Naomi, "Do you think that poor woman was the one we were expecting?"

The telegram Lydia had received a couple of days ago, using agreed-upon code words, had served as notice of their first arrival.

Before her friend could do more than nod, Russ strode back into the room.

"The nearest doc is eight miles away at Fort Greer. Ef, the blacksmith, is going for Whirlwind's nurse then he'll fetch the sheriff."

"There's no need for a nurse," Lydia protested. "Naomi can take care of me."

"Catherine's trained," Russ said stubbornly. "No offense, Miz Jones."

"None taken." She gave Lydia an uncertain look.

She knew Naomi didn't want to draw any undue attention to them and Lydia shouldn't do so, either. The safest and probably quickest thing to do would be to let Russ do as he wished.

The other woman relinquished her place and Russ took over again, pressing firmly on the towel. Lydia bit back a moan. She knew he was trying to be gentle.

Her mind raced, the injury throbbing now. "Is that woman really dead?"

"I'm afraid so," he said quietly, his blue eyes intent on her. "Did you know either of them?"

She couldn't meet his gaze. "No."

That wasn't strictly a lie. She wasn't *sure* if the dead woman was the one who'd been expected to arrive the following night.

Lydia tried to blink back tears. Seeing that woman's bruises, her lifeless body, brought back images of Isabel. Lydia's sister had died the same way, trying to run from a man who beat her.

The dead man had claimed to be Minnie's husband. He'd followed her here, apologized and cajoled in an effort to get her to return home. Even if he hadn't known that the place his wife sought shelter was a stop on the secret network for abused women, he could've told others she'd been headed to Whirlwind.

And Russ had killed the man, unwittingly protecting Lydia's secret. Protecting her.

She wanted to tell him the truth, but she couldn't. People's lives depended on her silence. She hadn't been able to save her sister, but she could save others like Naomi and the battered woman now lying dead in the hotel's lobby.

"How're you doing?" Russ's face held sympathy and concern. "Want something to drink? Water? Brandy?"

She would love a brandy or anything that might dull the

searing agony knifing up her arm, but she had to keep her wits about her. "No, I'm fine. Thank you."

Frowning, he sat on the bed keeping careful pressure on the wound with one hand. His other rested beneath Lydia's elbow, supporting her arm.

He lifted the towel to peer closely at the gash then let his gaze wander over her. This close, he could see the shadowy tips of her breasts beneath her gown. Russ broke out in a sweat, struggled to force his thoughts back to the problem.

She could've been shot in the chest instead of the arm. Killed. He replayed the incident in his mind. The gunman had fired on his wife, and even though Russ had his revolver trained on the man, the stranger had aimed for Lydia. Why?

"Russ?"

Glancing over his shoulder, he saw a beautiful, black-haired woman in the doorway and exhaled in relief. "Catherine. I'm glad you're here."

Expecting and barely showing, she moved gracefully into the room, carrying a leather satchel. The skirts of her gray-and-white day dress swirled around her feet. Her straight black hair was pulled back with a kerchief, concern plain in her blue eyes. "Ef told me what happened."

He stood and gestured to the woman in his bed. "This is my new partner, Lydia Kent, and her maid, Naomi Jones. Ladies, this is Catherine Blue."

He stood aside to let Catherine examine the wound. As she began to clean it with a mixture of carbolic acid and water, Lydia hissed in a breath. She squeezed her eyes shut and gripped Naomi's hand.

Russ watched Lydia. She had said she didn't know either of the dead people, but Russ couldn't shake the feeling that she knew *something*.

He wasn't sure she was involved in what had happened in the lobby, but his gut said she was. It also told him to stay, so he was staying. No woman was ever going to blindside him the way Amy had. Russ might want to wash his hands of Lydia Kent, but until he figured out if something was going on, he was planting roots in the hotel.

Chapter Three

∞◊∞

A couple of evenings later, Russ sat in his office with his brother and Ef. They had come back with him after speaking to Sheriff Holt again about the shootings. Davis Lee was still trying to find out if the man and woman who'd been killed in the hotel lobby had connections to anyone in Whirlwind.

The gaslight flickered off then back on. Russ shot a look at Matt, who was once again playing with the fixture just inside the door.

His black-haired brother was an inch shorter than his six foot five and a year younger than his thirty-one years. Matt peered closely at the gas-lit sconce, as fascinated as Russ with the newfangled light. "Noticed you finally got the glass for the third floor."

"Not me. Miz Kent."

"Is that so?" Sitting in a chair on the other side of Russ's desk, Ef's dark eyebrows rose. "How'd she manage that?"

Russ explained about her deal-making in Abilene.

His brother grinned. "She bested you? Now I really have to meet her."

He grunted, shooting a look at Ef when the blacksmith chuckled.

Matt leaned one shoulder against the doorjamb. "How's her arm? Ef said she was shot in that ruckus the other day in the hotel."

"Catherine put in a few stitches." Russ flashed back to the way Lydia had bitten her lip and how all the blood had drained out of her face. He'd offered to let her bite down on his razor strap, but she held on tight to Naomi and only a couple of moans escaped. "Miz Kent seems to be getting along fine."

"Word is all over town that she's one handsome woman."

"She is," Russ said. "Seems to have a good head for business, too. She contracted with Pearl to make desserts for the hotel."

A look of admiration crossed his brother's face as he ambled over to Russ's desk. "Involving Whirlwind's restaurant owner is real smart. Now Pearl will know y'all aren't going to try and steal her customers. Plus she'll have a stake in seeing The Fontaine succeed. I think I'll stay in town tonight and meet Miz Kent."

Russ didn't want that. Matt would ask her to dinner or to go for a walk or try to steal a kiss. For cryin' out loud! Russ wasn't even sure he liked the woman, so why did he care if his brother made her acquaintance?

He leaned back in his leather chair and propped both feet up on his desk. "You've been gone all week to the Stockraisers' Association meeting. Don't you need to get to the ranch?"

Dragging a hand down his face, Matt nodded. "I reckon. Pa said he didn't need me, but you and I both know he still has trouble getting around."

The constant guilt he carried snarled in Russ's gut. Dr. Butler from Fort Greer had said Pa was lucky. The accident could've cost him his life.

Russ was just relieved the doctor held out hope for a good recovery. Pa had been stringing fence down the side of a gully and fallen onto a protruding tree branch, impaling his thigh. He'd nearly bled to death before Matt and their neighbor, Bram Ross, had found him.

Stringing that fence had been Russ's job. If he had been doing what he was supposed to and not mattress dancin' with one of the girls over in Abilene, his pa never would've been in that gully. Never would've nearly died.

He shifted his thoughts back to his brother. "Did you find out if any cattle in other counties are being rustled?"

"Yeah, a few ranches up and down the border of Taylor and Callahan counties have lost stock."

"The same kind of cattle?"

"No. From what I've learned, no one except Pa is experimenting with that crossbreed of Hereford and longhorn. All the other cattle being stolen are longhorns. I figure ours and the Ross's stock are being rustled because we're two of the biggest outfits around here. The same's true for the ranches in Callahan County."

The Ross family of the Circle R were their closest neighbors as well as longtime friends. Russ knew Jake Ross, his brother, Bram and their uncle Ike had been working as diligently as Matt to catch the thieves.

"When I talked to Pa yesterday, he said we'd lost more than a hundred." Before the rustling, J.T. had planned to repay the banknote with money from the sale of the cattle, but being short so many head meant the loan couldn't be paid even if they got top dollar for the cattle they did sell.

Matt exhaled loudly and started for the door. "Which means I really should go on to the ranch."

Russ and Ef rose to follow.

Matt glanced over his shoulder. "Had any lookers to buy your share of the hotel?"

"One. I received a wire this morning from a Chicago businessman who's ready to deal." Russ had gone looking for Lydia several hours ago to tell her, only to learn she'd taken a buggy out for a drive. With the killings still fresh on his mind, his letting her know about the potential sale had been pushed out of his thoughts.

He and the other two men crossed the lobby, heading for the open front doors.

"If Miz Kent's as pretty as they say, it's a shame you'll be giving her up as a business partner," his brother said.

"There's more to her than looks."

"What matters more than that?"

Ef chuckled.

Grinning, Russ said, "Something about her makes me wonder what's going on in that head of hers."

Matt's gaze turned sharp. "Since when do you care what goes on in a woman's head?"

He didn't. Not since Amy. Russ wished he'd kept his mouth shut. "Since I partnered up with Lydia Kent. She sued a fella because he wouldn't marry her."

Ef's and Matt's eyes went wide, and they both halted in midstride.

"Sued? 'Cuz he wouldn't get hitched?" Ef asked in a low voice.

"They were engaged, but the man changed his mind. She sued him for breach of promise and won."

"Over that!"

Russ understood Matt's shock. "Evidently, she's not too forgiving about some things."

Ef shook his head. "If some man didn't want to marry her, you'd think she might want to keep that quiet."

"She probably wanted to get back at him for humiliating her," Russ said.

"Or show him that she didn't need him," Matt said darkly.

Russ glanced at his brother. "You thinking about Annalise?"

At the mention of the woman who'd broken his heart when she'd left him behind years ago, Matt's blue eyes went flat and his face closed up. "Anything you want me to tell Pa?"

"Nah. I'll have time to come out to the ranch tomorrow."

Russ continued with the men to the front doors. Matt lifted a hand in farewell then walked outside with the blacksmith.

As Russ closed the doors, a soft voice came from behind him. "Mr. Baldwin?"

He turned to find Naomi Jones on the other side of the staircase. "Miz Jones, how are you?"

"Fine, thank you." A dark kerchief covered her hair and a white apron draped smoothly over a blue calico dress. "I'm sorry to bother you, but I'm worried. Lydia—Miss Kent hasn't returned from her buggy ride."

Russ frowned. It would be dark soon. "Maybe she stopped off somewhere in town?"

"No, if she were back, she would have come straight here."

She *had* been gone a long time. After the shootings in the lobby, Russ could see why Lydia's maid was so concerned. He hoped nothing bad had happened. "I'll ride out and look for her."

"Thank you." Relief shone in the woman's coffee-colored eyes.

"Do you know where she went?"

"No, but I know she headed west."

"Don't worry. I'll find her." He hoped she was in one piece when he did.

"Thank you again." With a small smile, the woman started up the wide sweep of stairs.

He turned and went to his office to strap on his gun and holster, then strode out the back of the hotel and across to the livery where he'd left his gelding for the night. Heading west out of town, he kept his mount to a lope. He hoped he could find Lydia before it was full dark. And he hoped nothing had happened to the woman. Not three days ago, two people had been killed in their hotel and she'd been winged, yet here she was, going out past town.

He covered ground quickly as twilight settled over the land. After about two miles, he spotted a dark boxy shape in the knee-high grass. A buggy.

Relief eased the band of tension across his chest he hadn't realized was there. Giving his horse a little kick, Russ cantered toward the vehicle as a shape separated itself from the shadows. Just as he started to call out, he heard the snick of a gun being cocked.

"Stop!"

Yep, that smoky voice was hers. "Miz Kent?"

"Mr. Baldwin?"

"Yeah."

"I could've shot you!"

"Glad you didn't." At least she had brought her gun. He rode closer, and she stepped away from the carriage and into the moonlight. Now he was able to see the sleek curve of her body, the brief glint of silver as she released the hammer on her weapon and lowered it. "Good to see you know how to use that."

She placed the derringer on the buggy's seat and rested a hand on the horse's rump. "What are you doing out here?"

He wanted to ask her the same thing. "Miz Jones was

worried because it's so late and you hadn't returned. She asked me to look for you. Are you okay?"

"Yes, I'm fine."

Russ dismounted, noting that her hair was mussed, strands slipping out of the long dark braid hanging down her back. Her wide-brimmed hat hung there, too.

"I'm sorry to have worried her." She bent and lifted the horse's left back leg. "This mare picked up a rock or something in one of her hooves. She's limping."

Russ scanned the prairie, a blanket of shadow and silver light across night-dark tops of high grass, the dip of hills. Everything appeared quiet. "How long has she been hobblin'?"

"I noticed it a few minutes ago and stopped. After I checked her, I planned to unhitch her and lead her back to town."

He walked over and gently edged Lydia aside to examine the mare. There was nothing in the left front hoof, but when he ran his fingers lightly over the hoof of her right front leg, he touched a chunk of rock. He worked it out, murmuring softly to the horse.

Lydia's lavender scent was faint, but detectable beneath the stronger smells of horseflesh and grass.

"Her other hooves are fine," he said. "But it's still a good idea to let her follow instead of pull the buggy."

Lydia nodded, detaching the closest rein as Russ helped unharness the animal. He noticed she favored her wounded arm.

"You okay?"

She glanced up then saw where he looked. "Oh, yes, thank you."

In the amount of time Lydia had been gone, she could've driven to Abilene and back, so where the hell had she been? What had she been doing? "You get lost? I came looking for you right after lunch. You've been gone quite some time."

"Yes, I was lost," she admitted quickly.

So quickly that he wasn't sure he believed her. The way she answered made him think she was only agreeing so he wouldn't ask more questions. Russ didn't care for women who appeared to be keeping secrets, whether they were or not. "You're not that far from Whirlwind, about two miles. Good thing I came along. You might've been out here all night."

"Hardly. The mare knows the way back."

True. So, why hadn't Lydia let the horse guide them back before now? He stepped the animal away from the rig and slipped off the bridle, switching it with that of his gelding. His horse wasn't buggy-broke, but he'd do fine for the distance back to town.

While Russ unsaddled his mount, Lydia secured hers to the back of the vehicle. After hitching up his gelding, Russ put his saddle and gear on the lame mare. He helped Lydia into the buggy and climbed in beside her. Buggies didn't comfortably accommodate a man his size unless special made. As a result, Miz Kent was pressed tight between her side of the carriage and him.

Russ folded down the leather hood so he could sit up straight and not feel as squeezed in as a calf in a pen. Except the problem wasn't all due to a lack of space. The woman sitting next to him—almost on top of him—had him feeling bridled.

He couldn't escape her light scent. When she shifted, her breast brushed his arm and he had a sudden flash of her wearing nothing but him, his face buried in her dark, sweet-smelling hair. His jaw clamped tight.

He snapped the reins against the gelding's rump and the buggy lurched into motion. Russ noted Lydia hadn't been frightened when he'd found her, only cautious. The feel of her arm and shoulder burned into his side. And he couldn't understand why, out here on the open prairie, all he could smell was the lavender sweetness of woman. "Just how far did you ride?"

"A few miles west and south."

"There are two ranches in that area." The Circle R, Jake Ross's place and Riley Holt's ranch, The Rocking H. "You should've stopped and asked for directions back to town."

"I didn't realize I was lost at first," she explained in a strained voice as if trying not to lose patience. She glanced at the watch on her bodice.

How long had she been driving around out here? Had she been going in circles? Besides his friends' ranches, there was a pair of small farms in between where she could've asked for help.

"Glad you're okay." His gaze lingered on her finely sculpted profile, silvered by the moonlight. "Miz Jones will be happy to hear it, too."

His attention drifted to the full curve of her breasts, the small jet buttons on her pale blue bodice winking in the shadowy light. Tension wound through him and he tightened his grip on the reins.

"I'm sorry I worried Naomi."

"You're not sorry you worried me?"

She arched a brow. "*Were* you worried?"

"Yes," he admitted with some surprise. "Especially after what happened at the hotel the other morning. I told you before it's not a good idea to travel alone."

"I didn't intend to be gone so long," she said tightly.

Which was nowhere close to an acknowledgment of his warning. What if someone had come upon her? Her mouth alone could have a man thinking about trying all sorts of things with her. Impatient with his thoughts, Russ tried to shove them away.

He'd felt this kind of mind-addlin' attraction before, but this time he knew better than to let it get hold of him.

Lydia shifted, the left side of her body molded to the right side of his. She cupped a protective hand over her right upper arm.

"Sorry about the bumps. I know all the jouncin' must make your arm hurt."

"It's a little sore." She moved her hands back to her lap, her movement sending a fresh whiff of lavender mixed with the night air over him. "Why were you looking for me this afternoon?"

"I needed to talk to you about the hotel."

"All right." She waited expectantly, clasping her elegant, glove-clad hands.

"I've had a telegram from someone who's planning to buy my part of The Fontaine."

"What?" Her head snapped toward him. "You're planning to sell?"

"I have to."

"Why?"

Russ thumbed back his hat, trying to keep his attention on the conversation and not the soft feel of the woman beside him. Or the inviting smoothness of her pale skin. "My pa originally owned this share."

"I remember."

"He needed money to begin a cattle-breeding operation, so I bought it from him. But when he needed more bulls, he had to borrow against the ranch."

"And the loan is coming due?"

"Yeah. We probably could've repaid it with profits from selling the new hybrid stock, but we've been hit by rustlers so even if we sold every head for top dollar, we wouldn't get enough money."

"How many cattle have been taken?"

"More than a hundred. Several of those are prize bulls and some already breeding cows. My brother and some of our neighbors are trying to catch the rustlers, but so far, they haven't had any luck."

Lydia nodded. They rode in silence for a moment, the only sounds the whisper of grass against the buggy wheels and the distant howl of a coyote.

"So you posted a notice about the hotel in some newspapers and someone responded?"

"Yes. A Mr. Theodore Julius of Chicago. He's planning to come to Whirlwind in the next few days."

She hesitated then, "Will he move here? Live at the hotel?"

"You mean, will he stay out of your way and let you run things how you want?"

"I didn't ask that."

Russ had been teasing her, but the haughtiness of her reply set something off inside him. Maybe it was the frustration of needing some space from her or maybe it was his guilt over Pa that had him speaking sharply. "If you're so all-fired set against having a partner, why buy the interest in the hotel to start with?"

"I'm not set against having a partner."

"As long as they stay out of your way."

For a moment, she stared, then lifting her chin, she said in a cool, flat voice, "Yes, as long as they stay out of my way."

Russ wanted to grab her and shake her. Or kiss her. Do something to rattle that aloofness. After a few seconds of gripping the reins so tightly the leather burned his palms, he beat down the impulse and focused on getting to town.

The slight nip in the fall air carried the scent of wood smoke from someone's stove. He kept his attention on driving, working hard to dismiss the way Lydia's body rubbed and bounced against his every time they hit a rock or a rough patch of ground.

He was irritated as all get-out. Partly because he wondered what her creamy skin would feel like under his hands, his mouth. And partly because he wanted to know everything going on in her head. He wasn't sure which was more confoundin'.

Russ didn't want to be interested in Lydia Kent's mind. He wasn't going to figure her out. He didn't even want to try. No matter how much she intrigued him.

In the short time it took to reach The Fontaine, Lydia's arm was throbbing. Even worse, her nerves were vibrating. Partly from Russ catching her in a lie, but mostly from his being so close.

The buggy wasn't built for such a giant of a man and she was practically sitting in his lap! The man made her twitchy, restless. The one hand she was able to clamp on the seat didn't keep her from sliding against him as they drove.

Despite the dull ache in her upper arm, she could barely keep from looking at him. The night growth of his beard gave him a dangerous air, and he smelled of leather and a faint spice. When the moonlight slanted across them, Lydia caught a glimpse of dark hair in the open vee of his shirt.

"Whoa," Russ said, pulling back on the reins.

Against her arm, Lydia felt his muscles strain as he slowed the buggy at the hotel's back door. The coiled strength in his massive body had her heart thumping hard. Her skin went cold, then hot.

"I'll get this rig back to the livery." His words slid over her in a low rumble.

"Thank you." Somehow she managed to keep her voice

steady, but when he offered his hand to help her out, her pulse scrambled. Unsettled, she hurried inside and up the staircase.

Garner Kent had included Lydia in his business dealings since the time she was old enough to sit quietly and she had never been uncomfortable around men. Russ Baldwin made her uncomfortable every which way. Especially physically and not because his size was intimidating. It was the whole of him. The hard planes of his body that made a woman want to test his strength. The wicked blue of eyes that were sultry one minute, sharp the next. His mouth—

No. She refused to dwell on it.

She reached her rooms, switched off the gaslight in the hall and went inside. The night air was cool, but Lydia was warm. She could still feel the muscular line of his thigh against her leg, the heat of his palm through her glove. Her reaction to him was unfamiliar and quite disconcerting.

"Lydia?" Naomi rushed over from the velvet-draped window where she'd been standing, her footsteps muffled against the area's large rug.

Lydia reached out and squeezed the other woman's hand. "I'm all right."

"I was so afraid something had happened to you. Are you upset that I sent Mr. Baldwin to find you?" Naomi's brown eyes were troubled. "I was worried. We don't know the area and after the shootings—"

"It's fine. You did the right thing." In truth, Lydia wished her friend hadn't sent Russ, but she wasn't about to criticize. Naomi had lived with too much fear, and if Russ Baldwin helped relieve some of it, Lydia was glad. Even though the man put her on edge.

Her pulse finally steadied. Removing her hat, she walked to the walnut wardrobe along the wall which separated the sitting room from the bedrooms. She opened one of the double doors and hung her hat on a peg inside.

"How's your arm?"

"I don't think I tore any of the stitches, but it needs to be looked at."

"Your bandage needs to be changed anyway."

Closing the door with an elbow, Lydia reached back and undid her braid, threading her fingers through the strands until the heavy mass fell around her shoulders. The tension of her long afternoon began to ease.

The burning pewter gaslights illuminated the office and sitting room done in soothing colors of blue and cream. Touches of cobalt accented the large blue-and-cream rug.

"What happened?" Naomi's voice quivered. "Did something go wrong?"

Lydia knew how terrifying her prolonged absence must've been for her friend. Both of them knew all too well the danger that could befall them. Naomi was trying to remain calm, but Lydia sensed her upset.

"Except for having to stay so long at the second stop, everything went smoothly." She gave a reassuring smile as she unpinned Isabel's watch, laying it on the small marble table next to the wall. "The first stop was a ranch and the woman there, Emma Ross, was more than helpful. The second stop was a farm. That's the one where I had to wait. The family had guests so they couldn't talk to me until the people were otherwise occupied."

"Since your folks are the ones who told us about the stops, I wasn't worried about you being safe while you were there. It was the getting there and getting back. Did you get everything settled?"

"Yes." Lydia eased down into one of the sapphire velvet

chairs she'd arranged in a corner and bent to unbutton her black everyday boots. "For now, the signal will stay the same. When weather permits, the quilt is to be left outside if it's safe to approach the house. During bad weather, the quilt hangs in the front window."

Naomi knelt to pick up the shoes, but Lydia waved her off. "No, Naomi. I'll put those away."

The other woman rose. "Where did Mr. Baldwin find you?"

"About two miles outside of town."

"What did you tell him?"

"That I'd gotten lost, but I don't know if he believed me. My horse picked up a stone and was limping, so that might've helped the story."

"Do you think he suspects anything?" Naomi curled one hand over the back of the other chair.

Lydia stretched out her legs and wiggled her toes in her stockings, glad to be rid of her shoes. "I don't know, but we may not have to worry about that much longer."

"Why?" Moving carefully because of her bruised ribs, Naomi eased down into the chair beside Lydia's.

Knowing her friend's nerves had yet to calm, Lydia rested her head back against the chair, letting her muscles relax. Trying to get images of Russ out of her mind. "He's selling his share of the hotel."

The other woman's eyes widened. Lydia related what Russ had told her. "He's already received a response from someone who wants to buy. I plan to find out if the new partner intends to move to Whirlwind and stay here at The Fontaine."

"That must've been why he came looking for you after lunch."

"Yes, that's what he said."

"So, what about the telegram you received this morning?"

"That was from Daddy, about Philip."

At the mention of Lydia's brother-in-law, fear pinched Naomi's beautiful features. "And?"

"Daddy says the situation is grave, but he's still alive."

The other woman jerked to her feet, flattening a hand over her stomach. "He'll come after us! What if he finds us?"

"Shh." Lydia rose and took both of Naomi's hands in hers. "He won't find us. He probably won't survive. But if he does, if he tries to hurt us, we'll defend ourselves. Just as you did in the stables that night."

Tears streamed down her friend's face and Lydia hugged her, fighting not to cry herself.

As she did every time she remembered Naomi fighting off Philip, Lydia wished her sister had been able to do the same. But she hadn't. Isabel had already been weak and battered when her husband shoved her down the stairs. She died of her injuries.

People in Jackson knew how Philip DeBoard treated his wife, but most turned a blind eye. The DeBoards were an old family, wealthy and influential, so nothing had happened to the son of a bitch. He'd killed Lydia's sister, almost killed her sister's maid.

She couldn't hold back her tears any longer. Her arms tightened around Naomi, sending a jolt of pain up her arm. Lydia knew the other woman was reliving the same disturbing memories as she.

Months after Isabel's death, Naomi had finally agreed to leave the DeBoard plantation. Lydia had come, prepared to take her back to the Kent home outside of Jackson, and found her brother-in-law attacking the woman, kicking her in the head and torso. Lydia had drawn her derringer, but before she could shoot, Naomi had plunged a pitchfork into the man.

For horrible seconds, there had been only the sound of

Philip's low keening moan, then he'd choked out that he would kill them both. Lydia had grabbed Naomi's hand and taken off. Once they'd arrived at home, Lydia had told Daddy and Mama what had happened. They agreed she should leave at once for the hotel in Texas and take Naomi with her. So they had, arriving in Whirlwind two weeks earlier than Lydia had been expected.

Since then, Garner and Kathleen Kent had kept them well informed about Philip's condition. Infection had set in and DeBoard was hovering near death. After what he'd done, Lydia would feel just fine if he died. Lord knew, he wouldn't be arrested if he recovered, seeing as his cousin was the sheriff in Jackson.

She hugged her friend tight, her voice thick. "He won't find us, Naomi. We'll do whatever we have to so that he can't hurt you ever again."

"I don't want you to get hurt, either." The other woman drew back, wiping at her eyes.

"We're going to be fine. We are." Lydia fished in the pocket of her blue skirt for a handkerchief. Pushing the white linen into Naomi's hand, she opened the wardrobe and took another from one of five small drawers, drying her own tears. "How are your ribs?"

"A little better." Naomi smiled tremulously.

Lydia knew they probably still hurt dreadfully.

"Let me look at your arm."

Lydia unbuttoned her bodice to the waist and started to slip her arm out.

A knock sounded on the door, startling them both. She shared a look with her friend, hurriedly fastening her dress. As she walked to the door, she tried to smooth away signs of her tears.

She opened it to find Russ Baldwin and her chest tightened. Had he heard them crying? Lydia knew her eyes were probably red. If he noticed, she hoped he thought they were that way from fatigue.

His gaze slid down, down her body to her black stockinged feet then slowly climbed back up and lingered on her breasts. She glanced down and saw she'd missed a button. Skin heating, she fumbled it through the hole. His hot blue eyes had sensation swirling in her stomach and she curled her toes into the floor, hiding them beneath her skirts.

Holding his hat, he rubbed his nape. Fatigue lined his features and his blue eyes were bloodshot.

"Just wanted to let you know the mare will be fine."

"I'm glad."

He nodded. "Everything else okay?"

"Yes, thank you."

He looked past her. "Miz Jones?"

"Yes, thank you, Mr. Baldwin." Naomi's voice was steady. "Thank you for finding Lydia."

"You're welcome." His gaze returned to Lydia, lingering on the fall of her hair before doing one more slow pass down her body.

Her skin tingled and she struggled to remember her manners. "Thank you for all your help tonight."

"I'm glad you're all right," he said in a flinty voice, his features hardening. "After what happened to those people in the lobby, I'd think you would be more concerned about wandering off on your own."

Lydia opened her mouth to tell him she *was* concerned and she hadn't been "wandering" anywhere, but she caught herself. Biting back her retort, she murmured, "Perhaps you're right—"

"Things could've turned out a lot differently. It might be good to stay close to town for a while."

He was chastising her! That was quite enough.

Her eyes narrowed and she nodded sharply. "Good night, Mr. Baldwin."

"Miz Kent." He settled his hat on his head and walked away.

Irritated, Lydia closed the door, barely able to hear the hard tap of his boots above the pounding of her heart. Ooh, the man vexed her! When he looked at her with those piercing blue eyes, she felt completely undone.

As if he could see through her. Into her.

She didn't know what made her more nervous. That he might notice too much about the operation. Or about her.

Chapter Four

Asleep or awake, Russ couldn't get Lydia out of his head. Since the night he'd found her on the prairie, he'd been taunted by the memory of her thick raven hair sliding around her shoulders and that one undone button right between her breasts. Those images triggered more images. He dreamed about her, about that silky hair on his bare skin, about feeling *her* bare skin against his. He even thought he could smell her soft lavender scent.

He woke up hard and hurting. He didn't even remember the last time that had happened, and he sure didn't like it happening with Lydia Kent. It was time for that trip to Abilene he'd had to put off with her early arrival. He could work this heavy, hammering want out of his system with Willow or Sally. Or both.

It wasn't only the tempting thought of getting his hands on Lydia that made it impossible to get her out of his mind. It was also because when he had gone to her rooms that night she looked as though she'd been crying. Naomi had looked the same way.

Why? Did it have anything to do with Lydia's being lost? And why had his business partner gone out by herself, especially after the shooting in their lobby? The woman was confoundin'.

He tried to see her only about hotel business, hoping that would dim the vivid pictures in his head, but it didn't. Russ was plenty ready to sell his share in the hotel even though he wasn't leaving The Fontaine until he figured out what Miz Kent was up to.

Three days after Russ had found her on the prairie, he was at the stage stand between the livery and the saloon. Mr. Julius had taken the train to Abilene and was due to arrive in Whirlwind by coach. The businessman was coming to take a look at The Fontaine, but from his last wire, it sounded as though the visit was just a formality. He was ready to buy.

With one booted foot propped against a support post, Russ watched as Davis Lee stopped at every business across the street. Inside Ef's, the sheriff talked to the blacksmith a while before striding past the jail and on to The Pearl. In short order, he checked on the telegraph and post office as well as The Whirlwind Hotel.

Fingering his now-bare upper lip, Russ noted Davis Lee crossing to this side of the street. He worked his way down from the gunsmith shop past Haskell's General Store and the newspaper office.

Though this was the sheriff's morning routine, he usually did it between eight and nine o'clock in the morning, not a few minutes before noon.

Davis Lee joined Russ beside the saloon and shook his hand.

"Something going on today?" Russ asked.

"Nothing much. Why?"

"You're just now making your rounds. You usually do that first thing in the morning and last thing at night."

"I was taking care of Josie. She's been sick."

"I'm sorry to hear it. Is it catchin'?"

"No." A huge grin spread across Davis Lee's face.

"You sure look happy about it. How sick is she?"

"She's been sick every morning this week. *Every morning.*"

"Every morning? You might want to get Dr. Butler to come in from the fort."

"He's already seen her," Davis Lee said. "Said she'll probably be sick at least another two months."

"Two months!" *Sick every morning.* It dawned on Russ what his friend was saying. "She's expecting? Y'all are going to have a baby?"

Davis Lee nodded, chuckling.

"Congratulations." Russ clapped him on the back, pleased for his friends. Josie had suffered a miscarriage about three months earlier. "That's good. You telling everyone?"

"Just a few people right now."

"I'll keep it to myself."

"Thanks."

"Man, I hope y'all don't have a boy. He'll be hell just like you and Riley were, and Josie doesn't deserve that."

"Well, if it's a girl… What if it *is* a girl?" The smile faded from Davis Lee's face. "I don't know anything about raising girls."

Neither did Russ. "Well, Riley does since he married Susannah and adopted Lorelai."

"True." The sheriff relaxed a bit at the mention of his adopted niece.

A pregnant Susannah had come to Whirlwind under the impression that Riley wanted to marry her and he hadn't known a thing about the arrangement. He'd eventually fallen in love with her and her infant daughter, and married Susannah.

Davis Lee glanced back at the open door of the small stage office. "You waiting on somebody?"

"There's a man coming in from Chicago who's probably going to buy my share of the hotel." Russ had already told Davis Lee he needed to sell in order to pay off Pa's loan. "I told the banker in Abilene I might have the money early."

"Have you told your new partner?"

"Yeah." He didn't tell Davis Lee how she made no secret of wanting to get him out of there. "She seems fine with it."

Davis Lee nodded as one of the Baldwins' wagons rolled to a stop in front of them. Russ's brother and father called out a greeting. In a swirl of dust, Russ moved to help his pa out of the buckboard, guilt twisting inside him.

J. T. Baldwin was a big man, just like his sons. Though the accident had happened three months earlier, he still had trouble sitting for very long at a time so someone had to drive him where he needed to go.

"What brings y'all to town?" Russ asked as he waited for his father to maneuver his wheelchair to the support post where Russ had been.

"Pa's wanting some of Cora's peach pie and we both thought it was high time we met your partner." Matt's sharp-eyed gaze scanned the main street then rested on The Fontaine. "Is she out and about today?"

"I'm sure she is." Russ still wasn't all that keen on his brother meeting Lydia.

"That's her right now," J.T. said, pointing past Russ. "Spittin' image of her mama. Who's the woman with her?"

Russ glanced over his shoulder to see Lydia and her pretty black companion stepping off the hotel's front porch and angling across the dusty street toward them. "That's her maid, Naomi."

Lydia wore a deep green-and-blue-striped dress that fit

snugly across her full breasts, drawing his eye to the watch pinned to her bodice. Her hair was swept up beneath a small blue hat trimmed with a ribbon in the same blue and green as the dress. Naomi looked neat and fresh in a pale yellow skirt and white shirtwaist.

"Pretty don't come close on either one of them," Matt said appreciatively, shouldering his way past Russ and striding over to intercept the women.

Russ bit back the urge to tell his brother to stay away from Lydia. Away from both women.

A movement caught his eye and he looked across to the blacksmith shop. Ef stood next to his hitching post, staring at Lydia and Naomi as they walked toward the saloon.

Matt reached the women and the three of them talked for a moment, then Lydia laughed. He offered each woman an arm.

As his brother escorted the ladies over, Russ felt an unexpected bolt of jealousy. He didn't want Matt or any other man putting his hands on Lydia. What in tarnation was his problem? Russ had no claim on her, didn't want one.

As Matt drew the women to a stop, Russ and the others doffed their hats.

"Miz Kent, Miz Jones, I see you've met my brother. And you met Sheriff Holt the other morning at the hotel." Russ hitched a thumb over his shoulder. "This is my pa, J.T."

The big man rolled carefully around Russ and bent over Lydia's hand. "I didn't recognize you all grown-up, Miz Lydia, but there's no mistaking you for Garner and Kathleen's daughter."

"Hello, Mr. Baldwin," she said in a sweet smoky drawl. "It's nice to see you."

"I was sorry to hear about your sister."

"Thank you."

Despite her soft tone, Russ felt a sudden tension in her. In Naomi, too.

He remembered Pa telling him that Lydia's married sister had suffered a fall and died some months ago. J.T. released Lydia and bent over Naomi's hand. The woman said a quiet hello.

Davis Lee nodded to both women. "Ladies."

"Hello, Sheriff." Lydia smiled. "How's your wife?"

"She's just fine. I'll tell her you asked after her. How's your arm?"

"It's healing well, I think." Lydia glanced at Russ. "Are you gentlemen having a meeting?"

"Just visitin'," he said, drawing in a deep breath of her subtle flowery scent. He noticed Ef was still staring at the women.

Lydia's gaze found his. "We're headed to the restaurant to talk to Pearl about desserts for the hotel. Any requests?"

"Pecan pie," Russ said. There were plenty of the nuts around Whirlwind, thanks to the Eishens' pecan orchard.

She pulled her little book from her skirt pocket—was she ever without that thing?—and scribbled a note.

Matt eased up to her. "How about peach pie, too?"

"It's hard to beat Cora's peach pie," J.T. said.

"Is she a lady here in town?" Lydia asked the older man.

He nodded. "Cora Wilkes. Makes the best pie in the state."

"I'd love to try it sometime. Perhaps she would be interested in baking some for the hotel if Pearl wouldn't mind."

"Pearl gets her peach pies from Cora, too." Russ was taken with the gentle curve of Lydia's jaw and her dewy skin.

She caught him looking and a slight flush tinged her cheeks.

Closing her book, she turned away with Naomi. "Good day, gentlemen."

"Good day," they said in unison.

Russ watched as the women made their way across the street and disappeared into the restaurant. Forcing his gaze away, he noticed Matt was watching, too. And so was Ef, though his attention was only on Naomi. The blacksmith looked dazed, as if he'd been hit upside the head.

Russ grinned. He'd never seen his friend pay so much attention to a woman.

The rumble of hooves announced the arrival of the stagecoach. As it rolled into town and past the smithy, Ef stepped back into his shop. Wheels creaking, the coach pulled to a stop in front of the saloon. Pete Carter, who owned the saloon, also occasionally drove the stage, and today he was in the high seat.

"Hey, Pete." Davis Lee moved to open the door and a lone barrel-chested gentleman stepped out.

Russ thumbed his hat back. "Mr. Julius?"

The man's shrewd dark eyes flickered over him. "Mr. Baldwin, I presume."

"Yes, sir." Russ shook the man's hand and introduced his family, then gestured to Davis Lee. "This is Sheriff Holt."

"Sheriff." At least a half foot shorter than Russ, the man removed his bowler hat and rubbed his bald head. "Nice to meet you."

Pete had hopped down and now handed the visitor's valise to him. Mr. Julius pressed a coin into Pete's hand.

"Thank you, sir," the saloon owner/stage driver said.

"Would you care for a drink before we get started?" Russ asked the businessman.

"Maybe after."

"All right then. Right this way." He stepped around the horses and waited for his guest to follow.

"Nice to have met you, Mr. Julius," Davis Lee said.

"Thank you. Friendly town," he observed as he and Russ angled across the street to the hotel.

In front of The Fontaine, the other man stopped, eyeing the three-story structure built from pale sandstone. He indicated the arched doorways on the second and third stories. "This is very fine-looking."

"Glad you think so."

"Dignified, but not too fancy." He looked up at the second story balcony set off by a black railing. "The ironwork is some of the best I've seen."

"Our blacksmith, Ef Gerard, did that."

"He's very skilled." Leaving his valise, the businessman walked the length and width of the hotel. Then he went up the staircase on the outside wall closest to the livery. He strolled along the balcony then returned downstairs and picked up his bag, following Russ inside. Russ removed his Stetson and held on to it.

Placing his valise and bowler hat behind the registration desk, Julius walked carefully around the lobby. "You've done a fine job with everything, Mr. Baldwin. I especially like the rug you chose."

Russ grinned, making a mental note to tell Lydia.

The other man approved heartily of the dining room and spacious kitchen. He agreed with Russ that the second floor rooms didn't need to be completed before they opened for business, but the rooms would be finished soon after.

Russ figured he would close the deal with Mr. Julius that day and was surprised at the twinge of disappointment he felt over the fact that he would no longer be partners with Lydia.

"Impressive." On the third floor, Mr. Julius inspected the four rooms that each had their own facilities. "The beds look very comfortable. Not lumpy."

"My partner insisted on stuffing them with Spanish moss. Swears it makes a difference," Russ said.

"Very smart."

He examined the wrought iron stair railing on their way back to the first level, again commenting on the fine workmanship.

"Ef made the cookware for the hotel, too."

They reached the first floor and just as Russ turned to ask Mr. Julius if he'd like to step into his office to talk terms and have a drink, Lydia and Naomi swept in bringing a swirl of cool October air and lavender scent.

"Ladies," Mr. Julius murmured, removing his bowler hat at the same time Russ removed his Stetson. Interest sparked in the businessman's eyes as his gaze roved over both women then came back to linger on Lydia.

Knowing the man was going to be spending time with her, Russ didn't care for that look. His hands fisted on the brim of his hat. "Mr. Julius, this is my partner, Lydia Kent and her friend, Naomi Jones."

"Your partner?" The man bent low over Lydia's hand. "Do you live around here, Miss Kent?"

"Yes." She gave the smile that always grabbed a little bit of Russ every time she used it on him. "I live on the third floor—I'm the hotel manager."

"Indeed," the man murmured.

"Russ has probably answered all your questions, but if I can be of help, don't hesitate to ask."

The man nodded. His face didn't change, but Russ felt a sudden tension spring up.

Lydia smiled at both of them. "We won't keep you from your business."

She and Naomi swept past them in a soft rustle of skirts, headed toward the kitchen.

He turned back to Mr. Julius. "What about that drink now? I've got a good whiskey in my office. We can go there and discuss terms."

The man looked regretfully around the lobby. "I won't be buying your share of the hotel, Mr. Baldwin."

"What?" Completely taken off guard, Russ huffed out a laugh. "I don't understand. You seemed impressed with everything."

"I am, very impressed. I think you have a real money-maker on your hands."

"Then I don't follow."

"I assumed your partner was a man. It never occurred to me to ask." The man's gaze leveled into his. "I don't do business with women, ever."

Russ was so stunned he couldn't speak for several seconds. "You don't—"

"Do business with women."

He'd caught it the first time. He just couldn't believe it. "May I ask why?"

"It's a bad practice. Nothing good can come of it."

Fighting to keep the astonishment out of his voice, Russ said, "At least half of the ideas you praised are Lydia's. She is one smart lady."

"Perhaps."

"It was her idea to stuff the mattresses with Spanish moss."

"Hmm."

"That glass in the third floor windows? I tried for a month to get it delivered. Even the store in Abilene couldn't get the order. She figured out how to get it and did so in one afternoon. Plus she managed to gain free advertising for the hotel."

"That's admirable, but it doesn't change my mind."

Frustration churning inside him, Russ shoved a hand

through his hair. All he could see was the bank foreclosing on the ranch and him letting Pa down once again.

He struggled to keep his temper in check. "It sure seems shortsighted of you to turn down a profitable business. And it *will* be profitable. Lydia will be a big part of that."

"Or she might run it into the ground."

Russ might not know why she wanted him gone, but he believed she wanted the hotel to succeed as much as he did. And he believed she could make that happen. "She's got a good head for business."

"She has a good many things," the man said suggestively.

Russ stiffened.

The man gave him a pitying look. "You're probably blinded by her…other good assets, but having been around as long as I have, I can tell you, women don't do well in business. I'm sorry. I'm no longer interested."

Russ could argue with the man all day, but he could see Julius's mind was made up. "I think you're making a mistake."

"Maybe so." The other man shook his head. "I'll go on over to the stage stand and find out if I can make the return stage to Abilene."

If he couldn't, Russ would be happy to get the man out of town himself. He was surprised at how bothered he was by Julius's obvious prejudice against Lydia.

The man picked up his valise and walked out to the front porch. Russ put on his Stetson as he followed.

"It's a fine hotel." The businessman settled his hat on his head. "I just assumed the other partner was a man. That's what I get for not asking."

Russ let that stand, hands braced on his hips as Julius strode away. He'd never heard of anything so ignorant in his life. Lydia might drive him crazy, but he had no doubt her mind was every bit as sharp as his, if not more so. It sure as hell hadn't been him who'd come up with the idea to search out a man with an unfinished house for glass.

"Is he gone already?" Lydia's whiskey-and-honey drawl drifted to him from the door. "Did you close the deal?"

Russ turned, thumbing back his hat. "No, not in the end."

She looked disappointed, which got his back up. Couldn't she at least *try* to pretend she didn't want him gone? He opened his mouth to tell her *she* was the reason Julius didn't want to buy into the hotel.

"I'm sorry." She sounded genuinely concerned. "What are you going to do about your father's banknote?"

"I'll just keep advertising. Someone will come along. It's a sound investment."

"Are you sure you don't want to turn over the management of the hotel to me in the meantime? It would free you up to find another buyer."

"I'm sure." Why was she so all-fired set on that? Managing a hotel was no easy feat. Any person in their right mind would want help.

She walked back inside with him, her subtle scent stirring his blood. "He'd seemed interested when Naomi and I walked in."

"I thought so, too."

"Did he decide not to buy because he heard about the killings in the lobby?"

"No." Looking down into those velvet eyes, that angel's face, Russ felt a surge of protectiveness sweep over him. "Just said he wasn't interested any longer."

"That's odd."

Russ stared at the high crest of her cheekbones, the soft line of a jaw that could turn stubborn in a blink. He knew she had a spine of steel, but right now she looked delicate and vulnerable. "No accountin' for some men's tastes."

When she looked up at him and smiled, Russ knew he couldn't tell her the businessman's reason for walking away. He didn't know why he was being so careful of her feelings; she'd made no secret of the fact that she wanted him out of there.

Julius might have a problem doing business with Lydia, but Russ sure didn't. If anything, he added as his gaze lingered on her breasts, he might like it too much.

As far as he could tell, there wasn't one thing wrong with her, inside or out. She was smart and beautiful. Which was trouble all rolled up in one package.

After Russ had told her he wouldn't be selling his share in the hotel to Mr. Julius, Lydia saw him only once as he'd headed for the saloon. It was hours later, well after dark, when he returned to The Fontaine.

She was at the top of the stairs when he came in and very carefully shut the door, then slowly, unsteadily wove his way to his office. Even from here, she could smell the liquor on him. When he gave her the news about Mr. Julius, she'd briefly seen what she thought was panic in his eyes.

He had looked completely disheartened. Maybe the loan wasn't the only reason he needed to sell his interest in the hotel.

When he had first told her about selling his share, she had cautioned herself to be patient. She had thought she would likely have a new partner in less than a week, but that hadn't happened. She'd asked him again about turning over the management of the hotel to her and he'd said no. It wouldn't be long before more battered women arrived, and she would feel much better if Russ weren't so involved in the running of the hotel.

Well, if he thought they should continue making decisions together, she was happy to oblige him.

The next morning, she smoothed her white shirtwaist and rust-colored skirt, then walked to his office. She glanced at the timepiece on her bodice. It was eight o'clock and from what she'd observed he was usually up well before now, but she hadn't heard him moving around this morning. She knocked on his office door and a few seconds later, it opened.

Russ stood there, bare-chested, the ends of his thick hair damp, a speck of shaving soap just under his jaw. Lydia's cheery greeting slid right back down her throat.

His tautly muscled brown flesh had sensation curling in her stomach. Dark trousers molded to his lean waist then sleeked down long legs. Her gaze helplessly roved across his wide shoulders, over the dark hair on his chest, down the hard planes of his stomach. *Oh. My.*

A shiver skipped down her spine. She forced her gaze to his, noticing his bloodshot eyes and his haggard face. He was feeling the effects of his hours at the saloon.

She felt a twinge of conscience at bothering him and thought about coming back later, but his condition was an example of why he should turn over management of the hotel to her. "Good morning," she said tentatively.

"Morning." He scrubbed a hand down his face. "Something wrong?"

"No. I need your opinion on something."

He opened the door wider. "You want to come in?"

She shook her head. "I just need to know if you think the rug should stay where it is?"

He frowned. "The rug?"

She stepped back, pointing toward the hideous burgundy and gold carpet he'd purchased before her arrival. Her replacement would arrive soon. "See, right there. I moved it closer to the registration desk."

Russ stuck his head out the door and squinted. "I can't tell the difference. It looks fine there."

"Okay, thank you." She smiled up at him, compassion winning out for a moment. "Are you all right? You don't look like you feel well."

"I'm fine," he rasped.

"I heard you come in very late last night."

"And?" He scowled.

"And nothing," she soothed. "Can I get you anything?"

"I just need some quiet," he said pointedly.

"Very well. I'll talk to you later."

She turned away, hopeful it wouldn't take long to wear him down. A couple of hours later as she worked in the dining area, she heard Russ's heavy footsteps coming up from the boiler room. When he walked out of the kitchen, she took a few steps toward him. His color was better, though his eyes were still red.

"Could you take a look at the sconces in the lobby?" she asked.

"What's wrong with them?" He pulled a rag from the back pocket of his trousers and wiped his hands, leaving black streaks on the red fabric. "Do they need fixin'?"

"No. I don't think they're the same color."

He looked puzzled, but nodded. "Okay."

Once they were standing in front of the green tufted sofa, Lydia pointed to the left sconce on the wall above the furniture. "The shade of pewter on this one isn't the same as the other one."

"The shade," he muttered, staring hard at her as if making sure he understood.

She smiled hopefully.

His gaze shifted between the fixtures as he stuffed the rag back into his pocket. "You may be right."

"Should I order a new one?"

"Nah, I can put some axle grease on it, darken it up a bit."

"Axle grease!"

"Yeah." He turned toward the kitchen and its door that led outside. "I can get some real quick from Ef."

"No!" She fought to keep the panic from her voice. Axle grease indeed. "That won't be necessary."

"Are you sure? It won't take a minute."

"I'm sure." She stepped back, eyeing the sconces. "Maybe it's just the way the light hits it that makes the color look off to me."

"All right then." He picked his Stetson up from the registration desk where he'd left it and settled it on his head, walking out the front door. "I'll be back directly."

"Okay." Lydia followed to see if he was returning to the saloon. He went in that direction, but continued past the place and strode up the street to the mercantile.

He didn't seem impatient or fed up with her yet. Certainly not ready to turn over all the hotel management decisions to her.

She worked steadily with Naomi until lunch. An hour later, as they measured the long window in the kitchen for a curtain, Lydia saw Russ outside the blacksmith shop. Arms folded, he leaned back against the hitching post, talking to the smithy. Their conversation didn't appear to be serious.

Pulling a couple of napkins from the sideboard in the dining room, Lydia went outside and started toward the two men. As she neared, Ef glanced at her, then said something to Russ, who turned around.

"Miz Kent," he said in a scratchy voice, straightening to his full height.

His white shirt molded to his wide shoulders, reminding her all over again how big he was. As if she needed any prompting after seeing him half-naked this morning.

"Hello." She looked past Russ and smiled at the big black man who owned the smithy. "Mr. Gerard."

"Howdy, ma'am."

She glanced at her partner, who palmed off his cowboy hat. Because of the sun's glare, she couldn't tell if his eyes were still bloodshot. "Could I get your opinion on something?"

"Something about the hotel?"

"Of course."

She felt his gaze slide down every inch of her body before he said to Ef, "Give me a minute."

"Sure." The black man stepped inside his shop. "Nice to see you, ma'am."

Russ turned his attention to her. "What can I do for you?"

"I'm trying to decide on the table linens." She showed him the napkins. "Should we go with the white or the ivory?"

Settling his hat on his head, Russ looked down at the fabric then back at her, chewing the inside of his cheek. "They look the same to me."

"This one is cream colored." She held up the napkin in her right hand.

"The only difference I see is that one of them has fancy lace on the edge and the other doesn't."

"Maybe you can't judge it very well in this light."

His eyes narrowed on her then he cupped her elbow and steered her to the side of the smithy. "You know what I think, Miz Kent?"

"No," she said sweetly. "That's why I asked you."

He slyly maneuvered her against the wall of the shop and braced an elbow over her head. Lydia's whole body went hot. "You keep lookin' for excuses to find me. Makes a man wonder."

"Wonder what?"

"If you want to spend time with me, why don't you just ask?"

"If I *what?*" she sputtered, her spine going to steel. "I can assure you—Where did you get such a notion?"

He leaned close, his voice lowering in a way that had her toes curling. "This is the third time today you've sought me out. What am I supposed to think?"

"That I want your opinion. For the hotel." She tugged her arm from his hold. Foot, she had never imagined he would think such a thing. "And *that* is all."

Resting one shoulder against the wall, he studied her. "Everything you've asked me today has to do with decoratin'. You know good and well I don't know a damn thing about that stuff. Why don't you just—" He broke off, his eyes narrowing in suspicion.

"What? Why don't I just what?" A strand of hair worked loose from her braid and blew across her face. She pushed it back. "You said we should make all hotel decisions together, but if you don't want to do that…"

"You're right, I did." His silky voice slid over her like black velvet. He lifted her hands, his thumbs brushing the heart of her palms as he scrutinized the napkins. "Which is your choice?"

"I…don't know." His touch sent heat traveling up both arms. She found his nearness very distracting and eased away, too aware of his clean masculine scent.

"Hmm." He moved in until his dusty boots nudged her button-up ones. He bent his head, the brim of his hat brushing her hair as he considered the linens.

She pressed back against the wall, aware that her breasts

were nearly touching his chest. The scent of his spicy shaving soap slid into her lungs. Oh, why did he have to stand so close? She tried to edge back, but he kept hold of her hands.

His hot blue gaze touched every inch of her body, as if he were mentally stripping off her clothes. The thought put a quiver in her belly. She didn't find that nearly as improper as she ought to have.

He shifted, making her realize she hadn't been this close to him since he had carried her to his bed to treat her gunshot wound.

His breath feathered against her temple and she looked up to find him staring at her mouth. Her heart started pounding hard and she couldn't look away. For an instant, she wondered if he might kiss her.

Instead, he released her hands, a wicked satisfaction in his eyes that said he knew exactly what she'd thought.

He straightened, indicating the napkin with the lace. "How about this one? It's almost as pretty as you are, sugar."

Sugar? She narrowed her eyes at him. "Good choice."

"Where's your little book? Don't you want to write that down?"

"I'm sure I'll remember." She turned in a whirl of skirts and started for the hotel.

"In about an hour, I'll be over at the jail."

"All right."

"Then I plan to stop in at The Pearl for some pie."

"There's no need to account to me for your whereabouts."

"I reckon you might need me. To help make a decision."

"Thank you," she said brightly.

"I'll be back at the hotel by dark. In case we need to decide anything else," he added with emphasis.

"Very good," she muttered. The devil. He was on to her.

He laughed and she fought against the frustration burning through her.

Foot! It appeared she could forget about getting Russ Baldwin out of her way.

Chapter Five

⸻❦⸻

Russ had come close to kissing Lydia out there beside Ef's, and he wasn't near as blistered up about it as he should have been. The fact of the matter was he was feeling more regret over not kissing her than aggravation over wanting to.

A few hours later, he finally admitted that to himself which really blistered him up good.

The liquor was working its way out of his system and his head wasn't pounding as hard as it had been that morning when Lydia had come to his office. Sadly, the only other bright spot in his day so far had been her hunting him down with her nonsensical questions.

It had taken him a bit to figure out she was trying to maneuver him into turning over the running of the hotel to her. Russ didn't like being maneuvered—it dredged up memories of how neatly he'd been maneuvered by Amy—but once he had realized what Lydia was up to, he'd had fun giving it right back to her.

It had been a while since he had enjoyed a woman's company that much without a mattress. If she knew how funny he found her efforts at manipulation, she'd be madder than a wet hen.

Just thinking about the controlled frustration in her voice made him chuckle. She'd nearly had apoplexy when he offered to put axle grease on the sconce, but the best had been when he had asserted she just wanted to spend time with him. She'd been fit to be tied over that one.

Russ grinned just thinking about it. She'd blushed a pretty shade of pink and even though he knew it was from anger, it made him wonder if she blushed that pretty all over for other reasons. He wanted to find out, which was just a plumb bad idea.

Hell, breathing in her lavender and woman scent at Ef's had left Russ's body aching and half-primed the rest of the day, which boiled his water all over again.

Still, just because he wanted her didn't mean he had to do anything about it. Russ could only imagine what Lydia might try if she figured out he fancied her.

What he needed to do was get his mind off her. Off her pretty mouth, off that rosebud skin he wanted to taste, those full breasts he wanted to touch.

He would do better to set his mind to figuring out a way to get the money to pay off the loan. Thinking about the predicament the man's refusal to buy had put him in made Russ fume. What the hell was he supposed to do now?

He would continue to advertise for a buyer in the *Prairie Caller* and the *Abilene Reporter*, but he couldn't count on selling his interest too quickly. Most likely, there were others out there who didn't believe women belonged in business.

Last night, Russ had been cussing Julius up one side and down the other the whole time he'd been tipping the bottle at Pete Carter's saloon. He hadn't gotten that drunk since Pa's accident three months earlier. It was his fault Pa had nearly died and might never walk right. And it would be Russ's fault if the family lost the Triple B. He felt almost as helpless and guilty now as he had when he'd learned his father nearly bled to death before he was found.

Figuring out another way to get the money to pay off that loan wasn't all Russ had to worry about. The carpenter who had been hired to finish out the second and third floors had failed to show up two days earlier as they'd agreed. Something might have happened to delay the man, but there had been no word from him.

After leaving the blacksmith shop, Russ had stopped in at the telegraph office and had Tony Santos send a wire to the marshal in Abilene, asking if he knew of the man or knew if there had been any trouble.

In the meantime, Ef had agreed to help set up the last of the guest beds. Striding into the hotel, Russ tossed his hat on the registration desk and headed for the kitchen. Before he started work upstairs, he wanted a drink from the indoor pump and the last of Cora's peach pie.

Dragging a hand across his nape, he walked into the kitchen and found Ef lifting a large pot full of water onto a hook in the fireplace.

Naomi stood a few feet away, staring raptly at the black man's arms straining beneath his rough cotton shirt. She had covered her white shirtwaist and yellow skirt with a neat white apron. Her hair was pulled back in its usual bun, revealing a mix of wariness and interest on her dark, stunning features.

Ef turned back to the long counter next to the sink and hefted a second pot by the handle with both hands. Naomi hurried forward and swung out another hook from inside the fireplace. He hung the kettle there and turned to her.

"Thank you so much." Her drawl was quiet and as pronounced as Lydia's.

The blacksmith nodded, saying nothing, seeming rooted in place.

After a long moment, the woman looked down self-consciously. "I think that's everything."

Russ expected his friend to say something, but he didn't. Well, this just beat all. Sometimes Ef went with Russ or Matt to Abilene to visit the girls. Not once in all the years they'd been going had Russ ever seen his friend like this around a woman.

When the man just stood there, unable to stop admiring Naomi, Russ spoke up. "Miz Jones, Ef."

They both jumped as if he'd caught them in a compromising position. Naomi backed away and Ef looked almost apologetic.

"Miz Jones, I see you've met Ef Gerard, Whirlwind's blacksmith."

"Yes." She fiddled with a pocket on her apron, her gaze not meeting either man's.

"If you ever need anything and I'm not around, just lean out that door there." Russ pointed across the kitchen to the corner by the sink. "His shop is right there. All you have to do is holler and he'll be here quicker than you can bat your pretty eyes."

"Yes, ma'am," Ef said.

"Thank you. I'd best get back to work," Naomi said quietly, skirting Russ to walk out. "Goodbye."

"Goodbye." Ef stared after her with an arrested look on his face.

Amused, Russ ambled over to the sink. "I came in for some water and a piece of peach pie. You want to join me?"

"Yeah." Ef walked into the pantry and retrieved the dessert from the pie safe inside.

Grabbing a couple of tin cups, Russ pumped water into one. "Nice of you to help Miz Jones."

"She was trying to lift those pots by herself."

Russ had seen her do that very thing a few days ago so he knew she could, but he kept it to himself. "There's milk on ice down in the cellar."

"Water's fine." Ef set the pie plate on the table then found two forks in the drawer next to the sink.

After filling a cup for the other man, Russ joined him at the wide table that would be used mostly by the help.

They ate in silence for a minute, Russ savoring the burst of sweet fruit on his tongue.

Grinning, he slid a look at his friend. "Thought you weren't going to let the lady get a word in edgewise. Never seen you so talkative."

Flashing him a look, Ef shoveled a piece of pie in his mouth.

"Why don't you invite her to the Grand Opening?"

"I heard her and Miz Kent talking about Miz Jones doing the cooking that day."

"Well, ask her to dinner or something."

"You saw me," the other man said after washing down the dessert. "I couldn't get out more than two words."

"You just need to swap more than a howdy with her." Russ had seen the way Naomi had looked at his friend, and he didn't think Ef would have much trouble getting her to agree to spend time with him.

The black man glanced down at his homespun trousers and shirt. "A woman who looks like that ain't gonna give a man like me the time of day."

"What are you talkin' about?"

After a long moment, Ef said, "She's the most beautiful woman I've ever seen. She ain't gonna step out with a blacksmith who has rough hands and rough manners."

"Hey, there's nothing wrong with your manners. You never have any problems getting a girl in Abilene."

Ef glared. "That's 'cuz I pay *them*."

Russ chuckled. "You have your own business. Your reputation is good and solid."

Hope lit the man's dark eyes. "You think so?"

"Hell, yes. You're a good man, Ef. I trust you to have my back any day of the week." Russ swallowed another bite of pie. "You'll never know if you don't ask."

"I'll think about it."

"Don't let thinking be all you do about it."

Ef gave him a droll look and changed the subject. "Since that man from Chicago didn't buy your share of the hotel, what are you going to do now to get the money to pay off the loan? You either need something you can sell for a big sum or something that will bring in an income."

"Yeah, but what?"

"Dang if I know."

"I'll have to ponder it for a while."

The scuff of footsteps had Russ turning to see Miguel Santos, Tony's fourteen-year-old son, in the doorway. "Hey, Miguel."

"Hi, Russ. Hi, Ef. My pa sent me over with this wire. It's from the marshal in Abilene."

"Oh, good." Russ laid down his fork to take the message. "Hopefully the marshal knows why that carpenter has been held up."

"I'm supposed to wait and see if you want to reply," the boy said.

Russ nodded, gesturing at the pie tin. "Want the last of this pie?"

"Is it Miss Cora's peach pie?"

"Yep. Get you a fork over there." He pointed at the drawer. Russ read the note, barely aware of the boy returning to the table and cramming in the last bite of dessert. "Damn."

"What is it?" Ef asked.

"That carpenter's disappeared. And I'm not the only one he ran out on, either."

"What are you going to do?"

"There's no time to hire anyone else." He pinched the bridge of his nose, feeling swallowed up by worries for a moment. "I'll have to finish those rooms out myself. Our grand opening is in less than a week."

"If you didn't need money coming in right now, you could postpone the start of business."

Russ nodded soberly. It wasn't that he minded finishing the work upstairs, but he could've already been doing it if he'd known the lowlife carpenter wasn't going to show.

"I can help you some," Ef offered.

"Thanks. I'd appreciate any little bit."

Miguel jogged over to the sink and splashed water on his face and hands. "You want to send a reply, Russ?"

"Nah, just tell your pa thanks."

"All right." The boy left the way he'd come.

"At the smithy earlier, I heard some of your conversation with Miz Kent." There was a wicked glint in Ef's dark eyes. "You could hand the problem over to her."

Russ laughed. He wondered what she would think if he just shucked it off on her. The notion held appeal, but that wouldn't be right. He'd been the one to hire the carpenter so this problem was his to fix.

Besides, turning over the reins to her was exactly what she wanted and Russ just flat out wasn't going to give in to her. In fact, he wasn't even going to tell her.

Lydia was expecting two underground arrivals tonight. She had received a wire from her parents a week ago with an encoded message that said two parcels were en route, meaning she should expect two victims. She was going to do everything in her power to keep them from ending up dead like Minnie Dawkins. Starting with keeping Russ Baldwin upstairs until she learned from Naomi that the women were safely hidden away in the room behind the walk-in pantry.

Lydia had hoped her partner would be drunk again tonight or at least out of the hotel when the battered women showed up, but he was on the third floor, and from the sound of things, not going anywhere.

The *crack* and *thud* of hammers hitting wood had been steady for the last couple of hours. When she and Naomi had come back after supper at The Whirlwind Hotel, Russ had told Lydia there were some last-minute things to attend to. He must've been referring to whatever it was he was doing upstairs.

Once on the third floor landing, Lydia turned toward the rooms at the opposite end of the hall. The gaslights burned bright along the walls, giving off a sharp musty smell. Russ stood outside one of the guest rooms, holding a door in place while Ef screwed on a top hinge.

The white shirt Russ had worn earlier in the day was damp in places, down the middle of his strong back, around his collar. The fabric clung to him, lightweight enough to be almost transparent, revealing the deep tan of his back, the flex of sinew across muscles cut with definition. A funny feeling uncurled in her stomach.

He looked over his shoulder and the bold sweep of his gaze down her body told her he'd caught her staring. His blue eyes burned into hers.

Foot! She cleared her throat. "Hello."

"Miz Kent," Russ said.

"Ma'am." Ef peered around the door and smiled around a screw he held in his mouth.

"Did you need me for another decision?" Russ grinned before turning back to the wood panel.

Despite his orneriness, the wicked way his mouth hitched had her thinking about the kiss they'd come close to sharing earlier that day. Lydia swallowed hard. She'd told herself she was glad they hadn't, but ever since then, regret had pulled at her.

Regret? What a goose. The last thing she needed was Russ Baldwin kissing her. Or doing anything else physical. She had to keep their involvement limited to business. The operation was at risk enough with him being in the hotel, especially on nights like tonight when they were expecting secret guests.

Stepping closer, she caught the scent of pine and a hint of wood smoke drifting through the open windows. "Why are you hanging doors? I thought the carpenter from Abilene was going to do that."

"It's so close to our opening, I thought I'd give him a hand."

She frowned. "I never saw him come in."

"Hmm."

Ef suddenly seemed very interested in his boots.

"Did he eat supper?" Lydia asked.

"He didn't complain about missing it." Russ stepped halfway into the room, studying something intently on the other side.

Suspicion crept through her. "Is something wrong?"

He pulled slightly away from the door to look at her. "What makes you ask that?"

It occurred to her that Russ hadn't really answered any of her questions, just given statements which caused her to assume things.

"There's a problem with the hotel, isn't there?" she guessed. "What is it? The plumbing, the glass, the beds?"

She heard him curse under his breath, which only stirred her suspicion more. "Russ?"

"The carpenter's not gonna show," he muttered, meeting her gaze. Dammit. Russ told her how the man had welshed on their deal and others, as well.

Lydia's dark gaze shifted between him and the black man. "So, you and Ef are going to do the work?"

Russ nodded, bracing himself for what he knew was coming.

"If you'd allow me, I could take care of it, handle everything."

And there it was. What would it take to get her to be quiet about that? He bet he could shut her up if he backed her into the wall and kissed her. Which he wouldn't do because that would only bring him more grief.

"*I've* already handled it," he snapped, staring flatly at her.

Hurt darkened her eyes and her mouth tightened. He told himself to ignore her wounded look.

She fingered the watch over her bodice, drawing his gaze to her breasts.

He itched to touch her and felt like hitting himself in the head with a hammer. How could he want her? The woman riled him up faster than anyone he knew.

"If I might trouble you for a minute," she said coolly. "We need to talk about the Grand Opening."

If she held true to her pattern, she was going to be trouble for longer than a minute. "Talk away."

She hesitated. Did the man have to be so touchy about her offer? Lydia thought as she watched him close the door then swing it open. After an approving nod from Ef, both men moved across the room to the two empty window frames.

Lydia stepped inside, spying the narrow cut sheets of glass

against the wall. She remained silent as the two men carefully lifted the window and settled it in place. "Do you think we'll be ready by Saturday or should we postpone?"

"That gives me five days," Russ said. "These rooms will likely be finished and if they aren't, they'll be close. Let's stick with the original date."

She nodded, wrestling with her hurt over his snapping at her. And the realization she'd had earlier that if she hadn't asked questions about the carpenter, Russ never would've told her the man wasn't coming. "All right, then. I'll tell Mr. Prescott at the paper we don't need to change the advertisement."

Russ and Ef exchanged a look before Russ asked, "You haven't had any trouble with Quentin, have you?"

"Trouble?"

"He's a hard man. Can be mean, too."

"So far, there's been no problem." Though now that she thought about it, the wheelchair-bound man hadn't been nearly as friendly as the other people she'd met in Whirlwind.

Russ seemed satisfied with her answer. Since she hadn't seen Naomi yet, Lydia knew she had to stay up here and make sure the men didn't go downstairs.

"I thought we could begin the festivities at five that afternoon and serve samples from our menu."

"Is it too late to add something to the menu?"

"No." She dug her journal from her skirt pocket. "I imagine that will be an ongoing process. What would you like?"

"Possum pie."

"Possum pie!" Her pencil stopped midstroke as her gaze flew to his. "You're pullin' my leg."

"I wouldn't pull anything without your leave, Lydia."

The low timbre of his voice sent a jolt of sensation clear to her toes. Her breath caught, though she wasn't sure whether it was because of Russ's suggestive words or the glitter of frank male interest in his eyes. What was he about? Trying to put her off?

"If you or Naomi don't know how to make possum pie," he continued, "you can ask Pearl to make it."

"I think not." She wrinkled her nose in distaste, catching sight of his grin before he turned back to his task.

"Your idea about letting people sample the menu is good." He eyed the window critically as Ef leveled it. "Then what?"

"At seven, we can move the tables and open the dining room and lobby for dancing." She rubbed her injured arm, massaging the ache there. "Josie told me Cal and Jed Doyle are quite the musicians so I've asked them to play."

Russ and Ef nodded their agreement.

"And I hired Zoe Keeler as a maid today. Thank you for sending her over. I think she'll be a good worker."

"You can count on that with Zoe." Russ glanced at her. "Is your arm paining you?"

Lydia realized she was still kneading it and dropped her hand. "It's just sore from unpacking crates. The washbasins for the rooms were delivered and we also received our crockery and cutlery."

"Sounds like we're comin' right along then."

"Yes." Lydia wondered when their secret guests would arrive and hoped there hadn't been trouble.

"I'm glad you came up," Russ said. "There's an idea I wanted to talk to you about."

"Along the same lines as your possum pie?"

One corner of his mouth hitched up in a grin. "Better."

"That's…hard to imagine," she said wryly.

He cast a quick unreadable glance at Ef. "Because the deal with Mr. Julius fell through, I need a way to bring in some money. Even though there might be other buyers interested, they could change their minds just as Mr. Julius did."

"True."

He dragged an arm across his perspiring forehead, his sleeve coming away damp. "The solution needs to be something that doesn't take too long to get going."

She nodded, her gaze roving over the wide shelf of his shoulders, the hard belly hinted at beneath his shirt. The enticing scents of man and pine and the outdoors slid into her lungs.

The four-button placket of his shirt was open, revealing a tuft of dark chest hair. She tracked a trickle of sweat down his strong neck to the hollow of his throat. Why did that make her stomach clench?

"I want to open a gambling room."

"A gambling room?" She stilled. "Here? In the hotel?"

"Yes. There's plenty of space downstairs to accommodate one. We wouldn't need any cash to start, only cards and dice."

"And some tables," Ef added.

As if there weren't enough risk to her operation already in having to get around Russ and the hotel staff. "No, I don't think so!"

"Why the hell not?" He scowled. "It's the perfect plan."

"Perfect for you, you mean," she retorted.

"Well, yeah." He folded his arms, staring her down.

Her thoughts raced past the panic his announcement had sent through her. She knew he needed the money. She wasn't unsympathetic, but a gambling room?

Lydia softened her voice. "Russ, that would mean men coming and going into the late hours."

"And spending money."

"Naomi and I live here."

"I'd split the take with you. It's half your hotel, too."

"That's not what I meant."

"Then what are you getting at?" he growled, his biceps flexing beneath his shirt. "Spit it out."

"Two unmarried women living in a hotel with men stopping by frequently and often after dark? Our reputations would be ruined."

"Oh, hell, they aren't going to come up to your rooms."

"That's not the point and besides, you can't know that."

He unfolded his arms and took a step toward her. "Listen, my sale to Julius already went bust because of—"

"Russ," Ef interrupted quickly. "Miz Kent's right. It would look bad. People could get the wrong impression real easy."

Lydia was a little surprised his friend agreed with her. Russ dragged a hand down his handsome face and her heart twisted at the fatigue and frustration there. She wanted to help him, but she couldn't agree to this suggestion. Such an enterprise would threaten everything she and Naomi were working so hard to keep secret.

"I'm sorry," she started, feeling like a shrew. "I know you need the money. It's not that I don't understand."

He waved her off. "You're right. There's your reputation to consider, and Miz Jones's, too. That didn't cross my mind."

"Maybe together we can come up with an idea."

"No." He stiffened. "This is my problem. I'll figure out how to handle it."

He sounded offended, which hadn't been her intention. Couldn't the man accept her help for anything at all? "Russ, I—"

The heavy thud of boots echoing up the stairs had her pivoting. She knew that wasn't Naomi.

It was the sheriff, she realized, as Davis Lee Holt reached the landing. Lydia choked back a flutter of panic. She hadn't considered someone coming upstairs, had thought only about keeping Russ and Ef from going downstairs. Foot!

The tall dark-haired lawman swept off his hat as his long-legged stride closed the distance between them. Shadows danced around him as he passed the burning gaslights. "Miz Kent, how are you tonight?"

"Fine, Sheriff. And yourself?"

"No complaints. I think Miz Jones might be looking for you downstairs."

Hopefully that meant the women had arrived. "I should go down then."

"Would you mind waiting a minute?" he asked. "I found something in that dead man's saddlebags and I need to talk to you and Russ about it."

Ef moved toward the door. "I'll step out."

"There's no need," Russ said. "Unless Lydia has a problem with you staying."

"Not at all." Until she knew why Naomi was looking for her, she needed to keep both men upstairs.

The black man shrugged his big shoulders and returned to sanding the window frame.

Davis Lee reached into the back pocket of his brown trousers. "Since we buried Mr. and Mrs. Dawkins, I've been trying to find something to tell me if the woman was deliberately headed to Whirlwind or just stopping where she thought she had the least chance of being found. Their belongings have been locked up over at the jail and since no one's claimed them, I went through Dawkins's saddlebag. I found a letter."

Apprehension slithered up Lydia's spine. Touching her pinned-on watch, she struggled to keep her features blank. "A letter to whom?"

"A letter to Mr. Dawkins from a private investigator. Looks

like the missus was being tracked and had been for quite some time."

"So, our assumption that she was trying to escape her husband was right?" Russ asked, his eyes narrowing.

Davis Lee nodded. "And from the bruises we found on her, I think it's a safe bet to say the man was beating her."

Lydia winced, remembering the woman's bruised and bloodied face, her battered body. She could easily recall the same image of her sister. "Was there anything else in the letter?"

"Just a list of the places where the private detective had followed her. Looks like they started from Alabama."

"Hmm." Lydia's nerves wound tight. Had the private detective known The Fontaine was a stop on the underground network? If he had, had he put anything about it in the letter? Surely Davis Lee would've said so by now, but that didn't ease the worry churning in her stomach.

"I'll contact the law in some of these towns," the sheriff said. "And see what I can find out."

No! It took all Lydia had not to scream it out. If she protested, Russ wouldn't be the only one giving her those speculative looks when he thought she wasn't aware.

When the sheriff glanced her way, she nodded. "All right."

"I'll let y'all know when I get more information."

"Thanks, Davis Lee," Russ said tiredly as his friend strode to the landing.

"Yes, thank you." Lydia hoped she sounded sincere. She certainly didn't feel it.

As the sheriff started down the stairs, she heard him say, "Good evenin', Miz Jones. Nice to see you."

Naomi murmured something in return, and Lydia felt some of the tension across her chest ease. Her friend's coming to find her probably meant their guests were safely hidden now.

Lydia could go back down with the other woman and maybe stop thinking about Russ and his stubborn self.

Instead of waiting at the top of the stairs as Lydia expected, Naomi came toward her. She was surprised. Her friend typically kept her distance from men.

She stopped beside Lydia, smiling shyly.

"Evenin', Miz Jones," Russ said.

Ef made his way across the guest room toward them. "Ma'am."

"Hello." She took in the new door and windows. "This is fine work. Did the two of you do this?"

"We did," Ef said hoarsely.

Naomi was speaking to both men, but Lydia noticed she was looking only at Ef. He was looking at her, too. As though he couldn't quite believe she was there. He appeared... smitten.

Lydia bit back a smile, happening to catch Russ's eye. He raised a brow, letting her know he also thought there might be something between Naomi and the blacksmith.

For a long moment, Lydia found herself unable to look away from his deep blue eyes. She finally forced her attention from him and stepped back. "I'll leave you men to your work."

"I'll come with you." Naomi glanced at Ef. "Good night."

"'Night, ladies," Russ said.

"Good night," Ef murmured.

Lydia could feel both men's gazes as she and Naomi walked away. She had another worry now—Russ filling in for the carpenter.

A worker coming into the hotel for a temporary job probably wouldn't notice anything out of the ordinary, but her partner would.

Lydia was torn between being grateful he could do the

work and being nervous for the same reason. With him in the hotel even more, she couldn't do anything that might cause him to pay extra attention to her. Couldn't keep pushing him to let her take over complete management of the hotel. She and Naomi would have to be more careful than ever.

Chapter Six

Over the next few days, Lydia kept as far from Russ as possible. With so much to do before the opening, it wasn't difficult and she saw him only in passing.

Four nights after their conversation concerning the carpenter and learning about the letter the sheriff had found in Reggie Dawkins's saddlebag, Lydia crept down the stairs from her rooms. According to the tall grandfather clock next to the registration desk, it was just after midnight. Though she'd been in bed for a couple of hours, she'd been unable to sleep. They weren't expecting any new arrivals tonight, but the air was heavy, as if a storm were coming. If so, the quilt they used as a message to any arriving abuse victims should be taken off the clothesline.

She had waited until she no longer heard Russ working down the hall from her rooms. Picking up the skirt of her brocade wrapper, she moved quietly to the first floor without the aid of a candle or lamp.

The hotel was silent. Shifting bands of moonlight coming in through the bank of narrow windows on either side of the front door allowed plenty of light for her to make her way down the stairs.

She took special care to be quiet. Naomi had told her she had almost been caught by Davis Lee four nights earlier when she had sneaked their secret guests into The Fontaine.

Lydia's arm ached from days of unpacking crates of crockery and glassware, but her wound was healing, thanks to Catherine Blue's care. The nurse's advice was to keep it bandaged for at least another five days and continue to change the dressing twice daily.

Stepping out the back door of the hotel, Lydia made her way across the wagon-rutted patches of grass to the separate building about thirty yards away that housed the laundry. Two long, thick clotheslines stretched down one side of the limestone structure, with the distance between them wide enough for at least two people to work side by side. The quilt, a cheery nine-patch pattern done in squares of yellow, blue and red, fluttered in the wind.

She automatically reached up for the covering with both hands and her injured arm jerked in agony. Inhaling sharply, she lowered it and held it close to her body, waiting for the pain to ebb before trying again.

Using only her good arm this time, she managed to slide the quilt from the line one-handed. She bunched it into the crook of her opposite elbow and started back into the hotel, her arm throbbing.

During dry weather, the quilt hung as a signal that the hotel was a safe place to stop. In the winter or when it rained, the quilt would be hung in the front window and a lit lantern would be placed outside behind the hotel.

Lydia set a lantern beside the door then went inside and locked up. This wide area off the dining room had been designated for storage. Three large mahogany wardrobes stood against the opposite wall.

She awkwardly folded the blanket as best she could and opened the wardrobe on the far end, storing the quilt on one of the sliding shelves inside where extra blankets were kept.

The dull ache in her arm persisted as she made her way to the kitchen. Their guests from the other night, a mother and her married daughter, had been sent to the next station the night after they had arrived at The Fontaine. Lydia had received a wire this afternoon from her father that contained the coded message saying to expect two "loads of potatoes" in the next day.

Anyone intercepting the message would think nothing of the hotel's kitchen receiving an order of potatoes. Only a few people knew the message actually referred to victims escaping an abusive situation. Because Lydia's time for the next twenty-four hours would be taken up with final preparations for the Grand Opening, she wanted to make sure tonight that everything was ready for the two new arrivals.

She took down the lantern hanging on the wall inside the pantry and lit it, carrying it downstairs to the somewhat cool room beyond that she had requested for more food storage. To her left were waist-high cabinets and along the back wall was a long cabinet where canned goods could be stocked. It also offered more hiding space if necessary.

Walking quietly to the dark corner between the two sets of cabinets, Lydia opened the nearest cupboard and lifted the lantern. Though she kept the flame low, the hazy amber light was enough to show the thick pallets Naomi had made and hidden inside the storage space. The air was cooler here than in the hotel, but situating their secret guests on the wall closest to the boiler room would keep them relatively warm.

Satisfied, Lydia stepped back into the pantry, her slippers scuffing lightly against the floor as she backed out and carefully closed the storage room door. She extinguished the lantern and returned it to its place, fanning away a wisp of dark smoke that gave off the faint bite of kerosene.

Her arm burned like blue blazes. As she walked through the dining room and into a strip of pale light coming from the lobby, she glanced down at the injured limb. At the same time, a single gaslight flared to life.

Startled, Lydia jerked to a stop, but not in time to avoid running into Russ. She teetered, grabbing for him so she wouldn't fall. "Oh!"

"Whoa." He gripped her upper arms to keep them both from losing their balance and she cried out at a fresh burst of agony.

He cursed and dropped his hands, moving one to steady her with a firm grip on the elbow of her uninjured arm. "Sorry about that. I didn't see you until it was too late. Are you all right?"

The painful pulsing slowly lessened. It took her a minute to find her breath. "Yes."

He looked her over, pausing at her left arm. "I hurt you. I didn't mean to."

She gave him a weak smile, her nerves jangling at his unexpected appearance. "I'm fine."

"No, you're not."

"It hurts, but—"

"It's bleeding." He angled her toward the white glow of gaslight just inside the door.

Concern shot through her as she eyed the spreading red stain on her plum brocade and she clamped her hand over it. She had to have torn open the wound when she reached for the quilt earlier. No wonder it hadn't stopped throbbing.

"Lydia."

She blinked, realizing he'd asked her a question. "I'm sorry?"

"Sit down and let me have a look at it."

"I can have Naomi do it."

He arched a brow. "You're going to wake her up at this hour to tend your arm when I already said I'd do it?"

"Oh." His even tone made her realize how silly and selfish it sounded. "All right, thank you."

As she chose a chair at the closest dining table, he went to the sideboard on the nearest wall that held a few bottles of choice liquor.

She tuned in to the sound of his movements and the muffled sounds of the night outside the hotel. He brought a small glass and a bottle of brandy to the table then poured a liberal amount of liquor.

The soft white gaslight illuminated the curiosity in his blue eyes as he looked at her. "What are you doing down here in the dark?"

She sipped her drink, struggling to level out her pulse. Lydia reassured herself that Russ didn't suspect anything. He couldn't. Tonight, there was nothing to suspect. "I came down to get a quilt off the clothesline."

"A quilt?"

"The wind is getting stronger. I thought there might be a storm and remembered a quilt was still on the line. I didn't want it to get wet."

He pulled up a chair beside her and lightly touched the hand keeping pressure on the wound. "Slide your arm out of your wrapper and let me have a look."

She remembered what had happened last time she'd done that. "Not if you're going to cut off my clothes—I mean, my sleeve like you did last time."

"I won't," he reassured her then ruined it by murmuring, "unless you ask real nice."

Drat the man. A flush heated her skin and she shakily lowered her hand. For all practical purposes, she was covered from head to toe, but the intensity in his blue eyes burned right through her wrapper and pale pink cotton nightgown.

Suddenly, she was very aware that all she had on were her nightclothes. She had thought he was in for the night or she never would've come downstairs half-dressed.

After she slipped her arm out of the wrapper, she held the garment close to her body with her free hand. Now that she could see the area and the fabric plastered to her skin, she was startled at the amount of blood. No wonder her arm was paining her. She'd thought the burning had only been muscle soreness due to all her unpacking and storing things for the hotel.

The sleeves of her nightdress were loose enough for Russ to carefully push the billowy fabric to her shoulder. As his slightly callused fingers trailed up her arm, a shiver worked through her.

She felt light-headed and wasn't sure if it was because of his nearness or the brandy. She shifted uneasily in her chair.

"Can you hold this so I can get a good look?"

She gathered the fabric in her opposite hand, inhaling the dark manly scent of him.

"How did you reopen your wound?"

"It must've happened when I was getting the quilt off the line. I reached with both hands."

"Where's the cloth you've been using for bandages?"

"Naomi tore a sheet in strips. They're in the wardrobe out there." She indicated the storage area off the dining room. "Where we keep the linens."

He disappeared and returned shortly with a handful of cloth strips. Placing them on the table, he then went to the kitchen and came back with a small bowl of water, a soft cloth, a tin of soap and a pair of scissors.

After cutting away the bandage, he gently began to clean the area. "I haven't seen this since the night you were shot. It was healing well until now."

His strong hands, dark against her pale skin, moved over her tender flesh just as cautiously as they had the night she'd been shot. It amazed her all over again how such a big man could be so gentle.

Her next sip of brandy had a pleasing warmth spreading through her chest. She knew the alcohol was working when she found herself studying Russ rather than being distracted by the discomfort in her arm.

When she'd literally run into him, she hadn't noticed the state of his dress, but she noticed now. The white shirt molded to his wide shoulders was untucked and sprinkled with small bits of wood dust. There was a spot of white paint on one knee of his dark trousers. They sleeked down powerful legs to brush the tops of big bare feet. Even barefoot, he looked big and formidable.

His touch was easy, but when he grazed a place on her upper arm, agony stabbed at her. She sucked in a breath.

He stilled. "Sorry. I'm being too rough."

"No, you're not. It's just tender there."

One of his large warm hands cradled her arm as he used his free hand to rinse the bloody cloth and start again. He nodded toward her brandy. "Drink up."

She raised the glass to her lips, trying to hide that he put her off balance.

"Have you been unpacking crates by yourself?"

"Naomi has helped when she can."

"If there are any more, come get me to do that or ask someone else."

"I'm just doing my part. It doesn't hurt me to unpack them."

He looked pointedly at her arm. "What do you call this?"

"I told you, I think I did that when I was pulling the quilt off the line."

His head was angled over the wound and Lydia's gaze traced the strong bronzed column of his nape, the thick ragged hair that needed a trim. If she bent her head, she could brush a kiss against his ear.

The thought drew her up short and she squirmed in her chair. What was she thinking? She couldn't be kissing his anything.

She had tried to stay away from him, but here they were, alone and half-dressed in the flickering shadows of the gaslight. The scent of clean male and night air wrapped around her. The careful way he handled her put a longing in Lydia's chest.

She couldn't seem to settle her nerves. Nerves that she told herself were caused by the chance Russ might become suspicious of her late-night activities and not by the man himself.

He stared at her newly bloodied wound, his jaw tight. "You shouldn't be straining your arm."

"We all need to pitch in. I'm not doing any more than you are."

"It's not my hide that was dug out by a lead slug. This is no time for you to be stubborn and try to take over everything."

His words had her frowning. "I'm not."

"Now, why do I find that hard to believe?"

"Well, what about you?" she demanded. "You're working yourself into the ground, burning the candle at both ends in an effort to finish by tomorrow."

She hadn't been to the rooms during the times he was there, but when he wasn't around, she had stopped by a couple of times. Lydia had every confidence the rooms would be finished by the Grand Opening the next day. "You've got more than enough on your plate."

He considered her for a long moment. "Guess I was wrong."

"You were justified. I've given you plenty of reason to think I was trying to take the reins."

"Still, I was on a cold trail and I'm sorry."

When he looked at her that way, so intently, her body went soft. She moved restlessly in her seat.

Finished washing the wound, he laid the wet cloth on the table. As he reached for a clean dry strip of fabric, she turned her head to look at her arm and her hair spilled over her shoulder. Before she could push it back, Russ lifted the silky mass out of the way. He curled one strand around his finger, rubbing it between his fingers.

Lydia went very still and her breathing shallowed. He finally released her hair. He wanted to sink both hands into that raven hair, bury his face in it, but he began to wrap her arm instead.

With her lavender scent teasing him, want throbbed in his veins. The ribbon sash of her wrapper had come loose, and he could see her robe and nightgown had slipped down past the wing of her collarbone. All he could see was the silky slope of the place where her neck met her shoulder, and he wanted to put his mouth there. His blood heated.

His gaze flicked over the collar of lace that fell to the beginning swells of her breasts. He fought the impulse to reach out and cup one.

Touching her was a bad idea and he knew it. It had been too damn long since he'd had a woman. That had to be why he was thinking about peeling Miz Lydia out of her nightclothes.

She hadn't paid him any mind since he'd refused her offer for help the other night. She was probably only sitting here now because the brandy had relaxed her guard.

He focused on redressing her wound. Her skin here was as silky and fine-grained as that of her face and neck.

She fidgeted in her chair, which she'd done several times. "You look like you've had a lot of practice with bandages."

More than he wanted, thanks to his father's accident. His jaw tightened as he said gruffly, "I changed plenty of dressings after Pa was injured."

"What happened to him? You've never said."

There was a reason for that. Russ didn't cotton to telling anyone, especially Lydia, that J.T. had nearly died because of him. "He had an accident while stringing fence and his leg was impaled on a tree branch sticking out of the ground."

"Oh, my lands. It sounds awful."

"He almost bled to death." Russ didn't know why he was telling her anything about it. "We were lucky he didn't."

It was *all* luck and no thanks to Russ. When he tied off her bandage, he rubbed his thumb lightly over the area.

Lydia thought she could feel his touch through the dressing, which was ridiculous. She should get up and leave right now, but her legs wouldn't move. She couldn't seem to move anything. She wanted to lean into him, for just a moment.

Rattled, she fought the urge to squirm. "The wind is starting to blow something awful out there. Do you think it will rain tomorrow?"

"Hard to say. The weather could change in five minutes."

She stared in arrested silence as his thumb continued making small circles on the neat binding. Finally, he seemed to realize what he was doing and stopped, his gaze going to her mouth.

Oh, Lord! Lydia's pulse hitched. She nervously licked her lips and heat flared in his eyes.

He wanted to kiss her. The desire was plain in his eyes and set off a flutter of anticipation low in her belly.

As the silence pulsed between them, her breasts grew heavy and her nipples tightened beneath his regard. When his breath feathered across her lips, she realized only inches separated them and she jerked herself to attention.

She had to get away from him. Whether it was due to the brandy or the man, she felt as though she were slowly unraveling.

Unsteady on her feet, she rose and carefully slid her arm back into her wrapper. "I'd best turn in."

He stood, too, towering over her.

She jerked the belt tight. "Thanks for taking care of me."

"Happy to do it."

She managed to move calmly, deliberately to the doorway, but she really wanted to run. "Good night."

"Good night." His husky voice slid over her like dark velvet.

She felt his gaze following her, could still feel his touch. All the distance she had managed to put between them the last few days had dissolved in an instant when he had insisted on redressing her wound. And Lydia knew why.

She wanted him. Inwardly, she groaned. That was not good. The only thing worse would be if he found out.

Russ had known he wouldn't be able to get Lydia out of his head the night before and he'd been right. From the moment he'd startled her coming out of the kitchen, she'd been jittery, and he didn't think it was because he'd seen her in her nightclothes.

That was definitely one reason *he* was twitchy. All night long, he'd thought about her in her nightclothes, out of her nightclothes. Tangled sheets. Damp skin. And he kept remembering the feel of her thick cloud of raven hair. He wanted to put his hands in it again, his face, feel it slide over his bare flesh.

It wasn't just his body she had on low simmer. It was his mind, too. When he noticed her wound had reopened, he'd been stunned by an overwhelming need to take care of her. Russ hadn't wanted to take care of her or sit so close to her or touch her petal-smooth skin, but he had felt compelled to.

She had told him she was downstairs the night before because she was bringing in a quilt.

It wasn't her answer he found odd. It was the fact that she'd been coming from the kitchen rather than the back of the hotel. She could've been getting something from the kitchen, but she'd had nothing with her. And she'd been so skittish that he had wondered later if she might have been meeting someone. A man.

The thought had him clenching his jaw hard. He hadn't noticed her spending time with any one man since she had arrived in Whirlwind, but he supposed she could be keeping it quiet.

He didn't know why he cared if she had been meeting a man. She was the burr under his saddle right now, and it wasn't only because she had rejected his idea for a gambling room. He couldn't get her out of his mind and it was damn infuriating.

She had been flustered the night before and after Russ had almost kissed her, his calm, poised business partner had been even more flustered.

Every self-preserving instinct he had was screaming at him to spend as little time with her as possible, so that's what he planned to do.

By five o'clock that afternoon, he had washed up, shaved and put on his best suit. As he locked his office, he tried to turn his mind to more pressing matters than wondering why he hadn't seen Lydia all day.

He started toward the front doors. Except for a small amount of painting that remained to be done on the third floor, The Fontaine was finished. He was anxious to open to the public what he and Lydia hoped everyone would like. Russ figured the restlessness churning inside him was about the hotel. Until he saw her.

She glided down the stairs, looking like a vision. His chest went tight. Her gown of deep red was made from velvet and some stiff material that rustled slightly when she moved. The red bodice was cut low across her full breasts, so low he felt a jolt of anticipation that she might fall out of it.

His hands actually ached to get on her. In the next breath, he wanted to cover her up so no other man could see what he was seeing. Elbow-length sleeves hid the bandage on her arm and the bodice gloved her torso before flaring out slightly over her hips and the bustle in the back. Draped to one side, the red-striped skirt showed the solid red underskirt beneath.

Against the vibrant ruby of the dress, her skin glowed like pearls. Her upswept hair bared her dainty nape and showed off a pair of dangling diamond earrings. The chignon of soft curls on top of her head was wound intricately with a red and silver ribbon. Russ wanted to rip out every pin holding the silky raven mass in place.

They had to pass the next few hours together so he couldn't exactly avoid her this evening. Still, he didn't have to spend every minute with her.

As he got closer to her, he was able to breathe, but that didn't mean he could string together more than two words.

By the time she joined him at the now-open front doors of The Fontaine to begin greeting their guests, he had managed to find his tongue. And all he could think about doing with it was running it over every inch of her body, especially the luscious flesh swelling above her bodice.

Russ knew he wouldn't be the only man thinking such things once the others got a look at her and that didn't sit well.

She glanced at him, excitement sparkling in her eyes. "Hello."

"Hello." His gaze traveled from the top of her silky hair to the tips of her matching red slippers. "You look mighty fancy."

"It's a special day."

"You being in that dress makes it special for everybody," he murmured.

Surprise flared in her eyes and a slight flush tinged her cheeks. "Thank you. You look very nice, too."

She smiled, but beneath her outward poise, Russ felt a hum of anxiety. It was in him, too. Especially when he drew in a deep breath of her subtle lavender scent. "How's the arm?"

"Better."

"Does it still pain you? Did you do any more unpacking today?"

"No. And it doesn't hurt nearly as badly as it did last night."

"Good."

"Thanks again for fixing me up."

He nodded, studying her face carefully, looking for a sign of her nervousness from the night before. While he didn't see any unease, he did sense a tension that reminded him of the moment when he'd thought about kissing her. He wondered if she was curious as to why he hadn't. He sure was, because if he'd had a reason, it was gone now.

Before he could dig that hole deeper in his mind, Catherine and Jericho Blue arrived. The nurse who had tended Lydia's gunshot wound introduced her tall, dark-haired husband then asked after the injury. As Lydia explained to the expectant woman what had happened last night, Russ exchanged a few words with the former Texas Ranger before the couple moved on, making room for Jake Ross and his family.

Turning to Lydia, Russ introduced the rancher and his wife of less than a month, Emma, who held her year-old half sister.

Russ was used to Emma's blond hair now, but when she had first arrived in Whirlwind back in August, her hair had been dyed and was nearly as dark as his. That had been part of a disguise she'd used to try and hide the infant from Emma's abusive stepfather.

Jake's uncle Ike, and cousin Georgia, visited with Lydia then Russ. He overheard Bram, Jake's brother, ask Lydia to save him a dance later. She agreed, then encouraged everyone to look around the hotel, have some champagne and sample the menu.

She and Russ greeted people for close to an hour, including the man from Abilene from whom Lydia had bought their glass for the third floor.

As Russ and Lydia made sure the guests were serving themselves from the sideboards in the dining room and touring the hotel, the Doyle brothers began to play in the lobby. With Cal on the mouth harp and Jed on his fiddle, they started off the dancing with a reel to the music of "Durang's Hornpipe."

The dining tables and chairs had been moved against the far wall and the crowd spilled over from the dining room for dancing and mingling.

Several times Russ saw Naomi refilling food trays, dipping punch or pouring champagne. Ef stayed close to her, helping carry this or that. Russ had a feeling his friend's days at the bawdy houses in Abilene might be over.

He found himself watching Lydia as she whirled around the brightly lit room with different men. Color tinged her cheeks and her smile never wavered. Russ couldn't take his eyes off her, but she didn't look at him once.

As the evening wore on, he danced with Zoe Keeler and all four of Jericho's sisters as well as the man's mother. During that time, Lydia danced with Matt, then Bram, then Matt, then Mitchell Orr, who was Charlie Haskell's nephew. Then she was back with Bram.

Russ also partnered some of the older women around the floor, including Cora Wilkes. The tall feisty widow had already foregone a few dances to chat with Pa, who couldn't dance because he was still confined to his wheelchair.

Watching J.T., the old familiar guilt twisted inside Russ. Then quick as lightning, the emotion edged into something hot and reckless when he saw Lydia *again* change partners from Bram to Matt. Russ knew his brother, knew how he operated with women because he and Russ operated much the same way. Lydia didn't need to be finding that out firsthand, and she sure as hell didn't need to be learning it from Matt.

Observing them from the corner by his office, Russ's muscles coiled tight. His brother and Bram seemed to be engaged in a contest to see who could claim the most dances with her. Russ didn't like either of them spending so much time with his business partner so he asked her for the next dance.

Giving the excuse that she needed to check things in the kitchen, she said no. The next time he asked, she begged off claiming her feet hurt and saying she wanted to rest. Both Bram and Matt "rested" with her, each bringing her a glass of champagne.

During one song, she didn't dance at all. She stood beside Quentin Prescott's wheelchair, drinking more of the bubbly liquor and talking to the former railroad worker who now set type for the *Prairie Caller*. She was probably only answering Quentin's questions for the newspaper, but Russ didn't like that, either. She was talking to everyone except him.

He was supposed to be avoiding her. He *was* avoiding her. So why couldn't he stop looking at her?

Eyes narrowed, Russ watched his brother's hand move

lower to the small of her back. Without missing a step, Lydia guided Matt's hand to a more appropriate place. Russ thought about cutting in, but as the song changed to the fast-paced "Buffalo Gals," Bram swept her out of Matt's arms.

Jake Ross walked up beside Russ. "Looks like your brother's taken a shine to your business partner."

"Looks like your brother has, too," Russ said drily as he finished off another glass of champagne.

Jake chuckled. "This ought to be interesting."

It was downright aggravatin', but Russ didn't say so. He hadn't felt territorial over a woman since Amy. Just the thought of how that had turned out should've been enough to rein in the damn urge to stake a claim on another woman, but it didn't.

After another glass of champagne, he danced with Josie then Catherine, then Susannah Holt. The blonde woman, who was married to Davis Lee's brother, had taught Russ to dance a couple of years ago when she had arrived in Whirlwind. Several men had attended the charm school she ran out of Cora's house.

Despite his enjoyable conversation with Susannah, Russ couldn't keep his attention from Lydia. She was with Bram. Again.

The dark-haired rancher dipped his head and said something that had her smiling. The smile that made Russ's world go end over end.

He didn't know if Lydia's smile tripped Bram up the way it did him and he didn't care. She didn't need to be smiling that way at anyone else.

That was when he finally admitted he didn't want to avoid her at all. And he wasn't going to.

Chapter Seven

It was another twenty minutes before the musicians stopped for a break. Russ took advantage of the lull in the program and said a few words to the crowd then thanked everyone for coming. As Davis Lee made a toast, Lydia, standing across the lobby in the wide archway of the dining room, murmured agreement and raised a glass of champagne along with the others. Russ wondered how much liquor she'd had. He had lost count of the number of glasses he'd drunk.

When he saw her glance surreptitiously over her shoulder then duck into the dining room, suspicion shot through him. She had done that a couple of times this evening. What was she up to? Only one way to find out. He excused himself from his conversation with Jake.

He wove his way through the crowd, speaking to people as he went, but not slowing down. Several people were conversing in the dark-paneled dining room as he came to a stop in the kitchen doorway.

Lydia stood at the table, cutting a piece of pecan pie. Pie. The reason she had sneaked in here was because she was hungry, not because she was doing anything clandestine. Russ mentally smacked himself. What had happened before with Amy had made him paranoid. It didn't help that he'd had so much champagne.

Fading gold daylight from the window across the room outlined her profile. She lifted the fork to her mouth.

Russ braced one shoulder against the doorjamb. "That looks good."

She made a choking sound. Her silverware clattered to the table as she jerked toward him, pressing one hand to her chest. "You scared the fire out of me!"

"Sorry." He folded his arms and grinned.

The tip of her little finger rested on the swell of one breast and Russ wanted to touch her there, find out if her skin felt as satiny as it looked.

"I had to eat something." Dark eyes sparkling, she leaned toward him and said conspiratorially, "That champagne was goin' straight to my head."

Her honeyed drawl trailed over his body, sending a surge of hot hard want through him.

Turning back to pick up her fork, she slanted him a look from under her thick black lashes. "Want some?"

He damn sure did and he didn't mean pie. His gaze lowered from her face to her breasts. "What else ya got?"

At his suggestive tone, her eyes narrowed as she said sweetly, "Possum pie. It's at Pearl's."

He chuckled. "How do you think things are going out there?"

"Wonderfully!" She swallowed a small bite of dessert. "Don't you?"

"Yes," he murmured. It wasn't the lingering aroma of cooked meats and desserts that had his mouth watering. It was her.

Knowing she'd had a little too much to drink put all kinds of ideas in his head. "Why won't you dance with me?"

She blinked. "I don't think it's a good idea."

"Why not?"

"We're business partners." She daintily brushed a crumb from the corner of her lips. "Someone might get the wrong idea."

They sure would if they saw the avid way she was staring at his mouth right now. Tension coiled inside him.

The champagne had lowered her inhibitions. Hell, it had done the same to him or he wouldn't have followed her in here. He wouldn't be within five yards of her, let alone thinking about getting even closer.

A gentleman wouldn't take advantage. A gentleman would leave, but Russ couldn't make himself do it. Not when she was *still* looking at his mouth. No, he wasn't going anywhere.

He pushed away from the door and walked toward her, liking the way she went still as he approached. "Is that the only reason? Because someone might draw the wrong conclusion?"

She hesitated. "Yes."

He wondered if she were aware that she was backing farther into the kitchen. And that he was matching her steps. He drew in a deep breath of lavender and woman. "Nobody's watching us now."

"You want to dance in here?"

"Why not?"

She laughed. "There's no music."

Right then, strains of "The Blue Danube Waltz" drifted into the room. He grinned. "There is now."

He noted the rapid flutter of her pulse in her throat. She licked her lips nervously and his body went tight.

"Well, I—"

"My pleasure, Miz Kent." In one fluid motion, he snagged her hand and pulled her to him, curling an arm around her waist.

His touch sent a shiver through her. Lydia knew she

shouldn't be dancing with Russ, but she couldn't make herself pull away. The man smelled delicious, of spice and male.

She had been watching him all evening just as he'd been watching her. And drat it all, she'd dreamed about him the night before. About those big hands caressing her body.

He guided her smoothly around the kitchen, keeping perfect time with the song. Neither of them spoke. Russ's gaze stayed on her face, but Lydia was suddenly aware of her very exposed cleavage and the brush of his white shirt against her skin. A muscle twitch in his jaw.

The touch of her skirts against his trousers, the steel-hard arms around her, the solid brawny chest had her wanting to melt into him. Which would be the worst thing she could do.

She was on edge. His heavy-lidded gaze made her want to confess everything to him—about her, about the operation. That was just silly. Her mind skipped around for something to say.

"Bram told me Catherine met Jericho when he showed up at her house shot and near dead."

Russ stiffened. "Bram. You've danced half the night with him."

She tilted her head. Russ sounded as though it bothered him. Well, *he* bothered her. Yes, she had spent a lot of time with Bram, mainly in an effort to keep her attention off the devil in front of her.

It hadn't worked, regardless of whether she'd been with Bram or Matt or any other man. Lydia had been as aware of her business partner then as she was now. One of his hands huge and hot in hers, the other burning at her waist.

He pulled her closer, close enough that she could feel the hard muscle of his thigh through her skirts. It triggered another flurry of nerves.

"Bram said that after Catherine nursed Jericho back to

health, she learned he'd really come there to arrest her brother. That he had been spying on Andrew the whole time he was recovering. Is that really what happened?"

"Yes," Russ said tightly. "That's all true."

"Didn't she feel betrayed?"

"I reckon so. Wouldn't you? He lied to her for a long time."

She considered the circumstances for a moment. "I guess it *was* lying."

He snorted. "What would you call it?"

They were moving in smaller circles now. As they completed another turn, she said, "Since they're married now, it appears she forgave him."

"The woman's a saint." Russ eased Lydia an inch nearer, his hold firm. "Jericho was spying on her and her brother right under her nose. It would've taken me a while to forgive someone who was using me or my home to hide what they were really doing."

The way Lydia was using the hotel for abuse victims. Russ had put his life on the line for her and other women he knew nothing about when he had killed Reggie Dawkins. Lydia wanted to tell him the truth, confess to him that she was using the hotel for a secret cause and tell him why. But she couldn't.

Her hand tightened on the solid muscle of his shoulder. "Didn't Jericho think Catherine's brother was involved with an outlaw gang?"

"The McDougals, yes."

With every sweep of her skirts against his legs, Lydia felt more helpless to keep her body from straining toward his. "So, he stayed quiet because he was trying to catch the outlaws. He didn't want to tip his hand."

"He lied."

"You hold it against him even though he did it for a worthy cause?" She studied him carefully.

He had thought about Catherine and Jericho's situation more than once. "He did save people's lives. Some people, on the other hand, would lie because they were trying to hide the truth."

She tilted her head. "That sounds like the voice of experience."

Russ's past with Amy sometimes reared up when he least expected it, but his reaction wasn't a knee-jerk response. He splayed his hand wide on the small of Lydia's back, drawing her in even more. "Maybe it's just smarts."

They were chest to chest now, her breasts plumping up between them. Too close for propriety, Lydia knew, but she couldn't make herself step back. Even when he drew back and slowly ran a frank male look over her entire body.

"Beautiful." He lifted a hand, touching her dangling diamond earrings, but he was looking at her face.

Lydia could barely breathe. "They were my sister's."

The pad of his callused thumb grazed a sensitive spot below her ear as he moved his hand back to her waist. A delicious heat pooled low in her belly.

They had stopped moving. She didn't know if she had done it or Russ. Feeling the pantry door at her back, Lydia tried to get past his hypnotizing effect on her. She suddenly felt light-headed. "My head is spinnin'."

"Mine, too," he murmured.

The dark predatory look on his face had her nipples tightening. This man was dangerous. She tugged at her hand and he let it slip free. "Are you satisfied now?"

"No." His deep voice rumbled over her as his gaze lowered to her breasts. "I'm nowhere near having my fill."

Oh, lands! "What more could you possibly want?"

It was the wrong thing to ask. She knew it as soon as the

words left her mouth. She pressed back against the door, her pulse scrambling when he leaned slightly toward her.

His blue eyes glittered and the raw hunger on his face made it plain that he wanted *her*. He wanted to kiss her.

And she was afraid she couldn't—wouldn't—stop him. Her voice shook. "Don't. Don't look at me like that."

"Like what?" His muscular chest was an inch from hers, his legs spread wide to cage her in.

She knew she should push him away, duck around him, but she was rooted to the spot, trapped between a hard man and a hard door.

She could barely hear over the thundering of her heart. "You're looking at me like you want to—"

"Kiss you?"

Swallowing hard, she nodded.

His voice lowered as he slicked a thumb across her lower lip. "Afraid you'll like it?"

"Yes," she whispered.

Russ was done waiting. He settled his mouth on hers.

It was no soft exploratory kiss. It was hot and impatient and deep. He told himself to rein it in, but when she made a sound in the back of her throat, it kicked off something inside him.

His hands spread wide on her back and he pressed hard against her as need swirled savagely inside him. Her mouth opened and she let him in all the way, her tongue stroking his. Russ ached clear to his toes.

His thigh slipped between hers. He drew in a sharp breath, trying to control the desire raging through him. She tasted like hot sweet flowers. Her breasts flattened against him and Russ wanted to touch her there so badly his hands hurt.

She was gripping the lapels of his suit coat then it registered her hands were in his hair, fingers flexing against his scalp. He lifted his head. Breathing rough and fast, he realized he was holding her up off the ground.

Every inch of her clung to every inch of him. She sighed and opened her eyes. "Mercy."

At the dazed look there, he kissed her again, slower this time, softer, savoring the heated honey of her mouth.

She melted into him, her body curving to his like a shadow. Hell, this woman went to his head faster than Amy ever had.

Dragging his lips from Lydia's, he nuzzled her jaw, tipped her head back so he could kiss and lave his way down the elegant line of her throat. Her skin was as smooth as water under his tongue. He was headed for the deep fragrant valley between her breasts when she wiggled, pressing against his erection.

"Russ."

The breathlessness of her voice had him pulling back. She trembled against him, flushed, her lips wet from his, her breasts quivering. With one nudge, he could move that red velvet and bare her sweet flesh, have her in his mouth.

"What are you doing to me?" she asked shakily.

"What I've been wantin' to do for a long time."

She'd never been kissed like that in her life. And she didn't care one whit about anything except doing it again.

Russ let her slide down his body until her feet touched the ground. His blue eyes blazed as he bent for her mouth again. Lydia tipped her face to his, operating now on sensation, not sense.

He brushed his lips against hers then froze, saying in a low husky voice, "We've got company. Ef."

Completely absorbed in the man who held her, Lydia hadn't heard a thing. The black man's voice penetrated then.

She stiffened, her hands sliding from Russ's neck to his shoulders to push him away. She heard Ef and Naomi direct people away from the doorway.

Lydia's face burned. Hopefully, the only witnesses to the liberties she'd allowed were her friend and a man who Lydia believed wouldn't tell anyone. Still, she was mortified and shocked at herself. She had never lost herself in a kiss before, not even Wade's.

Russ's face was taut with desire, color streaking his cheekbones. "Sugar, that was worth at least five dances."

Oh, lands. He turned and strolled out as if they hadn't just…just devoured each other. The only way she was able to stand without his support was by flattening her hands against the door behind her.

As he disappeared from sight, Ef and Naomi glanced at her over their shoulders, both looking concerned. Lydia stood there, her face burning, unable to make her legs work for a long moment.

Overwhelmed, startled by her reaction to Russ, she opened the pantry door with shaking hands and stepped inside as if looking for something.

She could still feel the press of his mouth against hers, faintly taste the champagne from his tongue. Why had she kissed him? Why had she let *him* kiss *her?* There was no hiding now that she wanted him.

He had put an ache inside her no other man ever had. If he kissed her again, Lydia didn't think she could resist him. And she had to.

She had a purpose here, one that had nothing to do with Russ Baldwin. Getting involved with him was too risky to the operation, especially since he lived at the hotel. She had to think about the women she was trying to help. It didn't matter that she wanted him. She couldn't let her guard down again.

Russ had thought he'd gotten what he wanted from Lydia, but it turned out that one taste of her was not going to be enough. The next day as he helped his father and brother move cattle to the east pasture, he thought about that kiss. All damn day.

The fact that he couldn't get her out of his mind told Russ he shouldn't have kissed her, but the night before he'd been bested by an urgent driving need to feel her mouth against his.

There had been no thought, just keen thundering want. He might as well have been hobbled in place, because his legs wouldn't move.

The taste of her had spread through his system like slow, dark honey. If they hadn't been interrupted by Ef and Naomi, Russ wouldn't have stopped. And Lydia hadn't appeared to be of a mind to stop him. She had been enjoying it just as much as he had.

But the appearance of their friends had been a good thing. Russ had snapped to that realization once his body cooled down and his brain had reloaded.

Yes, he wanted Lydia—that kiss had practically singed his boots—but he was going to take his time over it.

He'd ridden out to the ranch today, not only to help with the cattle, but because he needed some space from her. Needed to be someplace where he didn't have to smell her stirring floral scent. Didn't have to see or talk to her.

Trying to get her out of his head had been as successful as covering a mare with a gelding. Lydia was still in his thoughts early that evening when he let himself in the hotel's side door close to his office. Cold air followed him inside.

Thinking about her was one thing. What mattered was that he did the smart thing. And smart meant not letting Miz Lydia Kent pull his trigger and tempt him into doing something stupid like kissing her again.

As he walked to his office door, he saw her in the lobby with Ef and Mitchell Orr. Lydia was telling the blacksmith and store clerk she wanted the old rug returned to the store and replaced with the one she had ordered.

Even in that plain blue day dress, she looked beautiful. Her hair was up, drawing his eye to the elegant line of her neck and making Russ want to press his mouth to a silky patch right below her ear. Or, well, anywhere. His body was just as primed as it had been last night.

Ef looked across the lobby and saw him, lifting a hand in greeting.

Lydia turned, a polite mask slipping over her face when she saw Russ walking toward her. "The new rug is here. Mitchell brought it over as soon as his uncle's store received it."

Russ nodded at the slender blond-haired man who worked for Charlie Haskell.

"Miss Lydia," Mitchell said. "Now that Russ is here, you let us take care of this rug."

"Oh, nonsense." She pushed back a loose strand of hair. "If we each take a corner, we'll have the old one rolled up and the new one down lickety-split."

Stubborn woman. It hadn't been two days ago that she'd reopened her gunshot wound. Dammit. He frowned at her. "What did I tell you about that arm?"

Her lips flattened and her eyes went as cool as black marble. "I hardly think—"

"Your arm is only one reason why you shouldn't be wrangling this carpet around," Mitchell said. "The other is you're a lady and we can't let you."

"All right then." She smiled sweetly at the young man.

Russ's jaw tightened. He palmed off his hat and laid his rifle on the registration desk. As he shrugged out of his duster, her gaze slid over him with the same heat he'd seen last night just before he kissed her. Tension coiled inside him. "Let's get this done."

She moved out of the way, standing between the sofa and registration desk. In short order, the men had the original rug bundled up and the new one unrolled.

As they arranged and placed and moved and rearranged according to her directions, Lydia and Mitchell kept up a steady dialogue.

About nothing, to Russ's way of thinking. More than once, he saw the way the blond man's gaze went over Lydia. As though she were his favorite sweet and he was trying to decide where to start nibbling. Judging from her unwavering smile, she either didn't notice or care how partial Mitchell seemed to her breasts. At least the woman was covered up today.

Hell. Russ forced himself to relax the knotted muscles in his shoulders. What Lydia did and with whom was none of his concern.

She was none of his concern.

Even so, he ground his teeth at how easy she seemed with Orr. Russ hadn't found one damn thing with her easy. Except maybe last night, which wasn't going to happen again.

Finally, the new carpet was arranged to her liking in front of the registration desk. Russ and Ef helped Orr load the old one into his wagon. When they came back inside, Lydia's gaze encompassed them all. "Thank you all."

Russ and Ef nodded, then the blacksmith took his leave.

Since Mitchell was still there, Russ didn't see any reason to stay. He excused himself and picked up his gun and coat then went to his office. Mitchell's voice reached him.

"You take care of that arm, Miss Lydia. If I can be of any service around the hotel or for anything, let me know."

Russ quashed the urge to say that the lady had him and didn't need any help. But he had no claim on her and he wasn't staking one.

"That's very kind," Lydia said. "I appreciate it."

"Well, I mean it. For any reason. Any reason at all."

"All right."

Her soft laugh had Russ tossing his hat onto the desk hard enough that it slid to the opposite corner. That woman could drive him plumb crazy.

"Do you have a minute?"

Surprised to hear her so close, he looked over his shoulder to find her in his doorway. He hung his duster on the wall adjacent to his desk. "Yeah."

When she stepped inside, he turned toward her, reaching down the inside of his leg to untie the leather thong of his gun belt. Her gaze followed his hands and the hungry way she watched had him clenching his muscles. He wanted to back her into the wall and kiss her silly.

He had no idea if she was aware of the invitation on her face, but he was aware enough for both of them. Dammit, if she didn't stop looking at him like that...

"You needed something?" he asked brusquely as he laid his gun and holster on his desk then opened the cupboard to his left for a bottle of brandy. Something told him he was going to need it.

"I wanted to talk to you about last night."

"What about it?" After she declined his silent offer for a drink, he took a slow sip. "I thought it went real well. You told Orr you thought it did, too."

"Not the party." She looked everywhere except at him. "I meant about what happened in the kitchen. With us."

Taken aback, Russ swallowed wrong. He barely managed to keep from coughing as the liquor seared a trail down his throat. Well, well.

Her mouth tightened. "The...kiss."

"Kiss*es*, actually."

She flushed. "It can't happen again."

Yes, he'd decided the same thing. He wondered what had made Lydia's decision. The out-of-control feeling he had experienced after kissing her had brought his past flooding back. With Amy, he'd let his body do the leading and that had been a big mistake.

Setting his glass down, he came around the desk and eased his backside against the edge. "You liked it."

"That isn't the point. I can't get involved with you."

Now this was an interesting turn of events. He hadn't counted on anything like this. Folding his arms, Russ crossed his feet at the ankles. He remembered how she had melted into him, how she had kissed him back just as ravenously as he had kissed her.

As he studied her, she edged sideways, putting herself behind one of his leather visitor's chairs. "We crossed a line last night I'm not comfortable crossing."

She'd felt pretty damn comfortable to him. He wondered what she would do if he up and kissed her right now. Not that he would.

"It isn't a good idea for us to get involved that way."

"Why not?" Just because he agreed didn't mean she had to know it. "Because we're business partners?"

"Yes." Though she stayed behind the chair as if it were a shield, there was no uncomfortable shifting, no squirming. Still, Russ saw the rapid flutter of her pulse in her throat.

"Okay," he said.

At his easy agreement, she looked startled. He wasn't fighting her on this. His head said steer clear and that's what he intended to do.

She moved to the door, putting even more space between them. Tension vibrated from her, and she looked as though she might bolt any second.

In the short time he and Lydia had worked together, Russ had learned there was always more to the story with her. And he would bet his interest in The Fontaine that it was more than their partnership that had Lydia broaching this subject. Because last night, she had been just as involved in the dancing *and* the kissing as he had.

To his way of thinking, she was more anxious than gunshy. It was as if she were trying to head him off at the pass, trying to keep something from happening. And that's when he realized. She was trying to "manage" him, just as she had with The Fontaine.

Lydia hadn't thought Russ might pursue her. She was trying to make sure he *didn't*. Now, why would she do that?

He quashed the urge to stand and walk over to her, trap her against the wall.

She glanced out his door and stilled. A frown puckered her brow as she brought her gaze back to his. "So, you understand what I'm saying?"

"Why, yes, ma'am," he drawled, irritation flaring. "And I even got your meanin' right off."

Her lips tightened at his sarcasm. She exhaled loudly as though he were trying her patience. She was damn sure trying his.

Her bringing up their kisses was behavior most females would consider too forward. Lydia's plain speaking told Russ she had been as rattled by what had happened between them the night before as he had. Otherwise, she wouldn't be trying to maneuver him in the direction she wanted.

She stepped outside his office, an urgency pulsing from her as though she were in a hurry. Why? Did she have somewhere to be? What did she keep gawking at out there?

"Do you disagree that we shouldn't get involved?" she asked.

"No." Arms still folded, he studied her.

"Then things can continue as they were before we… before."

"As far as I'm concerned." Maybe she was skittish because she had been spooked by the same reckless desire that had spooked him last night. But there was something else, too, though Russ couldn't pin it down.

Her attention drifting to a point outside his office, she asked absently, "So, you agree?"

"I said I did." His eyes narrowed. What was going on with her?

She gave him a faint smile. "Oh. Good. Thank you. Have a nice evening."

She turned in a whirl of skirts and Russ listened to the rapid tap of her heels against the wood floor as she walked across the lobby. Curious as to why she'd been so antsy to leave, he pushed away from the desk and peered around the door.

Lydia and Naomi were walking toward the dining room, their heads close together, their voices low.

What were they discussing? Was it about the hotel? If so, wouldn't Naomi be telling both he and Lydia?

He *wasn't* being paranoid and he wasn't imagining things. The woman was up to something.

He didn't care how delicious she tasted, how her scent tied him in knots, how intrigued he was by her. He'd had his iron in the fire before with a woman who hid things from him, and he wasn't doing that again.

He thought about how Lydia had shown up in Whirlwind early. How her being shot had seemed more a deliberate attempt than an accident. How she was trying again to keep him out of her way. And how twitchy she'd seemed just now.

He had gotten nowhere on his own in trying to figure out what she was up to, and he knew better than to expect answers from her. He needed help and he knew where to get it.

Chapter Eight

❦

Still as suspicious as he had been the night before, Russ was waiting at the jailhouse before the sheriff arrived. He rubbed his hands together against the November chill. He'd left the hotel before even seeing Lydia that morning. If she weren't his business partner, he would walk away right now. But he couldn't. However, that didn't mean he had to stay in the hotel with her every minute of every day. Or even in Whirlwind. He was making boot tracks out of town. Today.

The woman affected him far too strongly and he didn't mind admitting it. To himself. He wasn't only wary of getting involved with her physically. He was also concerned about his interest in the hotel. No woman was pulling the wool over his eyes again, not in love and not for money.

As the morning sun speared over the church at the east end of town, he caught sight of Davis Lee and Josie walking up the alley between Haskell's and the newspaper office. They lived behind the general store and every morning, Davis Lee escorted his wife to her thriving seamstress business, located in the back of the mercantile. While the couple said goodbye, Russ waited at the top of the wooden jailhouse steps.

His gaze moved from Haskell's, down past the newspaper office. Next door to The *Prairie Caller*, the saloon was closed, quiet except for Pete Carter's son, Creed, who was sweeping the porch before school.

Russ's attention shifted and he stared absently at the hotel. Its limestone facade glittered in the sunlight. His breath frosting the air, he stuck his hands in his trouser pockets to keep them warm.

A movement on the third floor had him looking up and squinting against the sun's glare off the glass. Lydia stood at one of her narrow windows, watching him. Russ's gut pulled tight as she tentatively raised a hand in greeting.

Her hair was down, swirling around her shoulders like black velvet, spurring that urge to bury his hands in it, his face. The sight of her put a funny ache in Russ's chest. One arm was wrapped around her waist. Her free hand lay across her chest and she fingered the watch pinned to her bodice. She did that when she was nervous. What was she nervous about?

He knew better than to think he'd find out from her. Russ tipped his hat then turned away.

Davis Lee called out to him as he crossed Main Street and started up the jailhouse steps. When the sheriff reached the landing and unlocked the door, Russ sent another look in Lydia's direction. Yep, she was still there. Watching him, pulling his muscles taut.

He followed the sheriff inside. As he closed the door, Davis Lee moved past his desk to a glass-front gun cabinet, making sure his three shotguns were locked inside and undisturbed. Davis Lee never took anything for granted. Russ didn't plan to, either.

"What brings you over today?" the lawman asked.

He didn't see any reason to pussyfoot around. "I need you to find out whatever you can about Lydia."

Davis Lee frowned. "What? Why?"

"She's hiding something."

The other man walked toward Russ, adjusting the gun belt that held his Peacemaker. "What makes you think so?"

"My gut," he said baldly. "She doesn't hem and haw when I ask questions, but even when I get a straight answer from her, it seems like there's more she *isn't* saying."

"I guess I could—"

"Being with her is like a dance and sometimes I'm not sure who's leading." He shoved a hand through his hair. "That bothers me. *She* bothers me. It's damn annoyin'."

Davis Lee leaned one shoulder against the wall behind his desk. "You sound intrigued."

He was, Russ admitted grimly. And that could only get him in a heap of trouble. "Are you going to help me?"

"Yes."

"Here's the kind of thing I'm talking about." Russ told the lawman about Lydia's early *unexpected* arrival, about all the telegrams she received, how she had been trying since her second day here to get him out of the hotel. "She wants to maneuver me. She's tried more than once."

The lawman eased down on the corner of his desk. "I can see why those things would make you curious, but none of them sound that suspicious to me."

"Well, they do to *me*. Something about her is…elusive. It doesn't sit right." Russ wasn't telling Davis Lee about the kisses that had turned him inside out and honed his wariness to a knife's edge. "And then there's her gunshot wound."

"What about it?"

"Dawkins shooting Lydia wasn't an accident. She wasn't

armed. I was, plus I had him in my sights. Yet Dawkins seemed to aim at *her*. Why didn't he shoot me? Or Naomi? Lydia said she didn't know him, had never seen him before."

"Good questions." The other man frowned. "I haven't learned anything new about the man and his wife since I came across that letter in his saddlebag. Do you think whatever Lydia's hiding has something to do with the woman who was killed in your hotel?"

"I don't know. It might. Might even have something to do with the reason Lydia was shot."

Davis Lee stood and moved around his desk to open a side drawer, pulling out a piece of paper and stubby pencil. "The first thing I'll do is send a wire to the law in her town. What do you expect me to find out?"

"I have no idea, but I'd lay money there'll be something."

His friend jotted a couple of notes. "Seems like you're just swinging a rope and hoping to lasso some answers."

"Maybe I am. The woman has layers and I want to know what's under them."

Davis Lee chuckled. "Are you sure her layers is what you're wanting to get under?"

If this conversation had been about any woman except Lydia, Russ would've grinned, but he didn't. "That badge gives you a better chance of finding out things. She sued her fiancé for breach of promise when their engagement was broken. That might be a good place to start."

"So, that's really true," Davis Lee murmured. At Russ's puzzled look, the other man said, "Josie heard tell of the lawsuit from Matt, but she wasn't sure she got the story right."

"She did," Russ said flatly. "Pa told me the man left Lydia standing at the altar. Can you find out more details about it?"

"I'll try. Are you sure you want to do this? What if you find out something you don't want to know?"

"There's no such thing. I want to know everything, down to the number of hooks on her corset and the brand of tooth powder she uses."

Davis Lee considered Russ for a moment. "You this itchy because of what happened with Amy?"

He gave a sharp nod, ignoring the look in his friend's eyes that said he understood Russ was trying not to fall for another deceitful woman.

"How urgent is this? You want me to hunt you down when I've got something? Or just send word to you?"

"Either way is fine with me." Russ rolled his shoulders against a sense of misgiving. He didn't understand that. It wasn't wrong to have Davis Lee do some nosing around. "You'll send a wire today?"

"Consider it done. She's from Jackson, Mississippi, isn't she?"

"Yeah."

"Learning anything helpful could take a while."

There was nothing to be done about that. "That's okay. I'm betting it'll be worth the wait."

"All right." Davis Lee walked outside with Russ, tugging his hat low over his eyes as he looked toward the hotel. "Does she know you're suspicious?"

"I'm not sure." Even if she did, it didn't matter. Russ wasn't going to be taken in by a woman ever again. A quick glance over showed she was no longer in the window. "And I'd prefer this stay just between the two of us."

"Absolutely."

"I'm headed over to Abilene and I'll be there for several days. Staying at the Texas Crown if you need to get a message to me."

Davis Lee nodded and Russ shook his hand before going down the steps and angling over to Ef's. Under a side awning, the blacksmith already had a fire blazing in his forge, which consisted of a raised brick hearth outfitted with bellows and a hood to let the smoke escape. The heat put off by the fire was tolerable today because of the cool temperature, but in the summer Russ found it unbearable even though it was outside. It never seemed to bother Ef.

If the other man were still working on the ironwork for The Fontaine's balcony or making wheel rims or other goods, his hammer would be banging out a loud and constant noise.

Today, Ef was using his hammer to anchor a piece of steel in place on the anvil. He was filing one side of already-tempered metal into what Russ recognized as the cutting edge of an ax head.

Knowing if his friend stopped in the middle of making the tool, the metal would cool and he would have to start over, Russ went to stand under the awning. He leaned against one of the support columns and propped one booted foot behind him.

Muscles flexed in Ef's forearms and shoulders as he glanced up from his anvil. Sweat glistened on his black skin. "Mornin'."

"Mornin'."

"Want some coffee?"

"No, thanks. I just stopped by to tell you I'm on my way to Abilene and I'll be there for a few days."

Ef smoothly stroked his file down the ax's edge then did it again before straightening. "Goin' for any special reason?"

Russ kept his back to The Fontaine. "The bank loan is due in forty-five days and I haven't found a buyer yet for my share of the hotel. There are a couple of businessmen over there who've expressed interest before in other ventures so I plan to talk to them about it. Depending on how that goes, I may meet with the bank officer about extending the due date."

"Good luck."

"Thanks."

The blacksmith dragged his arm across his perspiring forehead, drying his skin against his rolled-back sleeve. He set the honed ax head on a bench behind him and reached into the deep pocket on the front of his apron for a rag then wiped his hands. "You want me to keep an eye on the hotel for you?"

"Yeah, the *hotel*. Not just Miz Jones." Russ grinned at the pleasure that lit his friend's eyes. "Actually, I'd appreciate it if you would check on both ladies while I'm gone."

A smile creased Ef's dark features. "Happy to do it."

"I didn't figure you'd consider it a hardship," Russ drawled. "And let me know if you notice anything odd."

The other man frowned. "You thinking about something in particular?"

"No. Just anything that catches your attention, whether you think it's important or not."

"All right. You gonna tell me what's going on?"

"When I have an idea, yeah, I'll let you know."

"Good enough."

Russ stroked his bare upper lip. "One more thing. Would you mind telling Lydia where I've gone?"

Looking surprised, Ef swiped the rag over his knuckles. "Is there some reason you don't want to tell her yourself?"

"Just ready to get on the trail." Hell, Russ didn't want to go anywhere near her.

His friend's shrewd black eyes zeroed in on him. "Does it have anything to do with what Naomi and I saw the two of you doing in the kitchen?"

"She's not interested and neither am I." He scrubbed a

hand down his face. He was lying and Ef knew it. "The information about Abilene doesn't have to come from me. She just needs to know."

"Sure. I don't mind talking to her. What about your pa and Matt?"

"Tony Santos is going to ride out to the Triple B later this morning to tell them."

"All right then."

"Thanks." Pushing away from the wooden column, Russ gave him the name of the hotel where he'd be staying. "In case you need to reach me."

"Watch your back."

That's what Russ was doing. He shook hands with his friend then strode past the front of The Fontaine on his way to the livery.

There was no sign of Lydia in her window or in the lobby. A strange ache unfurled in his chest, but he dismissed it. He didn't want to see her. He sure as hell didn't want to talk to her.

If her sweet drawl and tempting scent were the last things on his mind before he rode out, he wouldn't be able to get her out of his head the whole time he was gone.

Russ was doing whatever he had to in order to keep Lydia Kent from getting to him, and if he had to leave town to do it, that was fine by him.

Lydia wasn't sure what to think when she looked out her window and saw Russ going into the sheriff's office.

Was he talking to Davis Lee about her? She couldn't dismiss the possibility. Not after last night when she had felt him watching her and Naomi like a hawk from his office doorway.

She had done the right thing by going to see Russ and addressing their interlude in the kitchen. By telling him they couldn't get romantically involved. The provoking man had agreed right off, which stung her pride.

Despite believing she had done what she should, it had left a hollow feeling in her chest, as though she had turned her back on something that could've been…more.

After leaving his office, she had been occupied with settling the travelers who had been delayed by a day. The two women had reached Whirlwind later than expected because one of them had broken an ankle the night they had fled their homes.

Lydia and Naomi had reset the bone and fashioned a crude splint. Tending to the woman had taken Lydia's focus from Russ for a while, served to remind her that these women were her priority.

But her focus came back to her business partner the following day when Ef delivered a message from him. Lydia stared incredulously at the blacksmith. "Russ did what?"

"Left for Abilene." Standing in front of the registration desk, the blacksmith ran his hat through his fingers. "He thinks he'll be there for several days."

"I see." Her heart sank. When she had asked the man for some distance, she never thought he would take her literally.

"He had to get going." Ef shifted from one foot to the other. "I told him I didn't mind gettin' word to you."

"Thank you. I appreciate it." Mr. Gerard was a sweet man, but Lydia knew from the couple of seconds Russ had looked at her this morning, he hadn't wanted to be around her.

"If you need to send him a message, he's staying at the Texas Crown Hotel."

Even though she had no right to feel hurt, she did. Her upset had nothing to do with being his business partner and everything to do with that kiss.

Regardless of them both agreeing it shouldn't happen

again, their relationship had shifted into a much more personal one. They were still partners, though, and Russ should've told her about the trip himself, she fumed. They generally discussed everything that concerned the business.

An unpleasant notion popped into her head. Maybe he wasn't going to Abilene for business. Maybe he was going for pleasure.

The thought put an ache in her throat.

"Did he say why he was making the trip?" she asked Ef.

"He's planning to meet with some businessmen."

"About buying his share of The Fontaine?"

"Yes, ma'am."

There was no reason Russ couldn't have told her that himself. He just hadn't wanted to. Lydia couldn't believe how vexing, and hurtful, she found that.

"He also said he might meet with the banker, depending on how things went."

The disappointment she felt was absurd. He was away from the hotel. That was what she wanted, wasn't it?

"I'll check by each morning and evening," the blacksmith said. "You or Naomi should feel free to send for me at any time."

"Thank you, Ef. And thank you for the message."

"You're welcome. It was no trouble."

As she watched the brawny man stride out of the hotel, Lydia told herself it was good Russ was gone. Now her full attention could be on the underground network.

Dismissing the heaviness dragging at her, she managed not to think about Russ until late that night when she was on her way up to her rooms. She found herself on the hotel's balcony looking past the town to the plains beyond. The November air sent a shiver through her and she rubbed her arms against the cold. The moon winked like a sliver of ice in the clear black sky, its light glazing the knee-high grass swaying in the slight breeze and the occasional mesquite tree.

Abilene—and Russ—was east of here. A long stretch of prairie separated her from him, and inside it felt as though the distance were even greater.

Lydia hadn't realized how much she had come to anticipate seeing him around the hotel. No matter how often he left during the day, he typically returned to the hotel for supper and to stay the night. The man's robust presence filled every inch of The Fontaine and now that he was away, everything seemed dull and flat.

There was no shortage of work to keep Lydia's hands and thoughts occupied. Helping Zoe Keeler clean the guest rooms, aiding Naomi in the kitchen. Washing and folding laundry, tending the guests, keeping the books.

Lydia would order herself not to think about him and before she realized it, she'd be lost in a full-blown memory— of him changing her bandage, of dancing with him. Kissing him. He wasn't even here and he distracted her!

His absence sawed at her, day in and day out. Wore away at her irritation over him not telling her about his trip.

She missed him, she realized one evening when his brother came to the hotel.

Matt strode through the dining room's wide archway and caught Lydia's eye from across the room, where she stood talking to a family of four. Upon seeing the youngest Baldwin, her heart kicked hard. Had something happened to Russ?

She excused herself and wove around another group of guests to the table Matt had chosen close to the kitchen. He eased his strapping frame into one of the dining chairs.

"Evenin', Lydia," he said when she reached him.

"Hello." She couldn't keep the apprehension from her voice. "Is everything okay?"

"Yes," he answered quickly. "Sorry if I alarmed you." He removed his hat and laid it on the chair beside his. "I didn't mean to cause concern."

"Have you heard from Russ then?"

"Not since he left. I guess you haven't, either."

"No." That didn't automatically mean there was trouble. Still, she felt wound as tight as an eight-day watch.

Matt grinned, flashing dimples in the same place as his brother's. "The real reason I stopped by was for a piece of Pearl's pecan pie and a cup of coffee."

"All right."

Steadying her pulse, Lydia returned with his order and placed it in front of him. "Let me know if you need anything else."

She cleared the dishes from an empty table then checked on him again. "Would you like more coffee?"

At his nod, she stepped into the kitchen and returned with a pot to refill his cup.

Matt shifted in his chair, his broad shoulders straining at the fabric of his shirt just as his brother's did. Both men were dark-haired and tall with muscular builds. Not as burly as Ef, but powerful and hard and sinewy.

He pushed his plate to the side. "That was real good. Nobody makes pecan pie like Pearl."

"Some of our guests have already requested special desserts from her."

As his gaze panned the dining room, Lydia found herself again comparing him and his brother. Matt's features were blunt, Russ's slightly more refined. Their eyes were the same dark shade of blue. Both were ruggedly handsome, but Lydia wasn't tempted to stroke her fingers down the solid line of

Matt's jaw the way she wanted to with Russ. "May I get you anything else?"

"Not right now." Matt took a sip of coffee. "Did you run a business back in Mississippi?"

Any mention of her home had tension coiling inside her. Why was he asking? "Yes, my father's shipping company."

"What does he do? Build barges and boats?"

"No. We own steamboats. Some people book passage for travel. Others hire us to ship their goods up the river."

She drew in Matt's scent of leather and the earth. Russ smelled like spicy soap and clean male. Oh, foot! Why couldn't she stop thinking about him? "I was in charge of schedules, paying the workers and pricing our fares."

Matt looked at her admiringly. "Russ said you were real smart."

"He did?" She tried not to pay too much attention to the pleasure that rippled through her.

"Yeah." Matt shook his head. "Have you run into problems before with businessmen accepting you?"

"A few times, yes. Not with your brother, though."

"Russ ain't no dummy. He appreciates smarts no matter how they come wrapped." He gave her an appraising look. "Of course, it doesn't hurt that yours are wrapped up so well."

Lydia laughed at his flirting.

"Too bad that man from Chicago wasn't so sharp."

Mr. Julius? she thought. "What do you mean?"

"His refusing to buy Russ's share of the hotel because you're a woman."

What? She barely managed to keep her jaw from dropping. Russ had told her only that the man wasn't interested, not that she was the reason why. She suddenly felt queasy.

"Said he didn't do business with women." Matt snorted.

"Some men are like that. Fools, if you ask me. One of the smartest businesspeople I know is a woman. Hell, she runs *two* whore—uh, two entertainment businesses out of Dallas."

Lydia barely noticed his glowing endorsement of the brothel madam or his following conversation. She was still scrambling to recover her mental balance.

If not for her, Russ could've sold his interest in The Fontaine and already paid off that bank loan.

He hadn't let on one bit that Mr. Julius had refused the deal because she was a woman. Even as she told herself not to, Lydia went all soft inside because Russ had tried to shield her feelings.

Oh, forevermore. His being a gentleman was nothing to get weak-kneed over. Still…she was touched. And charmed.

Just when she thought she could keep from falling for him, she learned something like this. How was she supposed to resist him now?

"Do you have any idea when Russ will be back?" Lydia asked.

"No, but I hope he has good news when he does."

When Russ did sell his part of the hotel, he would be moving out and the place would feel as dull as it had for the past few days. The idea didn't sound nearly as appealing as it had when she had first arrived. It niggled at her the rest of the evening.

Late that night, after the hotel was quiet, thoughts of Russ were interrupted by Naomi waking her with the news that the battered woman they had been expecting had shown up with two more victims.

Lydia pulled on her wrapper, her mind racing. There were already two women using the safe room. One had a broken ankle, so she and her companion had no choice but to stay on for a few days before making their way to the next safe station.

Now three more abuse victims had to be squeezed into the hiding area! Could they all fit?

Lord, as much as she'd missed Russ, Lydia was suddenly thankful he was still gone. And hoped he would stay away for a few more days.

Trying not to feel flustered, she worked beside Naomi to make pallets for the new arrivals. That done, she stepped out of the storage room, holding the lantern aloft as she walked to the pie safe at the front of the pantry. There was enough corn bread left over from tonight's menu for the new arrivals.

Lydia shifted the lantern to her other hand as she reached to open the cupboard holding the bread.

"Lydia?"

She gasped, whirling toward the door. She wasn't sure what surprised her the most. Seeing Russ standing in the kitchen doorway. Or the fact he had one arm draped around the waist of a willowy blonde.

Chapter Nine

Lydia nearly dropped the lantern. Framed by the pale gaslight coming from the lobby, Russ's shoulders looked as wide as the door. The sight of him in a black duster put a flutter in her stomach. In the wavering light, she could see that his black shirt and trousers were filmed with red dust, just like his coat and scuffed black boots.

Whiskers shadowed his jaw and he looked tired, but when his gaze met hers, pleasure flared in the blue depths. Then it was gone. She felt a tug of want deep in her belly.

Trying to compose herself, she said, "Welcome back. I— we weren't sure when to expect you."

"I wasn't sure when I was coming back." His voice was stiff and ragged. From fatigue? Or because he was reluctant to talk to her, just as he had been before he left?

The gladness she felt at seeing him was squelched as her gaze moved to the blonde plastered to his side. Something twisted in Lydia's chest. She'd been missing him and he had brought back a woman! She was swept with an urge to smack him upside the head, but somehow she managed to school her features into what she hoped was a blank mask.

After a moment, her irritation abated enough for her to notice more about Russ's female companion. He shifted so that the woman was out of his shadow and Lydia could see she was hurt.

Her curly golden hair was piled on top of her head in a wobbly knot and drew attention to her heart-shaped face. The blonde was pretty. And injured. Her lower lip was busted and bruises covered one side of her face. Lydia could make out the indentation of a ring on her bloodied cheek. Her pale blue eyes were bloodshot, one of them nearly swollen shut.

It was no accident that had caused those injuries. They were from a fist. And Russ was practically keeping the woman on her feet.

"Willow Upshaw, this is Lydia Kent." He looked at Lydia. "I told her you could help her."

"Me?" She frowned. Had Russ brought the woman here because she was trying to escape an abusive situation? If Russ had wanted medical care for her, he probably would've sent for Catherine. Or asked for Naomi.

Did that mean Russ knew about the underground network? Lydia tightened her grip on the lantern's handle.

"I told her you could help her get away from—"

Get away from…her abuser? Lydia's brain froze as she fought down a sudden panic. How had he found out? Was anyone's safety in jeopardy? It took a moment for his voice to penetrate her frenzied thoughts.

"Willow wants to get away from her old life and start over."

"I'm willin' to work hard, ma'am." The woman spoke carefully because of her swollen lip.

Lydia's legs nearly gave out in relief as she realized Russ wanted her to give the woman a job, not help her escape an abusive situation. He didn't appear to know anything about the underground network. Reminded of the need for secrecy concerning the women she had just hidden, she gestured toward the dining room.

"Have a seat at one of the tables and let me look at your injuries. The light is better in there."

She extinguished the lantern and hung it on the hook outside the pantry door. Hopefully, Naomi would realize the dousing of the light meant something was wrong and that it wasn't safe for anyone, including her, to come out of the storage room.

As Russ guided Willow to a dining table and pulled out a chair, Lydia hurried to the kitchen sink and pumped some hot and cold water into a bowl. She grabbed a small towel and moved into the dining room.

In time to see the too-familiar smile Willow gave Russ after he helped her into a chair. An intimate smile, in Lydia's opinion. Russ and the other woman were obviously well acquainted. *Sexually* acquainted, Lydia thought resentfully.

Pulling her attention from Russ, she sat in the chair beside Willow's. She soaked the cloth and squeezed out the water, carefully dabbing at the woman's cheek. "I'll try not to hurt you."

"I been hit worse than this before," the blonde offered.

Lydia's heart ached at how matter-of-fact the woman was about the beating. She gently touched the wet rag to the corner of Willow's swollen eye. "Are you hurt anywhere else?"

"Just my face."

"No bruised ribs, broken bones?"

"Not this time." She gave a raspy laugh. "I'm so tired I cain't see straight, but my face is the only thing busted. I really don't need no attention. Just a job."

Too caught up in the surprise of Russ's arrival and the added botheration of sensing the relationship between him and Willow, Lydia only now registered the other woman's ragged dress with its shockingly low décolletage. Her garishly made-up features. An ease with Russ that bespoke an unseemly familiarity with men. With *him*.

The woman was a prostitute. Lydia shot a look at her partner, who arched a dark brow in silent warning. Russ had said that Willow wanted a fresh start.

"Do you have any experience with the public?" As soon as the words left her mouth, Lydia realized the question was ill-phrased.

Before she could reword it, Russ made a sound halfway between a cough and a laugh. A flash of amusement in his blue eyes had her frowning at him.

Willow looked uncertainly at Russ. "Um. I worked at a saloon in Abilene, ma'am. I swept floors and did my own wash. I served drinks sometimes and men—"

"She understands." Russ laid a big hand on the blonde's shoulder, smiling down at her.

Yes, Lydia understood that Willow had served men's urges the rest of the time. Had Russ been one of them? Lydia knew he had, and she struggled to keep her tone even. "This is a reputable hotel, Willow. The work here will include things like cleaning and the laundry, not…entertaining men."

"Yes, ma'am. You don't have to worry none about that."

"She wants a new life, Lydia." With an edge in his voice, Russ gestured to the prostitute's battered face. "You can see why."

Still alert for any sound from the pantry, Lydia studied the woman in front of her. Willow held her gaze, doing some studying of her own. It was plain she wanted the job, but she wasn't going to lie about her old one. Lydia liked that.

She nodded. "We'll talk about your duties tomorrow."

"So I can work here?" The woman's pale blue eyes held a glimmer of hope.

"Yes."

"I can start right now, ma'am." She rose, gripping the edge of the table.

Lydia wondered if Willow were hurt in other places, despite her denial. "Tomorrow will be soon enough. Have you eaten?"

"Yes, ma'am. Russ fed me real good."

Of course he had. "All right," Lydia said softly as she got to her feet. "You go on upstairs now. Choose any room you want on the third floor. There should be a towel and cloth next to the washbasin beside the bed."

The pantry area and storage room remained quiet. It appeared Naomi had understood Lydia's signal.

"I really can do some work now, ma'am," Russ's guest insisted. "I don't want you to be sorry for taking me on."

"After all your travel today, you look as though you could use some rest. There will be plenty to do tomorrow."

Lydia followed the other two out of the dining room, not missing the way Russ's hand cupped his friend's elbow.

As the three of them made their way across the lobby, Lydia slowed her steps to match the injured woman's. "Did you anger anyone when you left Abilene? Will someone be coming after you?"

"No, ma'am. Eldon's got girls lots younger than me now."

"Good."

They all stopped at the foot of the staircase and Russ steadied Willow on the bottom step.

Lydia stepped forward. "Do you need *my* help getting up the stairs?"

Judging by the way Russ's eyes narrowed, he caught her subtle emphasis.

"No, ma'am. I can manage."

"There's indoor plumbing on every floor," Russ put in. "Take a bath if you want."

"Indoor plumbing. That's fancy." The woman smiled, revealing a chip on the corner of one tooth.

Had that been caused by the same person who had beaten her? Lydia wanted to help the woman, but she had to be clear. Her neck burned at the indelicate subject. "So, we have an understanding?"

"Yes, ma'am." Willow hesitated, then angled her chin. "I reckon your guests will find out what I used to be?"

"Not from me. As far as I'm concerned, your past will be just between us."

"And Russ," the other woman added, visibly relaxing.

"Yes, and Russ," Lydia agreed drily. And any other men from Whirlwind who had been her customers.

"You won't be sorry. I swear." Willow's eyes and face were hard from the life she'd lived, but she was sincere. "Thank you."

"You're welcome. Let me know if you need anything."

Willow leaned to give Russ a full-body hug, confirming Lydia's suspicions that she hadn't imagined the insinuation of sexual knowledge between them.

Although she tried to dismiss it, the thought set her teeth on edge. Oh, why did she care who Russ had been with?

Lydia watched the woman go up the stairs, moving slowly as she took in her surroundings with an admiring look. Now alone with the man she had missed this past week, Lydia could feel his attention fixed on her.

When she glanced over at him, Russ held her gaze. "Everything all right?"

"Yes, of course. Why?"

"As late as it is, I expected you to be asleep, not scrounging around in the pantry."

"It's a good thing I was up so I could meet your lady friend," she said brightly.

Russ gave her a considering look. "She really is finished with that life."

The words reminded her of his relationship with the prostitute and she said coolly, "That's good. Because when I said no entertaining men, I meant she couldn't entertain you, either."

"You think I'm going to visit Willow?" The words boomed in the large empty space.

With a quick glance up the stairs, Lydia hissed, "Keep your voice down."

"Why would you think that?"

"It's obvious you've...been with her before." A flush burned Lydia's cheeks.

"And that bothers you. Why?" He stared at her for a moment. "Because I've been with Willow a few times or because I might have been with her this past week?"

Yes, Lydia thought. Both. She had never felt jealous like this over Wade. It rattled her. And annoyed her. "Don't do...*that* in my hotel."

He opened his mouth as though to say something, then closed it.

"Well?" she demanded.

"Well, what?"

"Are you going to stay away from her?"

He didn't respond, just moved behind her and bent to pick up his saddlebag from where he'd left it inside the door. He slung it over one shoulder and strode for his office as though he couldn't get away from her fast enough. The thought stabbed her in the heart.

Over his shoulder, he asked in a gravelly voice, "Is there anything that needs my attention?"

Me! Lydia wanted to scream in frustration and was promptly horrified at herself. "Nothing that can't wait until tomorrow."

"Good. I'm dead on my feet."

Even as irritated as she was with him, she wanted to talk to him. About the hotel, his trip, Mr. Julius's refusal to buy Russ's share of The Fontaine.

Surprised by Russ's return as well as the fact he had brought a woman back with him, all thoughts of what she had learned from his brother had been pushed out of Lydia's mind until now. But the fatigue etched on his handsome features said he was too tired for that conversation tonight.

He opened his office door and stepped inside.

Mercy, the man was beautiful. She had missed him, wanted to kiss him. Foot.

Shaking away the thought, she moved toward him. "How was your trip? Ef told me you went to try and find a buyer for the hotel. Did you have any luck?"

"No, but I'll be out of your way soon enough."

"You're not in my way," she said sharply then softened her tone. "I asked because I know it's bothering you that you haven't discovered yet how to pay the loan."

He dragged a hand down his haggard face. "Couldn't find any takers for the hotel and the banker was out of town."

Her heart squeezed tight. "You're exhausted and I'm yammering on. I'll let you get some sleep."

He paused, his gaze sliding over her and causing her nerve endings to sizzle. "How's your arm?"

"Nearly healed." The intent way his gaze locked on her caused a ripple of heat deep inside. "The bandage is off."

"That's good. We'll talk tomorrow, all right?"

"Yes."

Knowing she should go, she said haltingly, "I'm glad you're back."

"Thanks." His eyes darkened with an intensity that reached out to her like a touch.

As his door shut, she forced her legs to move. She was glad he was back. And she wasn't. Not only because she was hiding six abuse victims right under his nose, but because it forced her to admit what she'd been sidestepping this past week.

Russ was as much of a threat to her heart as he was to her secret.

Though Russ had spoken only briefly to Lydia the night before, she was on his mind as he rode out to the Triple B to tell Pa and Matt that he hadn't had any luck in Abilene.

His leaving town had done the trick, seemed to have soothed the desire that raged in his blood since kissing her. While he'd been gone, he hadn't thought about her. Much.

Yes, he still wanted her, but he didn't feel as though the want were carving a hole in his gut. His belief that she was hiding something had been reinforced last night when he'd found her in the pantry at such a late hour. Because of that, it would be stupid to do something about the hot, almost reckless, impulse that came over him when she was around, and Russ was dead set against stupid. Good thing he had a tight hold on the whoa reins.

The sun was setting in a haze of golden-red when he returned to Whirlwind. He'd been able to talk to Pa, but Matt had been out in the pastures, patrolling their herd against rustlers as he'd been doing for months now.

While Russ had been out at the ranch, he'd had an idea

about how to make some money. Maybe not all he needed by the time the banknote was due, but a substantial amount. He had to run his plan by Lydia, but he'd studied it up, down and sideways. She couldn't find anything wrong with it. They both stood to profit. The woman would be a fool to say no and one thing he'd learned was that Lydia Kent was no fool when it came to business. Once he got cleaned up, he would find her.

After stabling his horse at the livery, Russ let himself into his office. He shrugged out of his duster, hanging it on the hook near the door then tossing his hat on his desk. One-handed, he pulled his shirt over his head and dropped the garment on the floor beside his bed on his way to the washstand.

Someone, maybe Willow, had left fresh water in his basin. Russ didn't fancy shaving with cold water so he started around the bed to get a clean shirt from the wardrobe, intending to go to the kitchen to pump some hot water.

"Russ?" A light knock sounded at the same time Lydia peered around his office door.

Upon seeing him, her eyes widened and she stared in arrested silence, tracking a path over his chest then lower. The unguarded desire in her eyes had his entire body going hard.

Damn, he should've made sure to close the door.

Looking flustered, she tore her gaze away. "I'm sorry. I didn't mean to intrude. With your door open, I assumed you were—" she gestured in his direction "—decent."

"You haven't compromised me, Lydia," he said wryly.

"I can wait until you're finished." She flushed a pretty shade of pink.

"Suit yourself. I had already planned to find you after I washed up."

"Oh?" With her gaze fixed on his belly, she drew her bottom lip between her teeth.

If she kept looking at him as though she were thinking about taking a bite, he didn't want her in here. He pulled his shirt on over his head and she returned her attention to his face.

"I wanted to talk to you," she said.

"About the hotel?"

"Yes. I can come back, though."

Best to get this over with. "Now is fine."

"All right." She moved slowly into the room and halted beside his desk. In one hand, she held her journal. With the other, she stroked the wood, making small circles on one corner.

Russ couldn't halt a flash of Lydia's fine-boned fingers petting him that way, gliding over his skin. She was so beautiful. The sight of her tripped all his senses. The loosely bound mass of her silky hair, the creamy skin of her throat. Every muscle in his body went taut. The night before, the only thing stopping him from giving in to the urge to kiss her had been Willow's presence.

Clenching his teeth in frustration, he gestured toward his desk. "You want to sit?"

"No, thank you."

He nodded, bracing a shoulder against a poster at the foot of his bed. "I wanted to talk to you about the hotel, too."

"All right." Her gaze settled on him, hot and interested.

Even with the several feet separating them, Russ caught a tease of her lavender scent. Sensation skated just beneath the surface of his skin and he folded his arms, asking gruffly, "Anything happen while I was gone that needs to be taken care of?"

"No. There were no problems. We've had several guests other than the ones still here. A couple from Taylor County and a family of five."

"Sounds like a good start to our business."

"Yes." She paced the length of his desk, sliding her fingers over the wood surface. "So far, we've had no problems. Everyone loves the steam heat and indoor plumbing."

"The heat sure was nice when I came in from the cold a bit ago."

She smiled, moving back the other direction and touching his dusty hat. What was the dad-blamed woman doing?

Russ shifted. "I've come up with another way to make money, so that I can pay off the banknote."

She stiffened. "Yes?"

"We lease some hotel space to merchants."

"Lease space?" She sounded as though he'd said they should get naked.

He straightened. "Before you get all het up, hear me out."

"I am not 'het up,'" she said coolly. "The idea is intriguing."

It was? He sure hadn't expected that. While Lydia was intrigued, he'd better spit out his plan.

"The way I figure it, we can split up some of our space on the first floor, like that unused area across from my office. I can put up some walls or whatever we need. We wouldn't be laying out any cash for new construction."

"What kinds of businesses?" she asked stiffly.

"Not Willow's kind, if that's what you're worried about."

"I'm not, but that's good to know."

Russ remembered Lydia asking him whether he planned to visit Willow. He could've told his business partner no. He hadn't been with the prostitute for quite some time and didn't plan to be again. But he didn't need to tell Lydia any of that. They had shared only a kiss. Nothing binding between them.

"A seamstress would be a good possibility."

"Josie."

"Yes. I think she'd be interested in the space. She's said a couple of times that she needs more room than she has in the back of Haskell's store." Russ touched his chest. "She made the shirt I'm wearing and she does fine work."

"Yes, I've seen some of her things. She's very good. What other types of businesses would you approach?"

Was she warming to the idea? Russ thought she might be. "A gunsmith."

"Mr. Doyle?"

"Jed has his own shop. I thought Jericho might be interested in opening one here in the hotel if he and Jed have enough business to split."

She nodded, looking thoughtful.

"And selling leather goods out of here might be a good idea."

"Tack?"

Russ nodded. "Jake Ross makes fine saddles. He does repairs, too, including boots. He probably wouldn't lease any space because he spends most of his time running his ranch, but we could sell some of his pieces for a commission."

"I don't know," she said.

Russ closed the distance between them, easing down onto the corner of his desk. He kept his voice easy, the way he would to soothe a stubborn mare. "It's a good plan, Lydia. We'd both make money. There's nothing to mar your or Naomi's reputations."

She touched the watch pinned to her bodice. "I agree."

His eyes narrowed. "You do?"

"Yes." She arched a brow. "You're surprised?"

"I'm surprised you don't want to go round and round about it first. Or scribble in that ledger."

"Nice to know you have such a high opinion of my business sense."

"It has nothing to do with that. You've definitely got a head for business. I just thought you might want more details before you decided."

She hesitated.

"See, there's something you don't like," he said.

"No, I like it. I'm just thinking it through."

"So you can naysay it?" He thought he saw a flash of hurt in her eyes. As though he had no basis for asking such a question.

She was silent, looking torn. He sure didn't understand that. He knew this idea would work.

"It's a good idea. Really good."

"Thanks." He felt sideswiped. That had been almost too fast.

She tilted her head. "This would allow you to get the money to pay the note on time."

"Probably not all of it, but it'll be a show of good faith to the banker."

"Whatever will help you is what I want to do."

"Don't you mean whatever helps get me out of the hotel?"

"No, that isn't what I mean," she retorted. "I want to help *you*."

"Well." She wanted to help him. And he had convinced her his idea had merit. Russ couldn't stop the satisfaction spreading through him. "All right then."

"I know it was because of me that Mr. Julius didn't buy your share of the hotel."

"What?" He stilled.

"He didn't buy your interest because he didn't want to work with a woman."

"Who told you that?" Russ got to his feet. He knew it hadn't been Ef.

"Does it matter? You were very sweet to shield my feelings."

"Well, it wasn't your fault," he said grudgingly. "The man was ignorant."

"That's what your brother said." Lydia gave him a sweet smile, a genuine smile that reached right inside his chest and grabbed hold.

"So, Matt's the one who told you."

Her brows drew together. "Shouldn't he have?"

"When was he here?"

"A couple of nights ago."

Russ should've expected Matt to come around while he was gone. "How many times did he stop by?"

"Just the once." She fiddled with the binding of her journal. "Is there a problem?"

That depended. "Did he need something?" Before she could answer, Russ asked, "Did he come to see *you?*"

"I think he came for some of Pearl's pecan pie."

Russ didn't like it. Just because he wasn't cozying up to Lydia didn't mean it was all right for Matt to do it. What else had his brother told her?

"Russ." Her voice was impatient, as though she had tried to get his attention more than once. "Is there some reason Matt shouldn't have told me about Mr. Julius?"

Yes, the fact that Russ didn't want her to know. "It's over and done. What's the sense in talking about it? It doesn't even matter now."

"It matters to me," she said, with the same soft look on her face that she'd worn after he kissed her.

Hell. Those velvety black eyes had Russ taking a step back. Then another. He might be in control of the fierce craving he felt for her, but there was no reason to tempt himself by standing so close to her.

Confound his brother! The next time Russ saw him, Matt

was in for a good thumping. A thought hit him and he watched Lydia's face carefully. "Are you agreeing to my plan because you somehow feel guilty about Mr. Julius's decision?"

The possibility bothered him. Russ wanted her to like his idea because it was good. Which it was. "His refusal to buy wasn't your fault."

"I know it wasn't directly."

"It wasn't, period."

She fingered her watch. "I agreed with the proposal to lease hotel space because it's a good idea."

"Damn straight." The tension in his shoulders eased as he directed the subject away from the Chicago businessman. "I plan to talk to Josie and the others as soon as possible."

"Very good. Is there anything you'd like me to do?"

He shook his head. "After supper, I'll—"

"Russ?" Matt stepped inside, grinning like a fool when he saw the woman talking to his brother. He swept off his hat. "Lydia."

"Hello." She gave him a warm smile.

Had Matt come here to see Lydia? Something big and hot swirled through Russ.

His brother looked her over, slowly. "You're the prettiest thing I've come across all day."

She laughed. "And where have you been today? With the cattle?"

"Guilty." He winked.

Russ rubbed his nape, telling himself that the sudden flare of displeasure he felt wasn't caused by the easiness between his brother and his business partner. Just how long had Matt stayed when he had come by the hotel while Russ was away? What all had he and Lydia discussed?

Lydia glanced at Russ. "Let me know what I can do to help."

He had plenty of ideas on that score and not one of them involved the hotel.

She gave him a steady look. "I mean it."

He nodded, watching the gentle sway of her skirts as she left. When he turned, he saw his brother doing the same thing.

He tamped down a quick flare of irritation and leveled his voice. "What are you doing here?"

Matt eyed him curiously. "Did I interrupt?"

"Just business."

"Pa told me you were back. I came to see if you wanted to get some supper."

That would take Russ's mind off Lydia. And he'd know where his brother was keeping company. Although that didn't matter, Russ told himself quickly. He had no claim on the woman and he wasn't making one. He did, however, have a bone to pick with his brother.

As they ate, Russ went back and forth about what to say to Matt. It shouldn't bother Russ that his brother had come around the hotel while he was away, so he wouldn't let it. But Matt's sharing confidences with Lydia was a different matter.

After supper, they stopped in at Pete Carter's saloon for a drink. They took a table in the far corner as Pete brought them a bottle of his good whiskey. The brothers sipped at the liquor, watching another of the countless arguments between Luther Grimes and Odell Pickett. At least they were still standing at the bar.

Neither was waving around a gun. Pete had learned long ago to collect their hardware when Luther and Odell came in.

The old men were harmless until they got full of liquor, then an old feud—no one knew about what—reared its head and they threatened to duel. Pete had already cut off their liquor supply, but the pair were spitting at each other like wet hens.

Russ glanced at his brother. "Lydia told me you came by to see her while I was gone."

"Yeah." Matt tossed back a drink. "She's quite the package."

Russ bit back the urge to tell Matt to stay away from her. "She also asked me about Julius's decision not to buy my share of The Fontaine. I was damn surprised she knew about that."

Matt frowned. "Was it supposed to be a secret?"

"It wasn't anything she needed to be privy to."

"Sorry. I thought she already knew or I wouldn't have said anything. Did I cause a problem?"

"No," Russ answered gruffly. The problem between him and Lydia had nothing to do with his brother.

The swing of the saloon door had Russ looking past Matt to see Davis Lee. The sheriff stopped to have a word with Luther and Odell, who still refrained from swinging at each other.

Davis Lee made his way over and eased into a chair beside Russ. He palmed off his hat, scrubbing a hand down his face. "How was your trip?"

"Not very successful."

"Sorry to hear it. Maybe I can give you a little good news." He slouched back in his chair. "I found out something about your business partner."

Russ couldn't decide if it was dread or anticipation stirring up his blood. "And?"

Matt looked from Russ to Davis Lee.

The lawman inclined his head. "It's all right for me to talk in front of Matt?"

Russ nodded. A sudden tension banded his chest.

"What the hell?" Matt muttered.

Davis Lee pinched the bridge of his nose. "She called off

the wedding and sued Wade Vance for breach of promise after he took off with a hefty sum of money her father thought he was investing in a business venture. To hear her tell it, Lydia hired a couple of private investigators to hunt down Vance and they found out the man had several fiancées. He had bilked all their families, too."

"So why did she sue him for not marrying her?"

"She stood a better chance of getting some of the money back and stopping him."

"That means everybody around there knew what had happened. She opened herself up to scandal and embarrassment." Matt voiced Russ's thoughts.

The woman had spine. Russ had to give her that. He found himself smiling inwardly. She was a piece of work. "I'll be damned."

"You knew I'd find something," Davis Lee reminded.

"Not anything like this." Russ had been hoping for a discovery that would make it easier for him to stay away from her, not harder.

Matt scowled. "You told Davis Lee to investigate Lydia? What's going on?"

"I don't trust her, that's what."

"Why not?"

Russ looked at the sheriff. "There's got to be more."

"Just getting this much information was like pulling teeth."

"That's not too surprising." Getting anything out of the woman herself was exactly the same. "I don't think whatever she's hiding has to do with her former betrothed."

"You want me to keep trying?"

"Yes."

"All right. I'll let you know when I have more information."

Matt waited until Davis Lee had stepped outside before

looking at Russ in disgust. "What the hell is wrong with you? You don't check up on ladies!"

"Why not? If I'd checked up on Amy, I could've saved myself a lot of misery."

"This isn't right. What is it you think she's hiding?"

"I don't know, but my gut tells me it's definitely something."

"Maybe I can find out."

"Leave her be," Russ said so quickly he realized he'd been thinking for a few minutes about warning Matt off. He'd been kidding himself to think he had his attraction to her under control. He didn't control anything.

A muscle flexed in his brother's jaw. "Why should I? You're not sweet on her."

The whole time Russ had been gone, he had told himself he wasn't thinking of her, wasn't missing her. It was a lie. She filled up his senses, enough to keep his chest tight since seeing her.

When Russ didn't answer, his brother prodded incredulously, "*Are* you sweet on her?"

"You just steer clear of those skirts."

"Why don't you call on her?"

There wasn't only one reason. And Russ didn't feel like sharing any of them right now with his brother. "I'm not sure that's a good idea"

"Then why can't *I* call on her?"

"Because I am sure *that's* not a good idea."

Matt grinned like a fool. "You want to court her."

"No, I don't."

"Well, you want to do something with her and I've got a pretty good idea what."

Russ couldn't defend himself against that. "Shut up," he muttered.

Nothing had changed. She still got to him faster than a whirlwind could snuff out a match. He wanted her until his back teeth ached and the fact that she was hiding something was starting to matter less every day.

Hell, he wasn't any better off now than he had been before going to Abilene.

Chapter Ten

Russ Baldwin made her head spin. It wasn't only because of the way her body reacted when he was near; it was also because of the way he had tried to protect her feelings. He could dismiss it if he wanted to, but Lydia couldn't.

The next day, she was still thinking about what he'd done for her. Russ had wanted to know if her agreement concerning his plan to lease space in the hotel was because she felt guilty about why Mr. Julius had refused to buy into the hotel. It wasn't, but it wasn't purely about business, either.

Knowing what she did now about the man's refusal to purchase Russ's interest made it impossible for Lydia to pretend otherwise. She felt something for Russ. Their kissing had sprung the lock on a curiosity about him she'd managed so far to keep in check.

Thanks to the friendship between their fathers, she knew he had never been married, but why? He liked women, all women.

And he seemed to feel it was his responsibility alone to pay off the banknote that would save his family's ranch. Granted, she didn't know the situation beyond what Russ had told her, but neither his brother nor his father seemed the type to put that responsibility solely on his shoulders.

His father used a wheelchair, but his accident hadn't affected his mind in the least. He was still as shrewd and capable as ever. Lydia supposed J.T. could be also trying to find a way to pay the banknote, but she had never gotten that impression.

She wouldn't let herself ask Russ for details. That would invite questions about herself, an openness she couldn't encourage.

Whether it was due to curiosity or his gallantry, she found herself wanting to see him, to be with him. More than once, she wanted to search him out for no reason. She managed to resist the urge. What she couldn't control was the hard tug of emotion she felt in her chest the couple of times she did see him.

With the hotel to comanage and the underground network to oversee, she had more than enough to keep her mind off Russ. Still, he was on the edge of her thoughts as she showed Willow around and explained her duties. As she served as lookout late that night when four of the most recent abuse victims slipped out of the hotel and headed for the next safe station.

It didn't help her resolve when she caught his gaze on her as she went about her business. His blue eyes were intense, speculative, as if he weren't sure what to make of her.

The temptation to ask his thoughts persisted, but she didn't give in to it. She managed to keep to herself until the next morning.

Standing on the hotel's balcony, Lydia struggled to contain her panic and a numbing fear. The sharp glare of the midmorning sun slanted across Main Street and the buildings on either side. She stared down at the telegram she had been handed by Tony Santos only minutes before. Philip had disappeared.

Her parents had kept her informed about her wounded brother-in-law since she and Naomi fled Mississippi. One of Lydia's parents checked on DeBoard every day, reporting on his still-serious condition. Yesterday, he hadn't been at the huge home her sister had managed, where her abusive husband had murdered her. Where Lydia had hoped Philip might die from the wounds Naomi had inflicted on him in self-defense.

Her parents believed he had hidden the extent of his recovery and had left under his own steam. DeBoard was missing and Lydia's father had no idea where the bastard could have gone.

She had to tell Naomi, but right now, Lydia felt as though her legs might fold like those of a new colt.

The cold air stung her cheeks as she stared absently at the people moving about Whirlwind. She stayed in the shadows, under the eaves with the limestone wall at her back for support. Another glance at the paper she held in her unsteady hand had her trying to breathe past the sharp tightness in her chest.

Upon reading the message, Lydia's first impulse had been to grab Naomi and flee somewhere else, but common sense won out. If Philip had disappeared yesterday, there was no way he could find them in Whirlwind today, even if he knew exactly where to look. Lydia knew she and Naomi needed a plan, then if they had to run, they could make a quick getaway. Maybe even hide at the hotel or another safe station.

She hated DeBoard for making her afraid, for what he'd done to Isabel and Naomi.

For an instant, rage engulfed her, then fear and a suffocating sense of being targeted crashed down on her. Tears stung her eyes and she tried to blink them away.

"Ah, I thought I saw you up here."

Russ. Foot! She quickly dashed a hand beneath her eyes. "What are you doing out in the cold?"

She turned to face him with a wobbly smile. He had used the door that led there from the second floor hallway. "Nothing."

His gaze shifted to Main Street then back to her, searching her face. "Are you all right?"

"Oh, yes." She gave a shaky laugh and hoped he didn't look too closely at her.

She had managed to keep him from finding out about the women hiding right under his nose. She could hide this from him, too.

He scowled. "Where's your coat?"

For the first time, she felt the chill sink into her bones. "I hadn't planned to be out here long."

"It's cold enough to freeze the horns off one of my pa's longhorns." Russ reached back to open the door. "Come inside before you turn blue."

"All right." She crumpled the message in her hand, fighting to compose herself.

She didn't want Russ to know she was upset. He would ask questions, and Lydia wasn't sure she could put him off. She pasted a pleasant expression on her face as she walked past him and into the hotel.

The hotel's moist heat made her aware of just how cold she was. Her skin felt tight as she rubbed her arms.

"Are you sure you're okay?" Russ swiftly closed the door.

"Yes." She smiled in his direction.

He looked doubtful. She headed for the staircase leading to her rooms on the third floor.

"I talked to Josie. She wants a space downstairs."

She turned on unsteady legs. "Oh, very good."

"Jericho's interested, too." Searching her face, Russ stepped closer. "In fact, Jed Doyle is thinking about selling his gunsmith business to Jericho."

"That's nice." She wished Russ would go away. He was too close, too strong, making her painfully aware that she was holding on to her composure by the skin of her teeth.

"Our new tenants want to move in as soon as possible."

Lydia nodded. She should've asked that, but her mind was on stall. All she could think about was Philip showing up here, trying to kill her and Naomi. Oh, why couldn't Russ leave her alone before she burst into tears like a ninny?

Looking solemn, his gaze slid over her. "I thought you'd be more taken with the news."

She felt as though she might unravel, the way she'd felt after she and Naomi had escaped Philip and they had finally realized the reality of what had happened. Her stomach churned.

If she didn't get away from Russ right now, she was going to come apart at the seams. She couldn't look at him or she would give in to the urge to blurt out what was wrong.

"It's wonderful news," she said over her shoulder, focused on reaching her rooms. "I don't mean to be rude, but I need to take care of something."

"All right," Russ said slowly.

A ball of emotion lodged in her chest, expanding until she felt as though her heart might crack open. She had one foot on the bottom stair when his big warm hand closed over her elbow.

"Lydia?"

A choked sound came out. She couldn't help it.

"What's going on?" Concern threaded his words.

She shook her head, angry at the tears blurring her sight, at herself for not being able to escape him before she started bawling like a baby. "Nothing."

"Bull."

He shouldn't be touching her. Not when even the smallest movement might destroy her crumbling control.

"You haven't drawn an easy breath since I found you. You're shaking." He gently, but firmly turned her toward him. His work-roughened fingers stroked up the back of her arm as he urged her closer. "What's happened?"

The question nearly broke her. She shouldn't tell him anything, but she couldn't face Naomi this way.

He lifted her right hand, looked at the paper she had wadded into a ball. "What is that?"

"It's a message from my parents." Fear pushed the words past her tight throat. "My brother-in-law has disappeared."

"Disappeared?" He frowned. "Do they suspect foul play? Is someone looking for him?"

"Oh, yes." Her voice was high and taut with the effort to keep from screaming out in pure rage. She couldn't stop a tear of anger. "I hope they find him and—"

"And what?"

Kill him.

"And what, Lydia?" Russ's hold tightened slightly. "Sugar, you're scared about something."

She looked into his blue eyes, coaxed by the concern there, the patience. "He killed my sister."

Russ ushered her into the nearest empty guest room. He closed the door, but he didn't release her as she expected.

Instead, he took one of her hands in his and placed both on his chest, then he splayed his free hand on her back. "Tell me."

"I don't like to talk about it."

"I have things like that, too, but telling somebody might be good." He thumbed away a tear she hadn't been aware of crying.

"It's about Isabel. When I talk about her, the pain starts

fresh all over again." And the loneliness, the guilt. Lydia looked down, touched the timepiece pinned to her bodice. "All I have left of her is this watch and the earrings I wore to the Grand Opening."

Russ squeezed her hand, waited.

Lydia knew she should step away, but she couldn't. She didn't want to. All the fear, grief and fury she had felt since Isabel's death crashed together in an overwhelming wave and she pressed closer to the big man holding her.

The words tumbled out. "My brother-in-law, Philip DeBoard, beat her. Isabel died after he shoved her down the stairs during one of his rages."

Russ brushed his thumb across her knuckles, listening quietly.

"The people who knew she was being abused looked the other way. The DeBoards are wealthy and well established in the area. Isabel wouldn't tell me the truth when I asked her about it. That's why I—"

"Why you what?" he asked softly.

She'd nearly told him about getting involved with the underground network. "That's why I...feel guilty."

He nodded.

"Naomi was her maid and she tried to help my sister, but there was only so much she could do. After Isabel died, my parents and I tried to get Naomi to come live with us, but she wouldn't. Finally, she agreed and the day I went to pick her up—" Lydia's voice broke.

Russ waited patiently.

After a moment, she continued, "Philip was beating her. He had tried to rape her and she fought back. Before Isabel died, I began carrying a derringer when I went to her home, but before I could shoot, Naomi stabbed him with a pitchfork."

As Lydia wiped away her tears, Russ reached in the back

pocket of his trousers and held out a worn black bandanna. "It looks ragged, but it's clean."

"Thanks." She took it, dabbing at her eyes as she continued her story. "We thought he was dead. Once Naomi and I got back to my parents' house, my father urged us to go on to Whirlwind."

"So, that's why you were here early," he murmured.

She nodded, drawing in his dark male scent. "We packed a wagon and left that night, stopping only when we had to. Naomi's ribs were broken so we couldn't travel very fast. When I wired my father to see what been done about DeBoard, he told me Philip wasn't dead, but gravely injured and not expected to live."

"So your father has been sending you wires keeping you updated on his condition."

"And my mother." She took a shuddering breath. "Philip showed some signs of recovery, but the doctor wasn't encouraging. My father went yesterday to check on him and Philip was gone, just disappeared."

"Maybe the doctor moved him?"

Lydia shook her head. "He came looking for Philip, too."

"If his condition is that critical, he couldn't have gotten very far."

"My parents think he's been lying about his progress. That he's well on his way to recovery."

"And your father thinks DeBoard is headed here?"

She nodded. "He thinks Philip will try to track down Naomi and me, and he's right. Philip will never stand for a woman getting the better of him, especially Naomi, whom he considers a slave. She isn't. She's free, but Philip has never treated her that way."

Russ said nothing for a moment, just held her. Her trembling ceased. She felt…relieved. She wished she could stay right here with him, just like this. Talking to Russ made her feel strong enough to face Naomi.

He dipped his head, his breath tickling her ear, making her aware of every hard line of his body against hers. "I'll do what I can to help you. I won't let anything happen to you or Naomi."

She looked up in surprise, his words putting an ache in her throat. Her gaze dropped to his mouth. "Thank you," she whispered.

He gathered her close against his solid muscular frame.

Touched by his solemn declaration, she laid her head on his chest. She drew in the his familiar scent, the spice of his shaving soap.

She hadn't planned to tell him about Isabel or Naomi or Philip's part in everything, but she had. For the first time, Lydia considered telling Russ the truth. All of it. And not only to relieve the guilt she still felt over his killing to protect her secret, a secret he didn't even know.

She knew she couldn't. She couldn't be as open about everything in her life as she had been about her sister.

Maybe she shouldn't have told him the things she had, but she wasn't sorry. She ignored the voice inside her that prodded her to thank him and step out of his arms. For the first time since Isabel's death, Lydia felt truly comforted.

Finding out about Lydia's former betrothed had made it difficult for Russ to stay away from her, but learning about her brother-in-law two mornings later made it impossible. When she told him the situation with DeBoard, Russ wanted to lock her up somewhere safe and go after the SOB, but he hadn't. Instead, he'd held her and listened.

Seeing her upset, feeling her body trembling against him

had rocked him a bit. He'd never seen Lydia intimidated or afraid, not even when she'd been shot in the lobby. Hurt, yes. Angry, yes. But not afraid. It was disorienting, as though he were stepping ass backward into the dark.

All day, he had checked on her while trying to act as though he weren't, updating her each time he spoke to one of their new tenants.

Since their kiss, Lydia had kept her distance. Her confiding in him showed the depth of her fear. He'd thought she might be aloof after sharing something so personal, but whenever she saw him, her eyes softened and she gave him a little smile that spoke of something private between them.

He'd learned something Davis Lee hadn't, although Russ could see why the lawman might not have been able to get this information. Lydia's father was probably doing his damnedest to keep secret any report about DeBoard so he could track down and deal with the man on his own.

Russ was glad he'd been the one to get the knowledge from Lydia. Otherwise, he wouldn't have seen the pure-dee terror on her face. Terror that clung to Russ like grit and sent him to the sheriff with a new request.

It wasn't betraying a confidence to alert Davis Lee about the DeBoard bastard. Russ didn't tell the sheriff why DeBoard was a threat to Lydia and Naomi. That was Lydia's story to tell or not. But the lawman was a friend. Just Russ saying the man was dangerous was good enough for Davis Lee to keep an eye out for him.

It might make Lydia as mad as a wet hen, but it would be safer for her and that was what he cared about most.

Was the fear and uncertainty about her brother-in-law what made Lydia so secretive? Daily updates on the man's grave condition would explain the frequent telegrams she still received.

Could the situation with her brother-in-law be what Lydia was hiding? It was hard for Russ to imagine that a woman who'd done the gutsy things Lydia had done could be involved in something unsavory, but that was just it. He didn't know.

Since the night he had found her on the prairie, he continued to watch her, to see if she went anywhere, did anything that might explain what she was up to. Except for the possibility that she may have done something during the week he spent in Abilene, she hadn't driven out of town alone again.

After learning about DeBoard, Russ had been real tempted to ignore the fact he knew she was hiding something. When he was close to her, her lush curves pressed against him, her subtle scent teasing his senses, it was easy to disregard everything except the feel of her.

As always, any dealings with her were underlaid with the awareness that put a hard throb in his blood. So far, he had managed not to act on his growing attraction to her. Well, except for kissing her in the kitchen.

Now that he was away from her, he had his wits about him.

Amy had torn him up like a twister. He wasn't letting another woman do such a thing again. Ever.

He wasn't so smitten with Lydia that he would turn a blind eye.

He had begun work on the shops that morning after seeing her. During the day, Josie and Jericho had stopped by to discuss how much space they would need. They liked his idea of having a large glass window in front of their shops to showcase their wares as well as anything Jake might want to sell.

Russ figured he could ask Lydia to take care of getting the glass. She'd already proven she was better at that than he was. Chuckling at the thought, he went in search of her just after dark.

When he didn't find her in the lobby or dining room, he checked the kitchen. Naomi stood in the pantry with Ef. They were close together, their voices quiet.

Russ grinned. "Sorry to interrupt."

Naomi jumped and Ef slid an arm around her waist. Knowing what he did now, Russ understood why the woman was so easily startled.

"Evenin', Russ." The black man smiled at him, still keeping his arm around Naomi's waist.

"Good evening." Russ smiled at the slender woman snuggled into Ef's side. "Hello, Naomi."

"Sir."

Russ had tried to get her to call him by his first name, but she wouldn't. "I'm looking for Lydia. Have you seen her?"

"No." The woman stepped forward. "She didn't tell me she was going anywhere."

Russ heard the anxiety in her voice. "She's probably in the hotel then. I'll check the other floors."

"Maybe I should help you find her." Naomi's lovely face was pinched with concern, her posture now rigid.

He could see the shadow of fear in her dark eyes. At the thought of the abuse she had suffered, Russ felt a surge of admiration for her toughness, then right on its heels a gut-twisting fury. She was gracious and kind, even with what she had been through.

He understood now why she always stayed in the background, tried not to bring attention to herself. But she was getting plenty of attention from Ef. Russ's friend wore his feelings all over his face and it was plain he was in love with the woman. Though Naomi's stunning features sometimes appeared aloof, Russ sensed she had the same feelings.

He smiled at the couple. "No need for you to help, Naomi.

I'm sure I'll track her down. Sorry I interrupted. If you see her, will you let her know I'm looking for her?"

"Yes."

"Thanks." He lifted a hand in goodbye and walked out.

She'd been on the balcony this morning, trying to hide her upset. Maybe she was there again.

He climbed the stairs to the second floor. As he stepped out into the cold November air, he saw her, but not on the balcony. She was in front of the livery in a buggy, driving out of town.

Remembering the other time she'd driven out of town after dark, Russ's eyes narrowed. He'd had to go after her then and when he had found her, she had claimed to be lost. What was she doing this time?

For a moment, he hesitated to follow. She had shared a secret with him earlier in the day. Maybe if he asked, she would tell him why she was venturing outside of Whirlwind.

He snorted. He wouldn't lay money on it. If he hadn't happened to see her so obviously troubled this morning, she wouldn't have told him anything. This opportunity might not come again. He had been suspicious of her excuse for being gone so long, out on the prairie. Maybe now he could find out the real story.

Inside of five minutes, Russ had his horse saddled and was riding out of Whirlwind.

It didn't take long to catch up with her. He kept his mount to a walk, staying far enough behind not to be heard over the creak of the buggy, but close enough to still see.

After a few minutes, he spied a wagon on the moonlit prairie. Lydia topped a rise and reined the buggy to a stop behind the buckboard. A shadow separated itself from the darkness. A man. He moved to Lydia and helped her out of the buggy.

Russ's blood was already starting to boil before the other

man stepped far enough into the moonlight for Russ to recognize him. Bram Ross.

What the hell! He had a torturous flash of déjà vu, just as when he had learned about Amy and her married beau.

Bram released his hold on Lydia as they moved a few feet ahead of the vehicle. They stood in the waving knee-high grass with their heads so close that Russ couldn't tell where one ended and the other began.

His face and hands were chilled, but that did nothing to check the unfamiliar heat shoving through his chest. He didn't want the rancher's hands anywhere on her, but the shadowy darkness and position of their bodies prevented Russ from being able to tell where Bram's hands were.

Why was Lydia meeting him out here? How many times had she done it? Was this the first time? Seeing her with his longtime friend had a stinging heat clutching at Russ's chest. It felt like…jealousy.

If he hadn't needed to be quiet, he would've laughed. Jealousy wasn't a problem for him. Ever since Amy had ripped his heart to shreds, Russ's philosophy had been that there were too many women in the world to be lassoed by just one.

But evidently, he was lassoed now because he burned to go up to Lydia and Bram, interrupt their…whatever the hell this was and demand to know what was going on.

When had they arranged this? Lydia had danced a lot with Bram at the Grand Opening. Had that been when they agreed to get together? The same night Lydia had kissed Russ stupid?

He thought his jaw might break in two. He must have unknowingly tightened his legs, silently commanding his horse to move because the animal started forward. Another command had the gelding turning quietly into a sparse stand of trees. As Russ forced himself to sit behind a pine tree and watch Lydia with his friend, anger pulsed in a white-hot wave.

It drove him crazy that he couldn't tell if Bram was touching her or kissing her or anything else. If Lydia was so damn afraid of her brother-in-law, what in tarnation was she doing out here *alone? After dark.*

DeBoard had disappeared the day before so he wouldn't have had time to get here, but he could have someone looking for Lydia and her friend, someone who could've been looking for a while and might be close.

Russ flashed back to her chalk-white face, the stark terror in her eyes that morning. Fear that deep-seated couldn't be faked. He knew in his gut she hadn't lied about her brother-in-law. Which meant her reason for being out here alone must be important enough for her to risk danger to meet with Bram.

Russ didn't like it. And he didn't like her being with his friend. Or any other man, he admitted grimly.

After a few minutes, the rancher helped Lydia into her buggy. Russ kept his horse still as she drove past his hiding place and back to Whirlwind. Bram left the opposite way, toward his ranch. Russ followed Lydia, directing his mount to stay to a walk.

He didn't know why she was meeting Bram Ross alone on the prairie this late, but Russ damn sure intended to find out.

Chapter Eleven

In the flickering amber light of a lantern, Lydia smiled at Pete Carter as he met her in front of the livery. Pete owned the stable as well as the saloon next door. The grizzled man helped her down, and after she paid him, he led the animal and rig to the back.

The smells of livestock, leather and hay mixed in the cold air. She tucked her remaining money into the hidden pocket of her navy serge skirt. Her thoughts drifted to where they'd been almost constantly. Russ.

She'd felt his arms around her all day. And all day, she wished she could've told him everything. Still, just sharing her uncertainty and her fear of Philip had helped tremendously.

Russ hadn't seemed suspicious of her story. He had listened, and the questions he asked were about her and Naomi's welfare, not probing or skeptical about what she'd told him.

Thanks to him, she felt safe for the first time since leaving Jackson. She knew it was probably his code of honor that had prompted him to offer protection, but not to hold her the way he had, not to listen so patiently. There was a new closeness between them.

A shadow fell across the pale amber light and Lydia angled toward the door, where the lantern hung. Expecting to see Pete, she was surprised to find Russ instead.

"Hello." She smiled.

He didn't return her smile, just stood there with his massive shoulders taking up half the doorway.

Behind him was a horse, the paint gelding she recognized as his. "What are you doing out so late?"

"I was just fixin' to ask you that," he said silkily.

The soft words had dread creeping up her spine. Before she could answer, he stepped closer. His eyes glittered like blue steel in the smoky light. "If you're so all-fired worried about your brother-in-law, why in the hell did you drive out of town after dark?"

"W-what?"

"You have no idea where DeBoard is or if he has someone on your trail. He could've hired someone to start tracking you right after you and Naomi left Mississippi. Why would you go out on the prairie? Did you stop to think about what risk you might be taking?"

His tone had her stiffening. "I'm not a complete idiot. I have my derringer."

His eyes flashed. "Why were you meeting Bram Ross?"

Her stomach dropped to her feet. "How did you— You followed me!"

And he had spied on her. No, no, no. Panic began to circle through her. Had Russ overheard her conversation with Bram?

She fingered the watch pinned to her bodice. Russ's eyes were too sharp, too piercing. She wanted to get away from him, but she needed to try and find out if he had heard anything. She knew he hadn't seen anything because the woman Lydia was supposed to pick up had never arrived at Bram's, concerning them both.

Just how close to her and Bram had Russ been? "Where were you hiding?"

"In a stand of pine trees behind y'all."

She thought she knew the spot. If he'd stayed there throughout their conversation, he probably hadn't heard anything incriminating. Hopefully. "How long were you there?"

"Long enough." Her partner shifted, positioning his muscular frame in a way that made it clear she wasn't getting past him. "What I want to know is how long have you two been carrying on?"

"What?" His question took her aback. She had expected him to ask about the secret network. In the stillness, her heart hammered so loudly she was surprised he couldn't hear it.

"You and Bram. How long?"

Russ thought she and the rancher were having a romance.

Her immediate reaction was to deny it, but she caught herself. If she told him her relationship with Bram wasn't like that, Russ would continue to press her for answers. He had just given her the perfect pretext.

She was hit with a mix of emotions. Relief that he didn't appear to know the real reason she and Bram had met. And distress that he believed she was involved with the other man.

After all the dances she and Bram had shared at the Grand Opening, Lydia understood why Russ thought the two of them might be seeing each other. Denying it would force her to come up with another reason for their meeting on the prairie and there was no good reason.

Frustrated, she admitted it would be better for the operation if she let Russ think she and Bram were romantically involved. Sometimes she got tired of putting the network first, but it only took one memory of her sister to renew Lydia's commitment to the secret operation.

It was a struggle to hide how bothered she was. "Why did you follow me?"

"Wouldn't want you to get lost again," he drawled.

Foot! A flush heated her neck. It was plain he hadn't believed her story from the night he'd found her out there alone. Tension arced between them.

He leveled his icy blue gaze on her. "What exactly were y'all doing out there?"

Still rattled, she shot back, "How would you like it if I questioned you about your…I don't know what to call them. Did you 'visit' Willow while you were in Abilene?" She wasn't only asking to distract his attention from her meeting with Bram. She wanted to know. "Have you visited her since you brought her to Whirlwind?"

A muscle flexed in his jaw. "She said she was out of that life."

That wasn't a denial or an answer, Lydia fumed. And she really wanted one. "She has a soft spot for you. Maybe she would make an exception in your case."

"She probably would," he said flatly.

That cut through her.

"I don't understand you driving out there. And it doesn't sound like Bram to ask it of you. He always treats women special. Why did you do that?"

Several explanations came to mind and they were all as flimsy as cheesecloth. She settled on the truth. "I promised I wouldn't tell."

Russ went stone-still. She thought she saw hurt in his eyes before it vanished and his gaze turned predatory.

"Is he in trouble? Someone in his family?"

No. Lydia didn't answer. She was deliberately misleading him, but she couldn't tell the truth. About the network or how Russ was the only man she wanted.

Angry color crested his cheekbones as he moved in on her. The wavering shadows made him appear even taller and more intimidating.

"I thought he was sweet on Deborah Blue. Dammit," he muttered. "Were you already seeing Bram when you kissed me blind that night in the kitchen?"

"No!" It hurt that he thought she would do something like that.

His gaze moved insolently down her body and back up, causing a prickle of sensation beneath the surface of her skin. Then, as though he couldn't help himself, "Did he kiss you?"

You're the only man I've kissed! Her stomach quivered. She wasn't sure if that was because of her anxiety or because of the way his voice had dropped, stroking over her.

"Answer me."

If she stayed much longer, she would end up telling him the truth. "What I did with Bram is none of your affair."

"Yes, it is. You're my partner."

"Which has nothing to do with my romantic life." He didn't appear to be any the wiser about her real reason for meeting Bram. Her apprehension edged into irritation. "Just because we own the hotel together doesn't mean you get to decide who I see."

He towered over her like a mountain. She tried to brush past him, and he finally moved enough for her to step outside.

"Lydia, wait," he said huskily, curling a big hand around her upper arm. "It isn't about that."

"Then what?" Hands on her hips, she faced him. "I'm hardly going to ask your permission to keep company with a man. You're out of your head if you think you can dictate—"

"It's about doing things behind my back."

"W-what things?" She froze, her spine turning to jelly. "What are you talking about?"

She stood only a couple of feet away, close enough to see

shadows in his eyes that she hadn't seen before. And a fleeting pain. Even before he released her arm, she planned to hear him out.

"I was engaged once."

Stunned, Lydia blinked. "You were?"

His face went carefully blank and she knew whatever he was about to tell her had hurt him deeply.

"She was carrying on with another man behind my back the whole time." He dragged a hand across his nape. His voice was quiet, ragged with an edge Lydia had never heard. "I was crazy about her, but Amy only got involved with me to hide her relationship with him."

Lydia could hardly take it in. Who wouldn't want Russ? Not only was the man as handsome as the devil, he was honorable and sweet and smart. He had a good heart. "How did you find out?"

"My brother caught them by accident. When she found out I knew, she dropped me like a hot horseshoe and hightailed it out of town with her lover. Her married lover. She took me for a complete fool. Looking back, there were things I should've questioned. So when I think someone is hiding something, especially my business partner, I start questioning."

"Perfectly understandable." That woman must have been a fool as well as a liar.

Lydia's stomach knotted. He had every reason to be suspicious, especially of her. Because Lydia *was* doing something behind his back. Maybe not something that would break his heart, but something that could put him in the middle of a fight that wasn't his. If he ever found out, if he ever looked at her with the same cold emptiness in his eyes right now, she wouldn't be able to bear it.

She realized she was brushing a thumb over her watch.

"Even though you and I aren't engaged," Russ continued, "we *are* partners. What you do affects me just like what I do affects you. If something's going on, I deserve to know."

"Yes, of course."

"I apologize. I shouldn't have bullied you."

"It's forgotten." Lydia could barely get the words out. He was apologizing when she was the one lying. The earnestness in his blue eyes made her feel lower than dirt.

And connected to him in a way she hadn't expected. She felt compelled to tell Russ about her past, as well. "I was engaged before, too."

He nodded. "My pa's talked about it."

"Wade was a first-rate con artist." When she thought about Wade Vance now, she felt more anger than hurt, but at that time, she had been skewered with pain. "He took me for a fool and tried to steal my father's money."

"What happened?"

Her gaze roamed over his rugged features softened by the hazy amber light. Glad she wore her gloves, she stepped back inside, out of the worst of the cold. "A couple of weeks before the wedding, I became suspicious. Something he said didn't add up and he'd taken a few unexplained business trips. Stupid me, I was still willing to give him the benefit of the doubt.

"So, I went to talk to him at the boardinghouse where he was staying. He and all his things were gone. Including the money my father had given him for an investment."

Russ cursed, moving closer.

Lydia caught the faint scent of leather and his own dark spice. She quelled the urge to walk into his arms and be sheltered by his brawny chest the way she had that morning. When she saw Russ's gaze was fixed on her breasts, she realized she was again stroking her watch.

She dropped her arm, retreating a step. "It finally occurred to me I'd been conned. I called off the wedding and hired a couple of Pinkerton men to find him. They warned me that they might not be able to get the money, so I was prepared for that, but not for what they found. During their investigation, they discovered he was engaged to three other women, all four of us at the same time. He'd stolen money from them and their families, too.

"My best chance of recovering any money and stopping him from doing this again was to sue him for breach of promise, so I did."

She told Russ how she had been the scandal of Jackson for about two weeks, until someone else publicly did something more interesting.

Russ's voice rumbled out. "Did he go to jail?"

"For a short time, but what made him stop were the warning posters the Pinkerton agency sent to every city or territory with law enforcement."

He nodded.

"I felt like an idiot for a long time."

"No way you could've known someone would do such a thing."

There was admiration in his eyes, which flustered her. "Neither could you," she said softly.

He shrugged.

"It's true. You didn't see what your fiancée was doing because you're honest. Straightforward. You believed Amy was that way, too."

"Doesn't excuse my being so smitten that I didn't figure out what she was doing. Matt's the one who found out Amy was lying and cheating."

"I blamed myself, too," Lydia said. "Sometimes, I still get

mad at myself when I think about it. It was hard to accept that I had been taken in by Wade's slick charm, but even my father was fooled and he's a shrewd businessman. Now I know it wasn't my fault. You have to know that, too. About Amy."

He nodded, reaching out to stroke a knuckle down her cheek.

She wanted to touch him, too, but she didn't. Closeted alone with him like this, it was tempting to believe this conversation was only about the two of them. Not the operation. Not his suspicion.

Still feeling the warmth of his touch, her common sense began to slip away and she stepped back. "All I'm trying to say is I understand how you felt. We both learned through hard experience."

"And now we're both cynical." Amusement glinted in his eyes.

"We're both *wiser*," she emphasized with a smile.

Russ's gaze trailed over her then came back to rest on her mouth. A shiver skipped up her spine. The memory of their kiss was there between them. Lydia could read it in the stormy blue of his eyes.

Tension arced between them and she couldn't help wishing he would kiss her again. But he seemed to be fighting it as hard as she was.

He made a low sound of frustration and stepped back, clenching his hands into fists.

She gave herself a mental shake. What was wrong with her? She'd just led him to believe she was involved with another man then nearly invited him to kiss her.

He broke the pulsing silence by tipping his head toward the livery's open door. "Let me walk you back to the hotel."

"What about your horse?"

"I'll tend to him in a bit."

"All right." She smiled and joined him outside. The air was sharp, the cold stinging her face even though the trip to The Fontaine was short.

They walked closely together. Lydia huddled into her gray wool coat, the hem of her skirts brushing against the leg of his trousers. They touched nowhere else and still she was aware of the warmth of his big body, his powerful arms, gentle hands. His mouth.

She wanted to feel the same sense of well-being she had felt that morning, but she didn't. The tension between them had eased somewhat though she wasn't naive enough to think it would stay that way.

Russ opened the outside door that was close to his office, propping it wide with an arm above her head. "Here we are."

"Thank you."

As she stepped inside, he touched her arm. "I plan to put a large window across the front of the new shops to display their wares."

"What a good idea."

"Would you mind taking care of the glass?" He smiled. "You seem to have a knack for that."

"I'd be glad to."

"Thanks."

The fresh scent of the outdoors clung to him. She wanted to get closer to him, bury her face in his neck. But he was looking at her expectantly, waiting for her to take her leave.

She did. "Good night."

"Good night."

Lydia watched his purposeful strides take him back into the darkness as he returned to the livery. When he was inside the small building, she pulled the door shut.

She'd been fooling herself all day, believing he was closer

to trusting her. His following her said he wasn't, and he had good reason not to. Not only because of her actions, but because of what his ex-fiancée had done to him.

She hated that he believed she was involved with his friend. As much as she despised the idea, it was better for him to think it. If he knew the truth, it could jeopardize the secrecy of the network.

A heaviness settled over her. The only man she wanted was Russ and she had probably just destroyed any chance of a relationship.

Because now, in addition to being suspicious of her, he believed she had a romantic relationship with another man. And she had to let him think it.

When Lydia told Russ it was none of his affair what she had been doing with Bram on the prairie, it had been all Russ could do not to back her into the wall of the livery and kiss the sass right out of her. She sure as hell hadn't looked kissed by Bram.

No reddened lips, no hue of arousal on her creamy skin.

She hadn't looked anything like she had after Russ had kissed her that night.

Not knowing exactly what had happened between the pair was one reason Russ hadn't been able to stop himself from asking all those questions about the other man. He'd been blistered up enough over seeing them, but the threat of danger to her had made Russ as angry as a teased rattlesnake. At her. At Bram.

Since then, his gut had been in a knot and he'd done everything he knew to get her out of his mind, working himself to exhaustion on constructing the new shops.

It took him four days, but when Russ stepped into Haskell's that afternoon, he'd simmered down. He stood at a barrel of nails, dropping a handful into the cloth bag he'd brought.

Hearing the thud of boots coming into the mercantile, he looked over his shoulder and saw Bram. By the time the other man walked over to shake hands, Russ had tamped down his resentment.

"Did you come into town to get some supplies?"

"Yes, and to pick up something Josie made for Molly."

Molly was Bram's adopted niece, half sister to his new sister-in-law, and Josie frequently made clothes for her and little Lorelai Holt, Riley and Susannah's daughter.

"She keeps them in the latest fashions," Russ noted.

"Emma and Georgia say it seems to help her deal with losing her and Davis Lee's baby."

Charlie Haskell interrupted to ask if Bram had a list, then he took it and went into the back for the items.

"Any cattle rustled from your place in the last week?" Russ asked.

"No, but I saw Matt and he said more of yours had been."

"Yes, we and the Rocking H lost some, too."

"Yeah, I heard that from Riley yesterday."

"Holt's been hurt as much as the rest of us by these thieves." Russ shook his head. "Matt's spent more nights with the cattle this month than with his lady friends."

Bram chuckled. "He must feel as though he's been doubly hit then."

"I reckon. You planning to stop by The Fontaine while you're in town?"

Russ had asked so he could gauge his friend's reaction. Bram gave away nothing by his face, but a sudden stillness came over him. "I might if I have time," he said carefully.

Russ figured the other man would *make* time. Judging by Bram's guardedness when Russ had asked, Lydia must not have told her beau that Russ knew about the two of them.

He remembered the wounded look in her eyes when he asked her if she and Bram had already made plans to see each other the night she practically kissed Russ out of his drawers.

The store's door opened and Charlie's nephew, Mitchell Orr, walked inside. He greeted Bram and Russ as he made his way behind the counter to help his uncle.

Russ had as many questions for Bram as he'd had for Lydia. How often did he plan to see her? What nights had they been together? Why in the hell was he keeping his relationship with her a secret? Did the other man know about DeBoard, and if so, why had Bram agreed to let Lydia drive outside of town alone after dark?

Russ had known Bram his whole life, and if the other man had seen the terror in Lydia's eyes that Russ had seen, he never would have asked or allowed her to go out on the prairie alone. He wanted to ask Bram about that, too, but she—*they*—were none of his concern. She'd made that plain.

A man and woman entered the store, prodding Russ to pay for his nails and say goodbye to Bram and Charlie.

As he strode down the planked walk past the newspaper office and cut across the street toward the hotel, he could feel himself getting lathered up again. The thought of staying inside the hotel right then, surrounded by walls, made him feel choked. After leaving the nails at his office, he made his way to Ef's.

The fire blazed in the forge, and Ef stood over a cauldron of water, dunking a freshly hammered horseshoe. The black man looked up as Russ moved under the roof.

The sizzle of water, the mixed odors of smoke and metal filled the covered area. "I came by to see if those hinges and locks for the new doors were ready yet."

"They need to cool a little longer." Ef dragged a forearm across his perspiring forehead.

Russ watched as the black man used a pair of tongs to rotate a bar of iron in the fire.

Wondering when Bram planned to visit Lydia was enough to make Russ grind his teeth to a powder so he shifted his focus. He wondered if Ef knew about Lydia's brother-in-law.

As close as the blacksmith was getting to her friend, it wouldn't surprise Russ if the other man did know. Before he could ask, his attention was snagged by the sight of Bram striding down the street toward the hotel.

"Russ?"

He looked over, only then realizing Ef had asked him something.

"Is something goin' on? You must've eyeballed the hotel ten times since you got here."

Russ wasn't going to admit to his friend that he had been waiting for Bram Ross to visit Lydia. As the rancher disappeared inside The Fontaine, Russ's gut started churning.

He dragged his gaze from the hotel's front doors and back to his friend. "I wanted to talk to you about Lydia and Naomi."

Ef straightened, wiping grimy hands down his apron.

"Has Naomi shared anything with you concerning their leaving Mississippi?" Russ asked.

"Some."

"About the brother-in-law?"

The other man nodded, looking relieved that Russ knew.

"Good, so you plan to keep an eye out for the bastard."

"Yeah. I'm glad you know. I promised Naomi I wouldn't tell anyone, but I feel better knowin' we're both aware of the threat."

Russ thought about Lydia and Bram on the prairie, wondered if Ef knew anything about the pair of them. Russ was curious as to what they were doing in the hotel. Talking? Did it have anything to do with DeBoard?

"You spend a lot of time with Naomi," he said to Ef. "Is she jumpy? It seems like Lydia is always at the ready, always looking over her shoulder."

"Naomi's the same way."

"Think it's all because of DeBoard?"

"Probably." A rare anger crossed the black man's face and his mouth tightened. "The bastard hurt Naomi and killed Miz Kent's sister. It makes sense for the two of them to be on guard."

"True." The more Russ thought about it, the more certain he became that the situation with Lydia's brother-in-law was what she had been hiding.

From the shadows of the smithy, Russ watched as Bram walked out of the hotel and back towards Haskell's mercantile. His visit with Lydia hadn't taken long. Maybe just long enough for them to arrange their next meeting.

Russ clenched his jaw. He hoped Lydia didn't drive out after dark again to meet Bram, because Russ would go after her, secrecy be damned.

A half hour later, he paid for his door hinges and said goodbye to Ef. He returned to the hotel to resume his work on the lease space, took a short break for dinner, then began again.

It didn't matter how long Russ hammered, he couldn't sweat out his frustration. Inhaling the scent of pine, he dragged an arm across his damp forehead and stepped back to eye the finished side of the door frame. The rest of the frame and one wall would complete this shop.

The sharp staccato footsteps coming across the lobby toward his workspace didn't prepare him for the angry flash of Lydia's eyes when she appeared in his doorway.

Cheeks flushed, she looked fit to be tied. "Do you know what's going on upstairs?"

"What are you talking about?"

"I thought we agreed on this," she said tersely.

"Agreed on what?" He tested the plank he'd just hammered and found it sturdy enough. She was downright agitated.

"I just saw—they went—" She fluttered a hand in the direction of the staircase. "They're up there doing…things."

Russ felt as confused as if he'd been kicked in the head by a horse. "Who's doing what?"

The flush streaking her cheeks deepened and her gaze skipped around the room.

He couldn't help but admire the fit of her deep purple day dress. The white edging at the neckline and cuffs drew attention to her chest and the way the bodice smoothed over her full lush breasts.

Tearing his focus from there, he asked, "Lydia, who's doing what?"

Her mouth flattened and she grabbed him by the arm. "Come with me."

Her hand slid away as he followed her. Picking up her skirts, she swept up the staircase ahead of him, giving him an impatient look when he lagged behind a couple of steps. She sure had a bee in her bonnet about something.

Seeing her all stirred up like that stirred Russ up, too. He watched the gentle sway of her hips, wondering what her undergarments looked like.

At the top of the stairs, she waited, hands on her hips as her gaze shot down the hall. Gaslight flickered on the walls and floors, moving as their shadows did. The air faintly smelled of fuel. When Russ reached the landing, she snagged his hand and dragged him around the staircase and down to a room near the end of the hall.

She came to an abrupt stop in front of the door and jabbed a finger toward it. "Listen."

After a moment, he shook his head. "I don't hear anything."

She tugged him right up to the wood. "There."

He leaned close and then he heard it. A long moan followed by a giggle and the steady rhythm of a creaking bed frame. Surprised, his gaze shot to Lydia. The rosy tint of arousal on her face started a low throb in his blood.

Cheeks streaked with color, she looked away. "I saw a woman, one of *those* women, going upstairs with a guest."

"She could also be a guest here."

Lydia gave him a look. "I asked Willow."

Yeah, Willow would know.

Another groan sounded, definitely a groan of pleasure. Lydia nearly jumped out of her skin. "Tell them to stop!"

It would be better for Russ's imagination and his body if he did, because his mind was stuck on wondering what it would take to make Lydia moan.

"You know that isn't supposed to be going on in the hotel."

He'd thought plenty about doing the same thing with her. In the hotel or anywhere.

Beside him, she shifted from one foot to the other, her fingers nervously playing over her sister's watch. Russ watched in fascination as her blush deepened and her breathing sped up. Hell, this was affecting her, too.

Another moan followed by a breathless "yes" had Lydia drawing her bottom lip between her teeth.

She flicked him a look from under her lashes and he couldn't take his eyes off her. The soft white light skimming her jaw, the graceful arch of her neck, the thick raven hair in a practical chignon. Russ wanted to take her hair down, shuck her clothes off.

Standing just behind her shoulder as he was, his gaze was drawn to the narrow patch of skin bared by the vee of her split neckline. He could see nothing except that tiny bit of flesh, not even a hint of the valley between her breasts. He broke out in a sweat anyway.

She tilted her head toward the door. "Tell them."

"Hell, no!" He stepped back. "I'll talk to them tomorrow, but I'm not busting in there."

"You don't have to bust in. Just knock and tell them to stop."

Russ shook his head, tension coiling inside him at the way her voice had turned husky.

"Other guests will hear them," she said in exasperation. "I heard them and I wasn't even in this hallway."

Watching the rapid rise and fall of her full breasts sawed at the lock on his self-control. If he wanted, he could bend his head and nip her delicate earlobe. He had to force himself not to reach for her.

"If you break up whatever's going on in there, you'll just be drawing attention to them," he said. "Other people probably won't even notice."

"How can they not? The two of them are loud enough to be heard clear to Ef's."

At his chuckle, she huffed out a breath. "I'll do it myself."

She raised a hand to knock. Russ hooked an arm around her waist and hauled her away from the door. "No, you won't."

She gasped in outrage and squirmed. It could've been the feel of her body moving sinuously against his or her reaction to those love sounds. Whatever it was had Russ operating on pure reflex. He carried her into the next room and shut the door.

Moonlight streamed through the window, making her features appear even more delicate. Her warm breath tickled his throat as she pushed at him. "What are you doing? Put me down."

He did. The second her feet touched the floor, he slapped

a hand on either side of her, caging her in with his body and covered her mouth with his.

He didn't hesitate, didn't think twice, didn't stop. He had to have another taste. He had to have *her.*

She resisted for less than the span of a heartbeat. Then with a soft breathy sound, her mouth opened to his and her arms went around his neck.

The same primal need he'd felt the other night clawed through him. He wanted to strip her naked, bare those lush breasts, get his hands on her. Aching, he took the kiss deeper, intoxicated by the dark sweetness of her mouth.

It seemed as though he had wanted her forever. When she melted into him, he moved his hands down the wall to bracket her waist. She buried her fingers in his hair as he dragged his lips from hers and nipped lightly at her earlobe the way he'd wanted.

The broken sound she made turned Russ hard as a poker. Her heart was beating so hard, so fast, he could feel her pulse beneath his tongue. Filled with the scent of warm woman and lavender, he murmured, "I wanted to do this the other night."

"Me, too."

Her words had him kissing her again. After a long moment, he pulled back, breathing hard. He wanted her and only her. She needed to know.

Her questions about him and Willow had nagged him since she had asked. It mattered what Lydia thought. He nuzzled her cheek, her ear, savoring the silky texture of her skin. "When you asked me about Willow, I wanted to tell you I haven't been with her in a long time. Don't plan to be ever again."

Her hands moved over his shoulders and she pulled him down, initiating the kiss this time. Russ wanted to taste all of her, touch all of her. Skimming his hands up over her rib cage to the undersides of her full breasts, he brushed his thumbs across her nipples. Beneath the wool of her bodice he felt them tighten.

Making a rough sound that echoed his own need, she shifted so that one of his thighs pressed between hers. Compelled by the frustration, the arousal, the concern he had reined in since seeing her with Bram, Russ moved his lips to her ear, down to the delicate wing of her collarbone.

He wanted to drink her up. She was soft and warm, honey-sweet beneath his tongue. He just knew she'd taste like this all over. The need to find out had him moving one hand to the buttons going down the front of her bodice.

He touched his tongue to each bit of skin revealed by the next open button then the next, unfastening the top to her waist. When he buried his face in the fragrant warmth between her breasts, she pressed hard against his erection.

"Russ," she said on a ragged breath that drove a spike of burning need through him.

He peeled the bodice back, his breath jamming in his lungs at the sight of her.

Her skin glowed in the silvery moonlight. The corset covering her low-cut chemise plumped up her lush breasts and they swelled over the satin edge of the undergarment. Looking wasn't enough. He had to touch.

Freeing the first few hooks of her corset, he loosened the tie of her chemise and pushed it off her shoulder along with her sleeve until he could cup her breast. The full weight of her in his hand frayed Russ's control. He licked the inner curve of her smooth warm flesh, nudging the fabric completely out of his way.

A breathy moan slipped out of her and she touched a shaking hand to his face, guiding him into another kiss.

Long seconds later, he lifted his head, wanting to rip the

pins from her hair, bury his face in its thickness, see it swirling like black satin around her bare shoulders.

Pulling away so he could see her velvety flesh, he continued to ply his thumb across her taut rosy nipple. She opened her eyes, and the desire smoldering in the midnight depths kicked off an urgency inside him. He bent again for her mouth.

The hard knock of the bed against the wall in the next room served to clear his head long enough for him to register voices in the hallway. Familiar voices.

Lydia made a needy sound deep in her throat, trying to pull him back to her. Breathing hard, he moved his hand from her breast to her mouth and listened.

She stilled, looking half-dazed then questioning.

"Ef and Naomi are out there looking for us," he whispered. Panic flickered in her eyes and he expected her to jump like a shot rabbit.

Instead, she pressed closer to him. Russ heard their friends move away down the hall, still searching. When he looked down to tell Lydia to be quiet a little longer, his knees nearly buckled at the heated invitation in her dark eyes.

The bed next door banged the wall again. And again. He could still hear the low murmur of Ef's and Naomi's voices, but the sounds faded as he lost himself in Lydia's dark eyes. He took his hand away, kissing her again, deep and hot and soft.

After a long minute, he pulled back. They were both breathing hard, her lips wet and swollen from his. He could barely gather up his common sense. This wasn't the place for what he wanted to do.

He should've romanced her before pouncing on her the way he had, but he hadn't been able to stop himself.

"You tear me up, Lydia," he said huskily.

She gripped the front of his shirt with both hands, trembling against him. He pulled up her chemise to cover her. The thought that she might have done this with Bram had frustration roiling through him.

She was his and he planned to have her.

"Sugar, if you can kiss me like that, you shouldn't be with Bram."

She stiffened, shock flaring in her eyes as though she'd forgotten about the rancher. Russ meant to make sure she did.

After she hooked her corset, he helped her straighten her bodice. As he watched her button up, he knew he had to leave that second or he was going to start all over with her.

Aching, he stepped back. "I'm going down first. You follow when you're ready."

After she nodded, he slipped out, relieved to see the hall was empty. His blood hummed as he started down the stairs.

He knew all of her secrets now. The only thing between them was Bram. And Russ was ready to do something about that.

Chapter Twelve

Sugar, if you can kiss me like that, you shouldn't be with Bram.

Russ was right, Lydia admitted the next morning as she stood in front of her vanity mirror. She wanted to tell him the truth about Bram, about everything. She was sick of lying to him.

After buttoning her bodice, she pulled her hair into a loose chignon. She hadn't slept much the night before. At first, because she had been too wound up. Her breasts, her entire body tingled from his touch, his kisses. And then, once her body had settled down, her mind wouldn't. She couldn't close her eyes because her thoughts were racing with ridiculous ideas like ending her pretend relationship with Bram.

Jake and Emma were part of the network. One of them could meet Lydia if and when necessary. She had gone back and forth all night about letting Russ know she wasn't having a romance with Bram.

She hated him thinking she would allow the liberties she had while supposedly seeing another man. And she hated that she had to let him think it. Of course, she shouldn't have let Russ touch her, *kiss* her the way he had, but she had been completely swept away. For the first time in her life, she had been focused on a man to the exclusion of everything else. That had certainly never happened with Wade.

Because Russ had seen her with Bram, she had explained to Bram that Russ believed the two of them were having a romance. Bram didn't like the idea of continuing the charade any more than she did. As Russ had mentioned in the livery, Bram was sweet on Deborah Blue. They weren't a couple, but he was working on it.

Even though neither Lydia nor Bram wanted to continue the pretense, they agreed it was best for now. Which only made it more difficult for Lydia to forget the feel of Russ's mouth and hands on her.

Exasperated at herself, she pushed the memories away. She had things to do. A few seconds later, she was on her way downstairs with her journal, her mind on the wayward guests from the night before.

She'd been angry when she had first gotten him upstairs, even more frustrated when he refused to intervene with the couple in question. Then in two seconds, her irritation had shifted to desire.

Listening to those noises on the other side of the door had made her pulse hitch, but nowhere near as wild as it had gotten when every inch of her had been pressed tight to every inch of Russ. Mercy, the man could kiss.

She reached the second floor landing and paused. Her partner had said he would talk to the couple this morning, so she knew he would. Still, she couldn't resist a look down the hall to the place where Russ had completely overwhelmed her senses. And there he was, in front of the guest room.

A blue shirt molded the powerful lines of his massive chest and shoulders. She knew she was staring at the strong thighs and long legs in denims, and she couldn't make herself stop.

He glanced over then a slow smile curved his lips. Even from where she was standing, she could see the blue of his eyes. Turning toward her, he braced one shoulder on the wall and fixed his full attention on her.

His gaze slid down her body and back up so intently it felt as though he were actually touching her. Her breath caught as sensation pooled low in her belly.

"Mornin'," he said, his low drawl enough to have her going soft inside.

"Good morning." She told herself to continue down the stairs, but her feet weren't moving in that direction. She walked closer to him.

Even without that wicked glint in his eyes, Lydia would've blushed at the frank male look he gave her.

"Did you think I'd forget what I told you last night?"

"No." She smiled. "I thought I'd check and see if you'd already done it."

"Nope." His gaze traced over her again. "You look pretty."

"I'm in my work clothes," she said drily.

"Still pretty."

Her nerves shimmered. He looked at her as if he wanted to finish what he'd started last night and get her all the way naked.

"Stop that," she ordered quietly.

"Can't help myself."

He sounded so silly that she rolled her eyes, biting back a smile. "Would you prefer I talk to these people?"

He chuckled. "Last night, you couldn't even say to me what they were doing."

A reluctant smile curved her lips. "This morning I'm feeling more bold."

"Maybe I should take advantage of that." His eyes flashed hotly, and Lydia knew he wasn't talking about the issue at hand. She felt a hard tug of desire.

"This isn't something a lady should have to do," he continued. "Besides, it'll be better if it's coming from me. The man will be embarrassed if a lady talks to him about it."

"All right." Relieved, Lydia retreated a step. "I'll make myself scarce."

"Don't go too far," he murmured.

The way his voice stroked over her gave her a shiver and she walked off, hearing him laugh softly behind her. Devil.

After one last glance, she started down to the lobby. She had to admit she appreciated his taking care of the matter, but her stomach was jumping. The man made her giddy.

She could hardly credit it. No man had ever affected her this way. If he hadn't stopped when he had last night, things would've gotten intimate. Lydia hadn't had the willpower or presence of mind to call a halt.

Her complete surrender frightened her. And excited her, too.

As she walked into the kitchen, she realized she was still smiling. She joined Naomi next to the stove where the other woman was mixing up a cake. Willow came out of the storage room and made her way over to them.

"How are they doing?" Lydia asked Willow in a low voice.

Last night, an abuse victim who hadn't planned a stop at The Fontaine had been forced to seek shelter here when she had gone into labor. Because Lydia had been upstairs with Russ, and Naomi was off somewhere with Ef, it had fallen to Willow to help the woman.

Willow had experience with childbirth, but she hadn't known about the underground operation. Now she did. She had sworn to tell no one and Lydia believed her. Anyone who could hide a woman in labor and deliver a baby without Lydia or Naomi finding out could keep quiet about the secret operation.

"Things looked grim at first." The blonde kept an eye on the doorway. "But it all turned out well."

"Good." Lydia noticed Willow's cuts and bruises were almost healed. She was even more beautiful than Lydia had first thought. She was glad Russ had told her last night that he didn't plan to be with the woman again.

"That boy was ready to come into the world," Willow said. Lydia smiled as did Naomi.

"The mother has stopped bleeding." The blonde closed her eyes for a second. "That scared me worse than anything."

"Should I look in on her?" Naomi asked.

"I'll keep an eye on her and if she needs a nurse, I'll let you know."

"Does the baby need anything?" Lydia asked. The victims who stopped here often traveled with nothing. "Does the mother need clothes?"

"The lady had a blanket and some little gowns she'd made, but nothing for herself. I loaned her one of my dresses."

"Willow, you didn't have to do that." Lydia squeezed the other woman's arm. "Naomi and I both have old ones to give."

"I wanted to do it. Y'all been so nice to me, I wanted to give something to that lady." She looked down, her voice gruff, "You're two of the finest ladies I've ever known, helping these women the way you do. There's so many women with no way out. I'm lucky to have a friend like Russ and a lady like you to hire—"

"Did I hear my name?"

Startled, the woman looked toward the door where Russ stood, his broad shoulders filling the space. He couldn't have been there long or Willow would've seen him. Lydia didn't think he'd heard anything, but what if he had?

Before she could think of something to say, Willow spoke up. "I was just tellin' Miz Kent and Miz Jones how lucky I am to have such a kind man as my friend."

At her words, a dark flush colored Russ's neck. He was embarrassed, Lydia realized with delight. Russ Baldwin, as big and solid as a mountain, was two shades of red. She found it endearing.

"And Miz Kent, too." The hotel's newest employee shifted her attention to Lydia. "My second chance is because of y'all and I thank you."

"You've thanked me every day since you got here," Russ said ruefully.

"Don't let it go to your head." The blonde grinned as she went to the pantry. "I'd best get busy."

The storage room door opened then closed. Willow was probably going to make sure the woman knew to stay quiet.

Lydia looked over at Russ. His gaze went past her. "How are you today, Naomi?"

"Fine, thank you." The black woman looked radiant, Lydia noted. No doubt due to a certain blacksmith.

"Lydia," Russ said. "Can I talk to you for a minute?"

"All right." She followed him a few feet into the dining room.

He took a step closer and said in a low voice, "That problem we discussed is handled."

"Was there any trouble?"

"No. And there won't be a repeat of last night's situation. The woman won't be back and if the man doesn't like our policy, he can find another place to sleep."

"Thank you." She had an overwhelming urge to kiss him,

but she wouldn't. Instead, she touched his arm. "Thank you for taking care of that."

"You're welcome."

When she would've pulled away, he folded his big hand over hers. "Would you spend the day with me tomorrow?"

"The whole day?" She should say no, as she should have the night before.

"I want to take you to the ranch, have lunch with Pa and show you around." His callused thumb brushed back and forth over her knuckles.

The smart thing, the safe thing would be to tell him to slow things down. "I don't know."

His eyes darkened. "Do you have plans with Bram?"

"No."

"All right." He grinned. "Say yes and I'll be at your door at nine in the morning."

It sounded wonderful. Being with Russ away from the hotel where there was always a chance he might discover something about the operation. Where the threat of her brother-in-law loomed over her.

She probably shouldn't agree to go, but she wanted to. Naomi could handle things here for a day. And Russ's family would be around, so there was no danger of them getting carried away the way they had the night before. "Russ, we can't do what we did last night. That's too fast for me."

"All right."

"Really?"

He lifted her chin. "I want you, Lydia, like hell afire, but I want to spend time with you, too. I can be a gentleman, even if it kills me."

She laughed. "I'd like to go—"

A screaming infant cut her off. Lydia froze. The baby!

"Was that a baby?" Still holding Lydia's hand, Russ moved back into the kitchen, angling toward the pantry. "That sounded like a baby."

Lydia threw a desperate look at Naomi. "It did."

Willow bustled out of the storage room, peering around the pantry's door frame. "I guess you heard the little fella."

"What's going on?" Russ's sharp gaze took in all three women.

Willow answered. "Last night, a woman showed up here, in labor."

"Why come here? Why not send for Dr. Butler or Catherine Blue?"

"She heard I had experience with childbirth. My ma had seven after me."

Lydia appreciated how Willow told the story although deep down, she cringed at keeping the whole truth from Russ. The wailing, muffled through the door, stopped.

Russ looked concerned. "Is the kid okay? It was making a lot of racket."

"He's fine," Willow answered. "He's just mad 'cuz he wants to eat."

"It's lucky you were around to help."

"That's what I told her." Lydia tried to direct some of Russ's attention away from the other woman. "I certainly don't know anything about babies, birthing them or raising them."

Russ frowned. "Why didn't y'all put her in a room?"

Lydia blanched. Willow jumped in. "Oh, there wasn't no time for that. That baby's head was already coming out and—"

"Uh, that's good." Looking horrified, Russ stepped back. "I don't need to know the rest."

At his typical male aversion to ladies' issues, Lydia shared a smile with Naomi.

Willow turned back toward the pantry. "I'd better check on them. The lady's probably strong enough to move now, so I'll put her and the baby in a room."

Russ glanced at Lydia. "Guess I'd better get busy, too. The new shops are close to done. I think I can finish today."

"That's good news." She walked with him into the dining room. "Is there anything you need me to do?"

"Don't change your mind about tomorrow."

"I won't."

"So, I'll see you in the morning? I want you to tell me again."

She laughed. "Since I work here, too, you'll probably see me before then."

"Yeah, but tomorrow you'll be all mine." He winked and strode away.

Lydia got a lump in her throat. Foot, she liked that man. Her anticipation about spending the day with him was dimmed by the guilt she felt at keeping the truth from him.

Naomi had been up-front with Ef about everything except the secret network, but that was little consolation. Lydia couldn't tell Russ the truth about Bram or the network.

She wasn't lying to him about either one. She just wasn't telling him everything. What she had told the whole truth about was wanting to spend tomorrow with him. She couldn't wait.

He was going to have a hard time keeping his hands off her, Russ thought for the tenth time as he and Lydia drove to the Triple B the next morning. Since the other night, when he'd had his mouth on her, he hadn't been able to stop thinking about having her.

But he'd given his word. He'd have to content himself with looking at her. For now anyway.

It wasn't a hardship, Russ thought as his gaze slid over her.

Her deep red day dress with black trim was covered with a black cloak, but that didn't hinder Russ's memory of how the bodice sleeked over her full breasts. Or what her plump flawless flesh looked like beneath. He hadn't forgotten how she tasted there, either.

Damn, he better rein it in.

Cold air swirled around them. Winter-brown grass made a shushing sound against the buggy wheels. He leaned forward, elbows resting on his knees, his hands controlling the reins.

The scent of lavender occasionally drifted in through the smells of earth and horseflesh. Russ told her how his ma and pa had helped establish Whirlwind. In answer to her question about his mother, he said she had died from a tumor in her stomach when he was ten.

Lydia talked about how awful her sister was about handling money. He laughed at her story of putting her sister on a budget. She'd been so pleased with Isabel and herself for following her suggestions. Until she found out Isabel was getting extra money from their father on the sly.

Russ itched to take down her hair, but with it pulled back the way it was, he could see her dainty ears, her cold-pinkened cheeks. She was so pretty.

As they drove, she held up a corner of the lap robe. "Are you cold? Would you like to share my blanket?"

"Just looking at you is keeping me plenty warm," he murmured.

She pushed at him as a blush spread across her face. "Oh, hush."

He pointed out where Baldwin land started and for a while they traveled a rutted road, then it turned to rough ground. After topping the last rise, Russ saw the herd of longhorn.

The cattle didn't typically graze in this pasture or this close to the house in the winter, but the threat of rustlers had changed that. Matt had moved the herd in an effort to keep a better eye on things.

Before Russ knew it, they passed the last two barns, and he reined the buggy to a stop in front of the sprawling house built of pine.

Her eyes lit up. "It's lovely."

"Glad you like it." He wanted her to like everything today.

A porch wrapped around the house so that there was a view of the vast land anywhere you stood. The front door, like everything else, was specially made for their size. The doorway was tall and wide enough for any one of the Baldwins to step inside without ducking or having to turn to the side. That had come in handy when Pa had ended up in that wheelchair.

Guilt bit at Russ, but he pushed it away. He didn't want anything to ruin this day.

The one front window, looking out from the kitchen, glittered in the sun. He hopped down and walked around to help Lydia out.

She studied the house with interest. "Did your father build this?"

"Yes. There's a big common room, the kitchen and three bedrooms."

"I'm impressed." Lydia took his hand and stepped out of the buggy, smiling at him in a way that made him want to put her back in the buggy and take her off somewhere alone.

The front door opened and J.T. rolled out onto the front porch, followed by Matt. His father's eyes, blue like his sons', twinkled. "If I'd known Russ was bringing the prettiest girl in town out to visit, I would've spiffed up."

"Hello, Mr. Baldwin." Her mouth curved.

"Call me J.T."

Russ's brother piped up, "You can call me Matt."

When Lydia laughed, he grinned like an idiot. Russ gave him a look.

The elder Baldwin gestured toward the barns. "Has Russ shown you around?"

"We drove straight here, Pa."

"I saw the cattle," she said. "That's a large herd."

"Used to be larger," Matt said darkly.

"Come in, Miz Kent," J. T. invited. "Lunch will be on the table in a bit."

"Are you the cook?" she asked.

"We all take a turn," Matt answered as he held the door open for his father.

J.T. rolled his chair inside. "It's nothing fancy, but we get by."

Russ watched the man who seemed imposing even in that chair. He wondered if he'd ever be rid of the kink he got in his gut every time he saw his pa in that contraption.

Matt hung back, gesturing for Lydia to precede him. Once she stepped inside, he stopped Russ and said in a low aside, "Stop beating yourself up."

"Leave off."

"He doesn't blame you. No one does, except you."

And Russ didn't know if he'd ever stop feeling the guilt, but now wasn't the time to ponder it. He didn't want anything to mar today. "Get moving."

He followed his brother inside, taking Lydia's cloak as she surveyed the rock fireplace and age-smoothed wood floor. A deer hide rug lay between two long sofas.

She gave him a warm smile and his gut knotted up for a whole different reason.

While Pa banged around in the kitchen, Russ walked her through the house, showing her his father's office then the bedrooms. Each room had a window, which she liked. He answered any questions she had, but all his attention was on her. How beautiful she looked, how thick and satiny her raven-black hair was, how badly he wanted to get his hands on her again. When they returned to the living area, she looked over at a stack of tools in the far corner behind the dining table.

Seeing her interest, Matt offered, "Pa's been fancying up the kitchen"

"For Cora Wilkes?"

"Cora?" Russ started in surprise.

Matt did the same. "Why would you think that?"

"I thought they were courting."

"No." Russ looked at Matt.

His brother frowned. "No."

Lydia's dark eyes danced as her gaze took in both men. She appeared to be fighting a smile as she asked Russ, "Have you seen them together?"

"Well, yes."

"Haven't you noticed how they are with each other?"

Feeling as dense as a rock, Russ shared another look with Matt. That had Lydia laughing outright. Could she be right? Russ and his brother had known Cora their whole lives. She and her murdered husband, Ollie, had been friends with their parents. Russ had never thought twice about seeing his pa and Cora together.

Matt chewed the inside of his cheek. "Remember that mirror we found in his saddlebag a couple of months ago?"

Russ nodded. "He wouldn't tell us who it was for."

"Maybe it was for her."

Russ remembered the times his pa and Cora had moved apart rather quickly when interrupted. He'd seen them together at a couple of dances, but outside talking. Not inside dancing.

He shot his brother a grin. "It would be good for him."

"It would be better for us. She can cook a whole lot better than any of us."

That got another laugh out of Lydia, which had Russ smiling as J.T. rolled out of the kitchen holding a platter heaped with ham. Russ pulled out a chair for Lydia, then helped his brother bring in the remainder of the meal.

The rest of the visit passed in a blur of laughter and conversation. It was almost evening when Russ bundled Lydia back into the buggy with a freshly heated brick in the foot warmer, and they said their goodbyes.

"That was wonderful," she said as they drove away. "Thank you."

Russ reached over and squeezed her hand.

Even through their gloves, he felt her touch. A warmth bloomed in his chest. "Do you mind if we stop for a bit on the way back? I want to show you something."

"Something like what?" Her eyes narrowed in suspicion.

He chuckled. "You'll just have to wait and see."

He steered the buggy slightly to the north and a few minutes later, they crested a rise. Russ parked the buggy alongside a deep gully. Out beyond the vehicle, the prairie rolled in a dip of hills.

"This is my thinking spot. I came here after Amy and Pa—" He caught himself. "After Amy."

She tilted her head, but instead of asking him what he'd been about to say about his father, she asked, "Are we here because you need to think about something?"

Not about you, he thought. *I know exactly what I want with you.*

The teasing light in her eyes captivated him. "This is also the best place on our land to see the sunset."

"You want to show me the sunset?" She looked skeptical.

"I swear, that's it. It's amazing, like the colors are coming up out of the earth."

She smiled. "All right."

He checked the sun's position. "We'll have to wait a bit."

"That's okay. I have a foot warmer."

Remembering the fetching smile she had given him when he surprised her with the foot warmer had something hot and scary unfurling in his chest.

She smoothed the lap robe. "Are you sure you don't want to share my blanket?"

He wanted to share more than that, but he was trying hard to respect the line she'd drawn between them. He wasn't sure how long he could keep to his side. Matt had asked him earlier if he was still suspicious of Lydia. Russ had said no; he knew her secrets now and she had good reason for keeping them, though he hadn't shared the stories with his brother. One thing he had told Matt was that Lydia was also seeing Bram. Matt was as surprised as Russ had been.

He relaxed into the soft leather seat, the hood of the buggy shielding them from the cold and an occasional gust of wind. This vehicle was a much better fit than the one he'd used to drive Lydia back to Whirlwind that first night he'd found her on the prairie.

Still, the buggy wasn't so big that they couldn't be close. Her lap robe touched the toe of his boot and their knees bumped often. His gaze roved over her face, taking in the fine texture of her skin, the pink in her cheeks, the delicate wing of her eyebrows.

She turned her head to look at him. "You're going to miss the sunset if you don't stop staring at me."

"It would be worth it."

He caught a smile as she looked away. She acted as though she had enjoyed herself so far. Russ hoped so.

Sitting out here alone with her, drawing in her sweet scent, tested Russ's willpower to keep from kissing her. When he realized he was staring at her chest, wondering how long it would take him to get all those tiny buttons on her bodice unfastened, he mentally reined up.

She looked at him then, heat flaring in her eyes as she licked her lips. That was all it took to bring back every torturously wonderful second of having her in his arms a couple nights earlier. The same thought was in her eyes, too.

Russ knew he couldn't stand strong against that soft want.

Trying to distract himself, he remembered something he had meant to tell her for a few days. "Thanks again for hiring Willow."

She frowned. "I didn't do anything you wouldn't have done."

"A lot of women wouldn't have hired her. Because of her past. Because of what she obviously was."

"I would've been like that once, but not now."

"What changed your mind?"

Golden light etched her refined profile. She was quiet for a long moment and when she spoke her voice was unsteady. "If just one person had looked past my brother-in-law's wealth and status to what he really was, what was really going on, my sister might not be dead."

The sadness in her eyes twisted at Russ's heart.

"I try not to judge a book by its cover anymore. I have lapses, but I still try."

Russ couldn't take his eyes off her face, softened even more by the hazy yellow wash of the setting sun. Peeling off his glove, he reached out to thumb away a lone tear.

"Oh." She dabbed at her eyes, looking embarrassed. "I didn't mean to do that."

"No harm done." He stroked her cheek lightly.

"The day has been so nice. I don't want to ruin it."

He tugged his glove back on. "You couldn't ruin anything."

She gave a little laugh. "I bet that's not what you said when I first arrived."

He grinned. "You've got me there."

The sun sank steadily, slowly painting the sky and earth in a warm gold then pink. Russ watched Lydia carefully. "Have you had any news about DeBoard?"

"My father says Philip still hasn't been found. No one seems to know what happened to him."

Russ fought the urge to twine a loose strand of her hair around his finger. "Does that make you nervous? Not knowing where he is?"

"Not when I'm with you."

"Good." Caught in the black velvet of her eyes, it was an effort to shift his gaze back to the sunset. "Look."

They sat silently as the sun hit the horizon. A burst of red and gold melted into the landscape then a line of fiery orange traced the line of the horizon. "Here it comes," he said quietly.

The sun dipped lower, almost hidden behind the hills. Then, for one instant, there was a separation between twilight and the bold colors of day's end. Lydia drew in a sharp breath. "It really does look like the color is coming out of the earth."

As they watched, the sun seeped into its own colors until it was a streak of glaring yellow at the base of blue-gray shadows. Dusk settled over the land.

"That was beautiful!"

Lydia looked so delighted that Russ laughed. "Worth stopping for?"

"Oh, yes."

He picked up the reins and clucked to the horse. "Glad you thought so."

As they drove, darkness settled over the prairie. Moonlight threw shadows across the tall grass, in the dips and rises across the land.

Lydia tilted her head. "Has anyone expressed interest in your share of the hotel lately?"

"Not yet." Was she still wanting him out of the hotel? His quick flare of irritation disappeared when he saw the genuine concern in her eyes. The caring.

"I hope my idea about the shops brings in some money," he said. "It's looking like that might be all I have to give the banker and it's not enough. We could lose the ranch, everything."

"What about your brother? Or father?"

"What about 'em?" He couldn't keep the edge out of his voice.

She looked taken aback at his tone. "I thought they might have some ideas."

"Matt and I have talked about it," he said gruffly.

"But you haven't talked with your father?"

What was she getting at? Why was she asking him about this?

Lydia clenched her hands tighter in the lap robe. Something was bothering him. There was a grimness in his tone that went beyond his frustration about not being able to repay the loan.

He'd been there when she needed to talk about Philip. "If you need to talk to someone, you can talk to me."

"Why would I need to do that?" he asked, sounding impatient.

She hesitated. "I overheard you and Matt talking when we

first arrived at your ranch. He said you shouldn't blame yourself for something."

Russ's handsome face closed up and he flicked the reins hard against the horse's rump. The animal hopped, jerking the buggy roughly.

He didn't say anything for a long time. Long enough that she tried to ease the tension lashing his big frame. "I don't want to spoil our day. Forget I brought it up."

"No, it's all right. It's just not something I talk about much."

Twilight drifted across the hard angles of his face and for an instant, he looked so anguished that Lydia's heart tightened painfully. She couldn't bear the look on his face. "You don't have to talk about it."

"You've told me all your secrets. I guess turnabout is fair play."

She swallowed hard. She hadn't told him *all* her secrets.

His face went carefully blank and she felt a twinge of compassion. Whatever it was had hurt him deeply.

"It's my fault Pa's in that wheelchair."

An instant protest sprang to her lips, but she didn't voice it. He needed someone to listen, not placate. "I thought he had an accident while putting up fence."

"He did. He was doing my work." Russ pinched the bridge of his nose. "I was the one who was supposed to be there."

"I don't understand. Does he blame you?"

"No, but he should. You know why I wasn't there? Because I was with a couple of whor—uh, with some lady friends."

Ladies of the evening. Even in the shadows, Lydia could see a dark flush on his neck. And the guilt and self-loathing in his expression.

"If I had been working at the ranch like I was supposed to, my father wouldn't have been doing my job. It was stringing that fence on the edge of the gully that caused him to fall and impale his leg on a tree branch. He nearly bled to death before Riley Holt found him."

Lydia's heart ached. She didn't think J.T. blamed Russ, but what she thought didn't matter. Russ believed his father held him responsible. There was nothing she could say or do to change that. It hurt. As much as the fact that he had opened up completely to her and she couldn't do the same.

After seeing the ranch, she knew how much he stood to lose, how much they all stood to lose. J.T. had borrowed against the ranch to continue a profitable cattle-breeding operation, but rustlers had hit the Triple B's herd so hard that now even selling every head of cattle wouldn't pay off the banknote.

She reached over and slipped her hand into his much bigger one. "Have you ever talked to your father about this?"

"Not since it happened," he said gruffly.

"Maybe you should think about it."

He stared at her for so long she felt her stomach hollow out. "I'm not trying to tell you what to do. You helped me with Philip. I just wanted to return the favor."

She also wanted to tell him the truth about the rescue operation and felt she couldn't. The guilt ate at her.

"It's not that. I don't mind talking about it with you."

He curved her hand in the crook of his arm. "It's just that I hadn't thought about discussing it with Pa. Seems to me I should take care of it."

"It isn't entirely your responsibility. Regret is a heavy burden to carry." In the darkness, his eyes glittered. "That's how I feel about my sister, because I didn't take any action at the time on her behalf."

Russ searched Lydia's face as her hand tightened on his arm. He considered her suggestion that he should talk to Pa before it was too late. The woman had gotten Russ to tell her something only three people knew. There was a time when that would've made him angry, but not tonight, not with her. "I'll think about it."

She smiled, leaving her hand where it was as they drove into town and up to the front of the hotel.

"You could've dropped me at the back."

He shook his head. "I'm walking you up."

"We'll probably both be downstairs later anyway."

"Don't care."

"All right." She looked pleased.

He helped her from the buggy and took her through the front doors, his hand resting lightly on the small of her back.

They encountered few people on their way upstairs. Gaslight burned bright down the hall. In front of her rooms, he stood to the side as she unlocked the door. Light glided over her perfect profile, played against the black satin of her hair.

She looked up, standing so close that her breath tickled his face. "Today was wonderful. Thank you."

"Sorry if I brought it down."

"I liked that you felt you could be open with me."

"One reason I got you out of the hotel is so you wouldn't have to listen to anyone's problems, then I—"

She touched a gloved finger to his lips. "Please don't regret telling me. I don't regret that you did."

He was starting to feel that way, too. He caught her hand, bracing one arm above her head. "So, you'll see me again?"

"Probably in less than an hour."

"You know what I mean." He played with her fingers.

"Maybe."

The flirty smile she gave him drew him up tight. He wanted to carry her to his room. Or hers.

"Thanks for going today. It did my pa a world of good to see somebody besides me or Matt. And it made my day."

"I'm glad."

"Good night." He lifted her hand to brush a kiss across her knuckles. At the last second, he turned her wrist and nudged aside the edge of her glove to touch his mouth to her pulse.

Her breath caught, and a long moment stretched between them before he released her.

She stepped inside her room and closed the door with a smile.

Russ stood there, fighting the urge to knock and ask her to let him in. Tension coiled in his gut. He'd managed to keep his hands off her, but he wasn't sure how much longer he could do it.

Chapter Thirteen

The guilt on Russ's face when he had told her about his father stuck in Lydia's mind and bothered her all the next day. She ached for him. Telling her had been plainly difficult. She'd seen a flash of vulnerability she never would've guessed he had.

He'd shared two of the most painful things she could imagine. While she had confided in him and felt some of her burden lifted, she hadn't told him everything. She couldn't stop thinking about telling Russ the truth.

About the operation. About Bram. Especially about Bram.

The decision weighed on her. She changed her mind a dozen times, cautioning herself that the fewer people who knew about the operation, the less risk there would be. But Russ had opened up to her completely. He deserved no less from her. He might be angry at first that she had been operating the network without his knowledge, but he would eventually understand. She was sure of that.

By nightfall, she knew she couldn't have this between them anymore. She went looking for him, deciding to try his office first. As she passed the hotel's front entrance, she noticed several people gathered in the street, talking. She wondered what was going on.

Russ's door was open, and she saw him gathering boxes of bullets and putting them in his saddlebags, quickly yet methodically. His rifle lay across the desk; his revolver was beside it.

Alarm skittered through her as she stepped inside. "What's happened? What's going on?"

Tension filled the room, a sense of urgency. When he turned to look at her, the grim set of his mouth had her heart skipping a beat. "Russ?"

"It's Matt. He found those rustlers and they beat him up."

She gasped. "How badly?"

"No broken bones, according to Riley. Whatever they did didn't keep him from following them a ways. He sent Riley to town with a message to bring a posse and meet him at a dry creek bed northwest of here."

Lydia's need to tell Russ about the operation faded. Apprehension slicked down her spine. "A posse? You're going after them?"

"Yeah." Russ yanked a shirt from his wardrobe and stuffed it in one of the saddlebags along with a pair of socks.

"Do you have any idea how long you'll be gone?"

"No."

After buckling on his holster, he slid one big hand down the inside of his thigh to tie the leather thong. The sight of his hand there had Lydia's mouth going dry. He shrugged into his duster, hefted the saddlebags over one shoulder and put on his hat.

Picking up his rifle, he started out of his office.

What she'd come to say would have to wait. His brother was hurt and people were waiting on Russ to travel.

He strode to the side door that led outside. "If you need anything, go to Ef."

She nodded, hurrying to keep pace with his long-legged strides, following him through the open doorway. The door thudded shut behind them and he frowned at her. "It's cold out here. You don't have a coat."

"I'm fine." Rubbing her arms, she went with him into the livery. The smell of hay had her nose itching.

Once inside, Russ eased the saddlebags off his shoulder and laid the rifle on the ground, facing away from them.

"Why isn't Ef going with you?" Lydia asked.

"A few men always stay in town to help the older ones guard the women and children. Tonight, Ef drew one of the short straws."

Lydia wished it had been Russ instead.

As if it weighed nothing, he plucked a worn black saddle and gray-striped saddle blanket from a sawhorse in the corner.

She moved quickly to open his horse's stall.

"Thanks." Russ had the gelding saddled and was leading the animal out in a couple of minutes.

He picked up his rifle and slid it into the scabbard then tossed the saddlebags over the horse's rump, adjusting them to distribute the weight evenly.

"Did you bring anything to eat?" she asked.

"Some of Naomi's corn bread and leftover venison."

"Good. I hope Matt's all right."

"He'll be madder than hell."

Her nerves twanged as she moved closer. The horse nudged her hip. "Please be careful. Ride safe."

He looked at her then, fully for the first time since she'd found him. "Nobody's told me that since my ma."

"You'd best do it." Lydia swallowed past a lump in her throat, but her voice broke anyway. "You won't be much use to me if you're shot full of holes."

In the dim light, with his hat pulled low and his jaw shadowed with stubble, he looked deadly, dangerous. The very real possibility that he could be hurt or worse tied her stomach in knots.

He palmed off his hat and hung it on the saddle horn, then reached for her.

One big iron-hard arm curled around her waist and he pulled her right into the hard power of his body. Before she could blink, he kissed her.

Taken by surprise, she froze for a moment.

"Kiss me back," he rasped against her lips in a voice that had her legs going to water.

Sliding her arms around his neck, she opened her mouth to his. She expected fast and hard; that's what she got at first. Then his lips softened and moved over hers with such tenderness that she melted into him. His free hand cupped the back of her head, keeping her where he wanted her. His tongue stroked hers and he held her tighter.

Then he pulled away, his eyes dark and serious. "Gotta go."

She could barely gather her thoughts. As she walked out of the livery with him, she saw Davis Lee and Josie standing several feet away with their heads close together. Jericho kissed Catherine, placing a protective hand on her gently swollen belly.

Charlie Haskell's wife, May, as well as Cal Doyle's Lizzie, stood quietly by.

"Is this everyone?" Lydia asked.

"We'll meet Jake and Bram on our way." Russ mounted and looked down, his blue eyes full of an indefinable emotion.

She laid a hand on his knee, feeling the heat and muscle of his leg. "Promise you'll be careful."

He covered her hand with his. "I promise."

Throat tight, she stepped away as he turned his horse and rode out with the others, heading west as she and Russ had done yesterday.

Ef and Naomi stood on the hotel's wide front porch with Willow. Lydia made her way over to Josie and Catherine. "If either of you would like to stay at the hotel tonight, there's plenty of room."

No abuse victims were expected that evening so Lydia had no qualms about making the offer. Both women thanked her, but neither accepted. Lydia made the same offer to the other women, who also declined, saying they would stay at their homes.

As she moved into the hotel with Ef and Naomi, she noticed Russ's office door was still open. She walked over and closed it, catching a whiff of his dark male scent.

There was a hollowness in Lydia's chest she'd felt only one other time. When Isabel died. She hoped Russ and the others would be all right.

Late that night, Lydia panicked when Naomi woke her. Her first thought was about Russ. No, Naomi said. There was no news about him or the others, but there was an unexpected arrival at the back door. Lydia threw on her wrapper and slippers, hurrying down the stairs with her friend.

"I was coming in from the laundry and she was lying at the back door," the black woman whispered. "She has no shoes."

They hurried through the dining room, the spill of light from the lobby enough to show the way.

Lydia noticed then that her friend was still dressed. "You haven't been to bed yet."

"Ef and I were talking."

Lydia nodded as she stepped onto the back porch and saw an unconscious woman. Coatless and barefoot, her skin was ghostly pale, emphasized even more by the dark streaks on her feet. Blood, Lydia realized.

Naomi tried to wake her, then Lydia tried, with no better luck.

"Is she dead?" Naomi whispered.

Lydia leaned down to listen to the woman's heart. "No."

Naomi grabbed the woman under her arms while Lydia lifted her feet. She was heavy and they could barely get her off the ground.

The black woman grimaced. "What are we going to do? She can't stay out here. She'll freeze."

They tried again to wake up the woman, but couldn't. Lydia sat on her knees, the cold seeping through her wrapper and causing her to shiver. "Even if we get her to stand, she can't walk. Her feet are torn up."

"What should we do?" Naomi's features were pinched.

"Maybe Willow—"

"She's nowhere to be found. I haven't seen her since Mr. Baldwin and the others rode out. Where would she go?"

"I don't know. We'll worry about her after we take care of this woman. She's going to freeze to death."

After another attempt to rouse the woman, Lydia stopped, a little breathless. "We need someone stronger than us."

"Ef," Naomi said quietly.

Yes. Lydia hesitated, but there was really no choice if they wanted to get the victim inside and her feet doctored. She didn't think this was what Russ had meant when he told her to go to Ef for anything. "Okay. I'll stay with her."

Naomi stood and ran the length of the building then disappeared around the corner.

Lydia shook the woman, patted her face. To no avail. "Please wake up."

From the corner of her eye, she caught a movement and

turned to see Naomi and Ef hurrying toward her. Ef was dressed, but his flapping shirttail and dangling suspenders testified that Naomi had woken him, too.

"Oh, thank you." Lydia kept her voice quiet, getting to her feet and moving back so the blacksmith could kneel beside the woman.

It took a couple of tries before he attempted to stand with her in his arms. His back and arm muscles strained at the fabric of his shirt.

Naomi held the door and Lydia followed as Ef went up the single step and carried the woman inside. Lydia hurried around him and into the pantry, opening the storage room door.

Naomi appeared with a match and Lydia lit the candle they kept at the top of the stairs. She held it high, leading the way through the shifting shadows down the stairs and around the large cupboard. Being so close to the boiler room took the chill from the air.

Ef laid the unconscious woman on the pallet Lydia indicated.

When he straightened, she noticed he was sweating, evidence of how hard he'd worked to get the stranger down here.

"Thank you." Lydia squeezed his hand.

When he turned, the safe station's lone occupant shrank back into the dark space behind the cupboard.

The blacksmith's gaze shot to Lydia. She walked with him to the stairs, keeping her voice low. "Did Naomi explain?"

"Some. She said the hotel was part of a secret network to help abused women escape bad situations."

Lydia nodded. "Most of them don't stay more than a night."

Ef's eyes were warm. "Naomi said you and she help because your sister died at the hands of her abusive husband."

"That's right."

"I'm sorry to hear it."

"Thank you."

"This is a good thing you're doing here." He started up the steps then paused. "Need me to fetch anything?"

"Some warm water, cloths and linen strips. Naomi knows where everything is."

The big man made his way to the top of the stairs. Lydia could hear their quiet murmuring. She was covering the new arrival with a blanket when Ef appeared with the things she'd requested.

As Lydia took the bowl from him, he smiled, admiration plain in his eyes. "Naomi's bringing some salve."

"Thank you." Wincing as she saw the cuts to the woman's feet, Lydia began to clean the wounds. Ef would keep silent about the operation. Lydia was sure of him. Russ would have, too; she was just as sure of that.

She'd finally revealed the secret, just not to the right man.

The days dragged with no word at all. Lydia's nerves were scraped raw and tension ran through the whole town.

Willow had shown up the next morning, sheepishly admitting she had fallen asleep in one of the hotel's bathtubs. Lydia was relieved nothing bad had happened to the former prostitute.

Neither woman who had sought shelter at the hotel was ready to travel so between hotel business and trying to help the new mother, Lydia had plenty to do, but Russ was constantly on her mind. Where was he? Was he all right? What about the others?

She must have replayed his goodbye kiss and the tenderness in his eyes a hundred times. She missed him even more than she had when he'd made that short trip to Abilene. Her feelings went much deeper than she had realized. That only made the time seem longer, the nights interminable.

Three days after Russ left, Josie Holt came looking for

Lydia. One look at the petite brunette's face and dread snaked through Lydia.

Word had come from a lawman in the panhandle. There had been a shoot-out between a band of rustlers and the posse from Whirlwind. Two men in the posse were injured, but the lawman hadn't given names.

Was Russ hurt? The thought made Lydia ill. Josie, Catherine and the other women were just as worried. Lydia tried to keep busy, but the slightest thing out of the ordinary rattled her. She couldn't concentrate, couldn't sleep. She held herself together, not only because she had hotel guests to see to, but also because the women taking shelter there needed her.

She prayed for word from somebody. Three grueling, achingly slow days after having gotten news about the shoot-out, she was on the second floor helping Willow change sheets on a guest bed when she heard the thunder of hooves.

Dropping the linens, she rushed to the window. Her gaze cut through the last light of day to the horses galloping into town. She easily found the black-and-white paint and...there was Russ! Her chest went tight.

Willow hurried to stand beside her. Lydia saw Matt, then Riley Holt. Riley wore a sling and Cal Doyle had a bandage on his head. Russ appeared to be unharmed. The relief nearly buckled her knees.

She steadied herself and flew down the stairs behind Willow, who loudly announced the posse had returned. Lydia moved outside to the edge of the porch, searching for Russ. Her gaze scanned the small crowd gathered between the saloon and the newspaper office. There was no sign of his broad shoulders, the gray shirt, dark hat. She couldn't find him.

Frustration streaked through her. Where was he—there! He straightened from examining his horse. Lydia couldn't tell what he'd been looking at; she didn't care. He stood with his brother, Davis Lee and Riley. A crowd jostled around the men, voices rising and falling in welcome.

His gaze cut through the group, locked on hers and relief overwhelmed her. Tears prickled her eyes.

Josie walked over to her. "Davis Lee said about half the rustlers escaped into Oklahoma Territory, with a couple of wounded."

"How many were there?"

"Eight. Or maybe seven. I can't remember exactly." Josie watched her husband with complete adoration. "I was more concerned with kissing him."

Lydia understood that. As the men continued to talk intently, a sudden thought chilled her. Keeping her eyes locked with Russ's, she asked the woman beside her, "They're not going out again, are they?"

"No. At least not yet."

Lydia wanted to go to him, to talk to him, but one look at the people crowding around him told her it would be better to wait where she was.

Torn between impatience and relief, she listened with half an ear as Josie shared more details of the chase. The posse had run the rustlers to the border. One of the men who had roughed up Matt was dead. Lydia was glad to hear the story, but she wanted to hear it from Russ, touch him and feel for herself that he was unharmed.

Red dust filmed his clothes, his horse. He hadn't shaved and lines of fatigue carved his face. He looked perfect.

He took off his hat and raked a hand through his hair. Even from where she was standing, Lydia could sense the restlessness in him. His brother said something and he nodded, then began walking toward her.

People kept stopping him to shake his hand or ask questions. Lydia knew they were glad to see him, too, but she wanted to talk to him. As he moved slowly in her direction, his attention rarely left her. Impatient, she wanted to grab him and take him upstairs.

When he was detained for the third time, Lydia told herself to go inside. He was unharmed. That was what mattered. Later, when things had calmed down, he would find her or she would find him, but she couldn't make herself leave.

A few seconds later, he cut away from the crowd and angled toward the livery, leading his horse. He caught her eye and tilted his head toward the hotel, a silent message to meet him inside.

She nodded, her stomach fluttering in anticipation. She excused herself from Josie, Naomi and Ef then went inside. Russ's office door was open and her heart began to pound hard.

Her hands were shaking, she realized in vague disbelief. *She* was shaking. Taking a deep breath, she tried to calm the tangle of emotions in her chest. Relief, gratitude, need. His coat and hat were thrown haphazardly across his desk, the saddlebags on the floor beside it. Red dust filmed everything.

She rapped lightly on the door and peered around it. He stood with his back to her across the room in a long-sleeved undershirt, his trousers and dusty boots. A huge hot sensation she didn't understand threatened to swallow her up.

He looked over his shoulder and saw her. Pivoting, he covered the distance between them in four strides. Pleasure lit his blue eyes.

Her gaze ran over him. He appeared unharmed, but she had to feel for herself. She moved to meet him. "Are you all—"

In one fluid motion, he swept her up, kicked the door shut and backed her into the wall, capturing her mouth with his.

Whatever she wanted to say was forgotten as his hands moved to cradle her face.

Lydia gripped his forearms, kissing him back just as fiercely as he kissed her. He lifted his head, slanted it another way and settled his mouth on hers again.

He made a rumbling sound from his chest. His body was rock-hard against hers. The scents of dirt and man and leather swirled around her. She needed to be closer. Her hands slid up his biceps then to his shoulders, holding tight because her body felt boneless. His tongue stroked hers.

It was a long moment before he drew back, still holding her face. "Sugar, you are a sight for sore eyes."

"So are you," she said breathlessly.

He gave a short laugh, trying to ease away from her.

She held tight.

"I'm covered in dirt and I smell like horses."

"I don't care. I'm so glad you're okay." Her lips were swollen from his. She smiled up at him and he groaned, taking her mouth again.

This time, when he lifted his head, he rested his forehead against hers. "I shouldn't start this here," he muttered.

"Why not?" She didn't want him to stop kissing her. His features sharpened with desire as his gaze did a hot slide down her body. A muscle flexed in his jaw and his eyes glittered with a predatory look. A shiver worked through her.

"Let me clean up, then take you to dinner."

She nodded. "Where?"

"You pick. I don't care. Here. Pearl's."

She wanted to suggest they stay in his office to eat. Or do other things. Her entire body vibrated with the desire pumping through her veins.

She wanted him. She didn't want to let go. If he put his

hands or mouth on her the way he had the other night, she wouldn't stop him. That probably made her a wanton, but she didn't care. She *needed* him. It was strange, something she'd never felt before, yet it was there.

He stared at her mouth in arrested silence, sending a thrill through her. She thought he might kiss her again; instead he released her. "Give me ten minutes, okay?"

She would give him whatever he wanted. Reaching behind her, she opened the door. "I'm so glad you're back and safe."

His eyes darkened and Lydia stepped out while she still could. She headed for her rooms, her pulse skittering.

Ten minutes later, a knock sounded on the door. Pressing a hand to her stomach to still the butterflies, she answered.

Russ stood there, looking big and strong and determined.

"Hi," he rasped.

"Hi." The scruffy whiskers were gone, the line of his jaw clean-shaven. The deep blue of his eyes glittered against his burnished skin. She drew in the fresh scent of his spicy shaving soap, a hint of his own darker musk.

She didn't care about eating. All she wanted was Russ. But he'd been riding long and hard for days. Who knew when he'd last eaten?

He stepped inside and closed the door.

She searched his face, shivering at the intensity there. "I thought you wanted dinner. What are you doing?"

"Getting ready to say something I never thought I would say again." His voice was hoarse, and his eyes were soft with the same tenderness she'd seen the night he left. He slicked a thumb along her lower lip. "Being gone this last week…"

He paused, slid a big hand across her lower back to her waist and pulled her to him. Her hands lay flat on his chest. He held her so tightly she could feel the buttons of his trousers.

And his arousal. The hard ridge of flesh sent a jolt of need through her.

Closing and opening his eyes, he started again. "Things didn't feel right…"

She'd never seen him have trouble expressing his thoughts. Bemused, she slid her fingers gently down his jaw. "What?"

Impatience streaked across his face, and he made a deep rough sound that sparked a delicious heat low in her belly just before he lifted her off her feet. "I have feelings for you, Lydia."

Chapter Fourteen

"Russ," she whispered, her midnight-black eyes dazed.

Setting his hands at her waist, he let her drift down his body until her feet touched the floor. He buried his face in her neck, filling himself up with her scent, her warmth. "I missed you like hell."

"I missed you, too." Her fingers played in the damp hair at his nape.

He lifted his head. In the soft white light, her creamy skin gleamed like a pearl. "I planned to tell you this earlier, but then I saw you and all I could think about was getting my hands on you, kissing you."

She laughed. "I felt that way myself."

Emotion rushed through him, the same emotion that had welled up every time he thought about her this past week. Widening his legs, he drew her between them. Her breasts flattened against his chest and his senses swam with the smell of flowers and warm woman.

"I never expected anything like you, like this," he said quietly.

"Neither did I." She touched a shaking hand to his jaw. "I've…never felt like this before."

"Not even with your ex-fiancé?"

"No."

Framing her face with his hands, he looked into her eyes. "After what Amy did, I never thought I'd let myself care about another woman, never thought I'd want anything except the physical, but the more I'm with you, the more I think about it."

"Really?" It wasn't disbelief on her face; it was pleasure.

"There's more to it than me wanting to get my hands on you. I can't remember what Whirlwind was like before you came, and I don't want to go back and find out."

He curved a hand around her nape, brushing his thumb along her jaw. Her pulse jumped in the hollow of her throat. "When I rode out with those men the other night, I was sorry I didn't tell you. I've been fighting these feelings for a while, but I can't do it anymore. I don't want to."

He pulled her tight into him, hard against his erection. "I want you so damn bad. If we don't go to dinner or get out of here, I won't be able to keep my hands to myself."

"Maybe I don't want you to."

"What?" A hush came over his body.

Her face was flushed, her eyes deep and hot with desire. "Ever since the night I dragged you upstairs to deal with…that couple, I haven't been able to stop thinking about being with you."

Her words drove a spike of pure burning need through him. He hadn't stopped thinking about being with her, either. He settled his mouth on hers, kissed her long and slow and deep.

When he lifted his head, she opened her eyes. The smoldering heat there had him dragging in a steadying breath. "I want you," he said hoarsely.

Her fingers skimmed his jaw. "I want you, too."

Russ froze, something he'd never done with a woman, but

this had never seemed so important before. He wanted to taste her, touch every inch of her wonderfully soft skin, feel her naked flesh against his. He didn't know where to start.

Watching her face, he pulled the pins from her hair. It fell in a tumble of raven silk, sliding around her shoulders and the gray-checked fabric of her dress.

He slid his hands into the thick tresses and kissed her. She moaned, sliding her arms around his shoulders. He went deeper and slower with his tongue. Aching, throbbing, he was nearly blind with the need to have her.

Trying not to ravage her like an animal, he gentled his kiss, dragged his lips from hers and gently scraped his teeth down her throat. She wiggled against him, making a deep breathy sound. He thought his legs might give out.

Scooping her up, he made it to the bed and eased down on the edge of the mattress, pulling her firmly into his lap. "This is about more than one night for me."

"Me, too."

Hell, yes. Her agreement unlocked something deep inside, knocked down the last of the wall he'd put up after Amy. Savoring Lydia's lavender scent, the powder-fine texture of her skin, he laid her down on the bed.

He came over her, threading his fingers through the silky raven tresses. Nuzzling her temple, he pressed openmouthed kisses to the side of her neck, nipped her earlobe.

She tugged his shirt out of his trousers and slid her hands to the bare skin beneath, pushing the fabric up to his shoulders.

He reached back and yanked the garment over his head, his hand going to her breast. Making a rough sound, he lifted up, muttering, "Buttons."

"In the back."

He groaned.

She laughed softly and pushed at his chest so she could sit up.

Propping himself up on one elbow, he closed a possessive hand on her hip.

As her hands went to the top button, his nostrils flared slightly. She stopped, suddenly looking alarmed. "Oh! Naomi could come back any minute."

Russ shook his head. "Ef's taking care of her."

"What do you mean? What did you tell him to do?"

"Whatever he wanted."

She swatted at him and he grinned.

"He's going to keep her busy, just like I'm gonna do you if you'll get on with it."

Flushing, she started on the buttons again. He lasted through three of them before sitting up and brushing her hands aside. An impatient sound rumbled out of him. Thumbing open the tiny buttons running down the back of her dress, he peeled back the fabric, nipping and laving her nape.

He dragged hot kisses from the top of her spine to the hollow of one shoulder blade. She shivered, making his arousal rock-hard.

She pushed the sleeves down, the dress falling to her waist as she reached for the front of her corset. Russ wrapped an arm around her and brought her back until she sat between his thighs.

She sent him a questioning look over her shoulder.

"Keep goin'," he said gruffly. "I wanna watch."

She blushed to the roots of her hair, but she turned her attention back to the task. Anticipation pulsed inside him, so sharp it was almost painful. He couldn't wait to see this, to see her. His mouth actually watered.

Gathering her hair in one hand, he pushed it to the other side and licked the shell of her ear.

She moaned and sank back into his chest.

He put his hands over hers. "Don't stop," he whispered.

He rested his chin on her shoulder, setting his teeth on a spot on the side of her neck and watched as she unhooked her corset then tugged at the satin tie on her chemise.

His breath sped up, grew rougher.

The ribbon gave, loosening the undergarment enough so that Russ could see the beginning swells of her breasts. He splayed his big hand on her stomach, touching the undersides of her breasts then brushing his thumb across her nipples.

She made a ragged sound and turned her head for his kiss.

When he dragged his lips from hers, he moved to the tender patch behind her ear, again tracing its shell with his tongue. She curled a hand around his neck, arching back into him. Her taut nipples pushed at the thin material of her undergarment. He couldn't wait any longer.

She inhaled sharply when he pulled at the gathered neckline of her chemise and slid the loose fabric over her shoulder and down her arm, tugging the garment off that side. The other shoulder of the chemise slid down and he pushed it to her waist, baring her.

"Damn," he breathed. He couldn't help cursing. She was so beautiful there. Everywhere.

Her nipples were rosy and tight, her breasts full, begging for his touch, his tongue. His hands covered her and the sight of his work-roughened hands on her plump, perfect flesh had his mouth going dry.

She squirmed in his lap, pressing against his erection, driving a hard-edged need through him. He shifted her so he could stretch out beside her.

Enthralled, he brushed his thumb along the curve of one lush breast. "Sugar, you are gorgeous."

He lowered his head, curling his tongue around her nipple. His name spilled brokenly from her lips.

Urged on by the rush in his blood, Russ dragged her dress and chemise down her legs, catching her petticoats, too, and dropping them all to the floor. Soft white light played over the flat of her belly and she quivered beneath his gaze. For some reason, that got him even hotter.

She slid her arms around his shoulders and pressed into his touch. Skimming her hands down his chest, she flexed her fingers in the hair there. He pulled the tapes on her drawers, pushed them down, tugged off her boots at the same time.

He swept a hand up her thigh, his thumb drawing lazy circles on her bare hip. She shifted restlessly beneath him, moving a hand down his stomach into his trousers. He clenched his muscles as his mouth returned to hers.

She undid the top button of his trousers, then the next and the next, until she could slip inside and close her hand around him. He squeezed his eyes shut, muscles coiling as he reached for control.

Raising his head from her breast so he could see her, he coasted his palm down her stomach then between her legs, delving a finger into her silky heat.

Her body went soft as his thumb circled the sensitive knot of nerves between her legs. She gave a small cry and her muscles tightened around him.

He levered himself between her legs, nudging her thighs wider with one of his. She touched his back, his flanks. His mouth closed over one breast. Easing inside, he paused when he felt a barrier of flesh.

He went still. "You've never?"

"No." She stared up at him, flushed, her eyes soft with desire. The thought that he would be her first made his insides tighten and throb, released some primitive ferocious urge. It took considerable effort not to bury himself in her completely right then.

He moved his mouth to her other breast and her body opened to his. When she relaxed around him, he stroked a hand through her hair. "This will hurt the first time."

"I don't care."

Nuzzling her breasts, he teased her with his tongue, his fingers, not going further until he felt her body go soft around him.

She lifted her hips against his. "It's okay, Russ."

Need hammering at him, he kissed her, long and slow, then smoothed her hair away from her face. Her eyes were closed, her face glowing.

"Look at me."

She did and the complete surrender there nearly set him off. Holding her gaze, he growled, "You and me, Lydia. No one else from here on."

She clasped his face and kissed him. Holding her hips, he thrust hard. She winced, shying away from him. "Sorry," he whispered.

"It's okay," she said breathlessly. "I'm all right."

He brushed kisses across her eyelids, her cheek, her forehead. Careful not to move until she relaxed around him, he dipped his head and drew one nipple into his mouth. Finally, he felt her tight flesh give around his, and he began to move in slow, deliberate strokes.

When she melted around him, he slid his hands beneath her hips. He tilted her, his body touching the nerves at the apex of her thighs with each stroke. The little sounds she made sawed at his restraint, but when she caught his rhythm and moved with him, Russ knew he couldn't last much longer.

He swept a hand down her hip, lifted her thigh just a tiny bit so he could go deeper. "C'mon, sugar."

She moaned his name and came apart in his arms. He went over the edge with her. She held him tight as he stilled and buried his face in her hair.

Giving her a soft kiss, he rolled to his side, taking her with him, settling her against him so he could feel every inch of her, soft to his hard, curve to his muscle.

They lay like that a long time. He felt wrung out and at the same time, energized. The feel of her bare skin against his was intoxicating.

He couldn't believe how much he still wanted her. The longer he had kept her at a distance, the more he realized he wanted something with her that he hadn't wanted with any woman since Amy.

Lydia was a woman he could make promises to. What he felt for her was stronger than anything he'd experienced for anyone before. Now that he knew her secrets, he could admit to himself what he'd known for some time.

He'd fallen and fallen hard.

Lydia's legs tangled with his as she relaxed against him, boneless and content. Russ grabbed the edge of the counterpane and pulled it up the side of the bed, covering both of them against the chill. He put off enough heat for two people and Lydia was plenty warm.

"You all right?" His voice rumbled above her.

"Oh, yes," she sighed. Her fingers flexed in the hair on his chest. A fine sweat dampened his skin and hers, too.

Her entire world narrowed to the man who had come to mean so much to her. The deep male scent of him, the hard muscle of his chest.

He trailed his big hand from her shoulder to her hip. She lifted up and kissed him, her hair sliding across his torso. When she pulled back, he smiled and slicked his thumb across her bottom lip. His eyes blazed with such naked emotion that Lydia felt her heart turn over.

She was so relieved he was okay, that he was back.

Russ stroked his hand up and down the curve of her waist. "You sore?"

"A little." She smiled up at him.

He settled his hand on her hip. He was hard, but he didn't try to do anything about it. If possible, her heart melted even more.

"It'll be lots better next time," he said huskily.

"It was pretty wonderful this time."

He lifted her chin, searched her eyes as though making sure she really thought so. Making a deep rumbling sound, he combed his fingers through her hair.

They lay in languorous silence, comfortable and easy. Lulled by the strong feel of his arms around her, she drew in the musky scent of their lovemaking.

"You're not sorry, are you?" he asked quietly.

"No." She lifted her head, staring into his blue eyes. "Are you?"

"Why would I be sorry?"

"Maybe it wasn't as good for you. I've never done this before."

"Knowing I'm the only man you've ever been with about blows my boots off. Before, I never thought about it much, but I have to admit I like knowing there's been nobody but me. That makes you different from any other woman I've ever known."

She was his and only his. It was special to her, too.

They lay there quietly, kissing, sometimes soft, sometimes deep and hot. His hand trailed down to the curve of her hip.

She drifted off, coming awake when she felt something brush her temple.

Opening her eyes, she found Russ dressed and sitting on the edge of the bed. He leaned over her with one hand on either side of her body.

"Where are you going?" she asked drowsily.

He kissed her softly. "To the kitchen to scrounge up something to eat."

"Oh, I forgot all about that."

"So did I. When I was getting dressed, it occurred to me that someone might see me leaving your rooms. If you want me to leave now, so as not to compromise your reputation, I will."

"I don't want that." She ran her hands up his arms. "You'll just have to be sneaky."

"Okay, you've talked me into it." After another kiss, he asked, "Want me to bring you something?"

"I'll get dressed and come down."

He slowly tugged the sheet until he uncovered the swells of her breasts. "I can help."

"I don't need help getting my clothes *off*."

The tenderness in his smile made her feel shivery inside. His gaze drifted over her face, the heat there stirring her up even more.

"I'll be quick," she said. "Go on down. You're probably starving."

"You sure? I don't mind waiting."

"I'm sure."

He helped her out of bed, dropped a kiss on her shoulder and walked to the door.

"If there's pecan pie, don't eat it all," she warned.

"You better hurry." He opened her door, checked the hallway then stepped out, winking as he shut the door.

Lydia left her corset off. It was late enough that she wouldn't run into anyone. After slipping into a dress she could button in the front, she started downstairs. The hotel was quiet, still.

Being with Russ felt right. Looking back on her life before, something about Wade had always nagged her, but never hard enough for her to be able to figure out what it was. Now that Lydia was with Russ, she knew.

Wade hadn't cared about her the same way Russ did, completely and wholly.

There were no guests on the second floor or in the lobby. Unable to stop smiling, Lydia walked into the kitchen. She didn't pay much mind to the open pantry until she realized Russ was nowhere in the kitchen.

A half loaf of bread and a knife sat on the table. Her heart skipped a beat.

He could've stopped at his office for something. Or to look over the new shops, but Lydia knew—she just knew—he was in the storage room.

Dread punched at her. This wasn't how she wanted him to find out. She wanted to be the one to tell him. With the way the storage room was designed, the guest currently down there wouldn't be immediately visible.

Lydia moved through the pantry, apprehension choking her. She stopped just inside the open door, able to see through the lantern light that he stood with his back to her.

His voice was quiet. "Do you need food? Some kind of help?"

He'd seen the women. Lydia winced.

"Feel free to stay as long as you need," he offered. "I'll tell my business partner so she'll know what's going on."

Those words drove into her like a spike. What he'd said made her painfully aware that he was planning to do what she hadn't—tell his partner what was going on in the hotel.

His voice was kind, not measured or suspicious. Maybe he hadn't guessed the truth about those women and the secret operation. That hope shriveled and died when he turned to start up the stairs.

Something in her face must've given away the fact that she already knew about the women because his features turned hard, his eyes cold with anger and hurt.

He stalked up the stairs and past her through the pantry. She closed the door, following him out. "Russ—"

He clamped a hand on her upper arm and towed her out of the kitchen, across the lobby.

She almost had to run to keep from tripping. He dragged her into his office and slammed the door, dropping his hold on her as though he couldn't stand to touch her.

"Tell me what the hell's going on right now, and don't even think about putting me off or lying to me."

Chapter Fifteen

Lydia's heart slammed into her chest. Where did she start?

"Why did you go in there?"

"I'm asking the questions." Fury vibrated in the air between them. "Those women I saw looked like they'd been beaten."

"Yes." When she hesitated, the dark look that came over his face pushed her on. "The Fontaine is a stop on their way to another safe station."

"Safe station? Like the underground railroad?"

"Yes, but for abused women."

"How long has this been going on?"

Wary of the leashed anger in his voice, she asked, "Here?"

"Yes, here." He kept his massive body in front of the door, blocking any escape.

She felt trapped. "Since we arrived."

"We?" His voice was measured, controlled. "Naomi, too?"

"Yes." Lydia clenched her fists to hide her shaking hands.

"How many women have you helped?"

"A dozen or so." She had to tell him everything now. The issue was no longer that she might not be able to trust him. It was that he didn't trust her.

"How does it work?"

"We receive word from other safe stations when a person has left there to come here."

"Some of those telegrams you receive aren't about your brother-in-law. They're telling you when to expect someone."

"Yes."

"The women stay here for a night or two, then move on?"

"That's usually how it works, not always."

"Like the lady who had the baby isn't able to leave yet."

She nodded.

His eyes went flinty with suspicion. "That woman who was shot in the lobby? You said you didn't know her. Was that a lie?"

"No." Lydia tried to hang on to her temper. He had every right to be angry, to feel betrayed. "I didn't know her, but—"

"But she was coming to the hotel because she knew it was a stop on your...network."

"I think so, yes."

"When I asked you that night, point-blank, if you knew her, you said no. You made it sound as though you had no idea, didn't know why she would be here, but you did."

"I didn't know for sure."

"You had a good idea, especially when you saw she was battered." His features hardened. "Naomi knew, too."

"Neither of us have ever known if Reggie Dawkins figured out the hotel was a safe station or if he thought his wife just happened to stop here for shelter."

"He knew. That's why he shot at you and not *me,* who had a gun trained on him. It makes sense now. He knew you were trying to help his wife," Russ said savagely. "And Dawkins could've killed you or Naomi."

"You probably saved our lives that night. At the very least, you protected the operation. I've wanted to thank you a hundred times."

He gave her a flat stare. "Who else?"

She blinked.

"Who else knows?"

"Willow."

"The baby she delivered." Lydia could see Russ putting it together. "The woman didn't come here because she had heard Willow had experience with childbirth."

"That's right. She stopped here as part of her escape route, then went into labor."

"What else haven't you told me?"

"That's all."

His furiously disbelieving look slammed home just how much she'd hurt him, how much she had ruined by not telling him about the operation. "I promise. That's all."

He gave a harsh laugh. "Do I look like I'm going to fall for that twice? I don't know why I think you'd tell me now. I have to be the dumbest SOB walking this earth. Here I've been believing that I knew your secrets, that I knew exactly what was going on. I didn't know a damn thing."

The scornful look he leveled on her knotted Lydia's stomach. "That story about your brother-in-law. Is that true?"

"You know it is," she said hoarsely, her throat burning with regret.

He looked ready to explode. "I know the story about your ex-fiancé is true because Davis Lee checked it."

She gasped. She had no right to feel betrayed, but that didn't lessen the hurt at his mistrust. "You had Davis Lee checking on me?"

"Damn straight. Evidently I didn't have him go far enough."

"You could've jeopardized the network!"

He pushed away from the door and took one step, towering over her. "Don't put that on me, sweetheart. If you'd told me, that never would've been an issue. And that's another reason you should've told me. What if I *had* unknowingly put the operation at risk, or one of those women? It's obvious they really need help and any threat to them would've been because of me. As it was, I scared them out of their minds."

She angled her chin in false bravado, but she was shaking. "I did what I thought I had to."

"And what about Bram?" Russ shoved a hand through his dark hair. "Will your seeing him put him and his family at risk? Are you lying to him like you've been lying to me?"

Her stomach dropped. "Bram knows about the operation."

"He knows the truth?"

She nodded miserably.

The hurt and cold anger in Russ's eyes had her choking back a sob. "Does everybody in Whirlwind know about this except me? Are you really seeing him?"

"I had to let you think that."

"You *had* to let me think that?" His voice was dangerously quiet. "That you were seeing another man?"

A dark flush of anger colored his neck and the volcanic fury on his face had her taking a step back. "I didn't want to."

The thought of losing him pierced her like a blade. This numbing hollowness was the same she had felt after she had lost her sister. A giant fist closed around her chest, cutting off her breath. "Bram and his family host one of the safe stations."

"How the hell do they know about it?" In the next breath, a look of comprehension swept across his face. "Emma."

"Yes, that's what Bram said. That his sister-in-law had been abused by her stepfather so she took her half sister and ran. She refused to let the little girl endure that. They ended up in Whirlwind at his family's ranch."

Taking a step closer, she thought about touching him until he fixed a glacial stare on her. "Letting you believe I was involved with Bram nearly killed me. He didn't like it, either, but you saw us together. We couldn't tell you the truth."

Russ folded his arms across that wide chest, eyes glittering. "You could've told me about *our* hotel being a safe station."

"Then I would have implicated Bram. Letting you assume he and I were a couple was the smartest, safest thing to do, but it hurt the most. I knew I had feelings for you."

"Feelings?" The word lashed the air like the crack of a whip. "If that were true, you would've told me what you were doing."

She pressed a hand to her trembling lips to keep from crying.

"I don't have a problem with you helping these women. I do have a problem with you not telling me you were using the hotel to do it. The Fontaine is part mine. As your partner, your *lover,* you should've trusted me enough to tell me the truth."

"At first, I didn't know if I could trust you. Then later, after I got to know you, I planned to tell you. I just didn't do it soon enough."

"You never tried to tell me," he accused bitterly.

"Yes, I did."

"Really?" His lips twisted.

"The night you rode out with that posse, remember I came here, to your office? It was so that I could tell you about the network, but you were getting ready to leave. Your brother was hurt. That wasn't the time for me to tell you."

"What about when I got back?"

"It didn't even cross my mind," she admitted, hoping he would see the truth of her feelings. "We heard two of the men had been injured. All those days you were gone, with no word, I didn't know if you were dead or alive. I was so afraid something horrible had happened. And when you got back and I saw you were all right—" her voice cracked "—all I cared about was being with you."

He went very still. Something about his suddenly rigid stance had a cold fist of dread closing around Lydia's heart.

"Why was that?"

Confused, she frowned. "Why did I want to be with you?"

"Yes."

"Because I—" *Love you.* She cut off the words. "I have feelings for you."

"Is that really why?"

"Why else?"

He arched a brow.

It took her a moment, but when she understood his inference, pain ripped through her. He couldn't really believe it had been about the network. "It was about us and only us."

"Did you think if you got me into your bed, there would be less chance of me questioning things you did? Easier to get me to believe your lies?"

"You know that isn't why!" Her voice shook. "You're angry and I understand that, but what happened between us had nothing to do with anything except you and me. It was special."

"You can see why I have a hard time buying that." His eyes narrowed to slits. "All you've done since you got here is try to manipulate me."

"That's not true!"

"First, you tried to get me out of the hotel. Telling me you could manage things on your own, then trying to frustrate me so much with small decisions about the place that I would turn it over to you."

She couldn't deny any of that. The already-thick tension drew tighter.

"Then after that kiss in the kitchen, you tried to 'manage' me, to see if you could keep me from taking things further. Now, I wish I'd given you what you wanted."

The blow of his words nearly choked the breath from her. Her own temper spiked. "I'm sorry I hurt you, Russ, but I slept with you because I wanted to, because I have feelings for you and you know it. What I told you earlier was the truth."

If possible, his face became even harder.

"Do you think I didn't want to tell you? There were several times when I did."

"What matters is you didn't," he said baldly.

Wrapping her arms around herself, she tried to explain. "Whenever I considered sharing the secret with you, I thought of my sister and women like her. Women like the one who was killed in our lobby because she was willing to risk it all in order to get away from someone who likely would've killed her at some point. Just like Philip did to Isabel. These women trust me to keep them safe. If I'd told the wrong person, they would all have been in danger."

"And when you knew I wasn't the wrong person, you still didn't try to tell me." With a curse, he jerked open the door and stalked out.

Alarmed, Lydia followed him just outside his office. No one was around, but she tried to keep her voice low anyway. "What are you doing? Are you leaving?"

The look he gave her was brutally cold. "You wanted me out? You got it."

He pushed through the side door and left her feeling devastated and alone, throbbing with regret.

* * *

Russ went straight to the saloon, where Matt had said he would be. He was standing at the bar, but not drinking, just talking to Pete.

Russ was so mad all he could think about was getting a drink. Shouldering his way inside, he stalked to the spot beside Matt. His brother and Pete were the only two people there. All the other men who had been in town earlier had gone home.

Russ tossed his hat onto the bar and requested a bottle of Pete's good whiskey.

"The good stuff?" Matt, his face swollen and bloody from the beating he'd taken, looked over in surprise. "What's going on?"

A bottle and two glasses appeared on the scarred surface in front of Russ. He sent the saloon owner a grateful look.

Pete walked out from behind the bar. "Gotta go to the livery for a minute. Be right back."

Matt watched as Russ poured them both a drink. "What is it?"

"Lydia."

"What did she do that's got you looking ready to go for your gun?"

"You know I told you I thought she was hiding something?"

"Yeah. Did you figure out what?"

"Yes," he said through clenched teeth, seething.

"It must be pretty bad to make you this mad."

"The woman's been lying to me."

"Like Amy?"

"No, the one thing I know Lydia isn't doing is seeing another man behind my back."

"She's not seeing Bram anymore?"

"No." Russ did believe that her pretend courtship with his friend had been just that.

The way she had looked at him when they'd been in bed

together had Russ second-guessing his anger and doubt about her feelings. A woman didn't give herself to a man she didn't care for. She especially didn't give him her virginity.

Lydia must have feelings for him, as she had claimed, which made it even harder to forgive her for not telling him what she was doing in the hotel. *Their* hotel. His anger flared again.

"So, if she's not having an affair, what is she doing?"

Russ tossed back his drink and poured another.

"Does it have something to do with what you were asking Davis Lee to check into?"

"No, it's about—" He broke off. He couldn't talk to Matt about this!

Dammit to hell and back. What he had just learned needed to remain confidential. Russ knew his brother would never tell a soul, never let on that he knew about any underground operation going on at The Fontaine, but Russ had told Lydia she could trust him with the secret. He was furious with her, but he had to think about the women who were trying to flee abusive, possibly deadly situations.

"What?" Matt demanded. "Are you gonna tell me or not?"

Russ's fist tightened on the liquor bottle. "She…hasn't been shooting straight with me about the hotel."

"Whatever she's hiding must be a doozy. I haven't seen you this lathered up since you found out Amy was cheating on you."

"I don't know if I've *ever* been this mad," he muttered.

"If you're this het up, you must have some pretty deep feelings for Lydia. Are you in love with her?"

"No." Russ hadn't let himself think it before. He wouldn't now, either.

"Are you going to tell me what she's done?"

Russ might be torn about telling his brother everything, but he couldn't do it. Suddenly, he got a flash of how conflicted

Lydia must have felt while keeping the secret from him. *If* she had told the truth about wanting to confide in him. For some reason, that made him clench his jaw so hard he thought it might snap in two.

His brother eyed him speculatively. "Well?"

"I can't talk about it. I said I wouldn't."

"What the hell?" The youngest Baldwin didn't look inclined to leave it alone, but to Russ's surprise, Matt didn't badger him. "So, what are you going to do?"

"Try to stay away from her, although until I sell my interest in the hotel, I won't be completely shed of her." He took in his brother's cuts and bruises, realized Matt was standing upright mostly because he was leaning against the bar. "Let's go sit down."

Taking the whiskey and glasses, they chose the closest table. Just as Russ started to sit down, he saw Ef at the swinging doors.

Looking grim and concerned, the black man motioned Russ outside.

Tension coiled inside him. Why was Ef here? Why didn't he want to talk in front of Matt? Had something happened to Lydia?

In the next breath, Russ ruthlessly dismissed the thought. She wasn't his responsibility. Still, the possibility nagged at him as he told Matt he'd be right back and walked out to meet the blacksmith.

Russ wanted to ask his friend if he was aware of what his lady love was up to. The women who sought shelter at the hotel weren't the only ones in danger; Lydia and Naomi were putting themselves in harm's way, too. Another reason Russ was furious that Lydia had kept the information from him.

Ef stepped down into the street, his features visible in a wedge of light thrown by one of the lanterns from inside the saloon.

Russ couldn't keep the edge out of his voice. "What's going on?"

"You and Miz Kent had a falling-out."

Trust Ef to cut right to the heart of the matter. "How do you know about that?"

"Naomi and I came in a while ago and saw you leave. Both you and Miz Kent seemed upset. You looked ready to spit smoke."

"It's blowing over," he said tightly. Frustration layered in on top of everything else. If Russ couldn't tell Matt what was going on, he couldn't tell Ef, either.

His friend glanced around as though to make sure they wouldn't be overheard. "Naomi's worried about you and Miz Kent. So am I."

"No need to be. We're both fine. And we're done."

"You sure about that?"

"Yes. She's been keeping something from me, something big." He cursed, part of him wishing he'd never gone into the storage room. "I knew better than to get involved with a woman who acted as skittish as she did, but I did it anyway."

"I can see how you'd be angry, especially because Amy hid something from you." Ef paused, then seemed to make a decision.

He leaned a shoulder against one of the saloon's support posts. "One night while you were out with the posse, the ladies came to me for help."

"That's what I told Lydia to do." Russ frowned, unsure where this was going. "I assumed the problem was taken care of. She never mentioned anything."

Of course, Russ reminded himself, there was a lot she hadn't mentioned.

The other man lowered his voice. "What I helped them

with was a woman, a battered woman. She was in bad shape, her feet torn to shreds."

Russ's eyes narrowed. His friend was talking about one of the women he had seen in the storage room, which meant—

Hell. A hush came over his body. "So, you know their secret."

The black man nodded.

Russ had thought he couldn't get any madder, but his insides burned as though they were boiling. The cold temperature didn't even touch him. They—*she*—had told Ef and not Russ.

Ef's being the only one who could help at the time meant he needed to be told. Russ understood that. But Lydia should've told him, too. She could've done it earlier that night after he'd returned from chasing those rustlers. But she hadn't.

Another thought slammed into him, this one just as infuriating. "Did Lydia send you out here?"

"No." Ef shook his head, saying ruefully, "The two of you are a pair. I told her I was going to talk to you and she didn't want me to. Said you'd think exactly what you just said. Finding you was my idea. She had nothing to do with it."

Russ felt empty and numb. It had been bad enough when he thought Lydia was doing this right under his nose and everyone else's. But finding out that Ef knew, that she had told the blacksmith and not Russ, had raw fury slashing at him. He wanted to hit something, someone.

Ef looked worried. "Hey."

"I appreciate you checking on me. I need to get back to Matt."

His friend frowned. "You know I couldn't tell you?"

"Yes. I wouldn't have told you, either."

"Want to have a drink, vent your spleen?"

"No, that's all right. You get back to Naomi."

In the amber light, the man studied Russ uncertainly, but finally shook his hand and returned to the hotel.

While Russ had talked to Matt and Ef, he hadn't known what he was going to do. He did now.

Ten minutes later, he had his brother settled in a room at the Whirlwind Hotel, waiting for Catherine Blue to check Matt's injuries. And Russ was back in his office, gathering his things.

A black fury pulsed inside him. He thought he'd been so smart, following up on his instincts that she was hiding something, but once again lust had clouded his judgment.

The feelings he had for her made the mistake even harder to stomach.

Wearing his gun belt and duster, he hefted the saddlebags over one shoulder just as he had when he'd left a week earlier and walked to the hotel's front door.

"Russ?"

He froze at the sound of Lydia's voice, telling himself to keep moving. He didn't trust himself not to explode all over again.

"Are you going somewhere?"

He turned, wishing he could ignore the hurt in her eyes, the redness there that told him she'd been crying. Knowing he'd put that hurt there tugged hard at Russ, dimmed his anger. He didn't want to feel anything *except* anger. "I'm going to Dallas."

"You're going all the way over there?"

"I need to get away from here." *And you.* He didn't say it; he didn't have to.

The flash of pain in her eyes said she knew. She wrapped her arms around her middle. "What are you going to do there? Try to find a buyer for the hotel?"

That was exactly what he intended, but he'd already talked to her more than he wanted. "When I return, whether I've sold my interest in the hotel or not, I'll be moving out. You can finally have the hotel to yourself, just like you've wanted all along."

"No, Russ." Picking up her skirts, she rushed down the stairs toward him. "I don't want you to move out."

His eyes narrowed on her. She must have gotten the message not to come closer because she stopped a few feet away.

Her face was chalk-white and bleak with hurt. In a quiet voice, she offered, "It might take a little time, but I can try to relocate the operation."

Now that he knew about the work she was doing, he could see how a move might cause problems. He damn sure wasn't going to feel responsible for that.

"Move it or not. I won't change my mind about staying. My problem isn't with what you're doing. It's with you."

Refusing to soften at the way her face went even more pale, he turned and reached for the door.

"Where will you stay tonight?" Her voice trembled.

He wasn't telling her anything but he'd probably stay at Ef's. "No need to concern yourself. You'll have free run of the hotel."

He couldn't take her wounded look anymore or the anguish in her face. Russ walked out of The Fontaine and closed the door.

He couldn't ride out for Dallas tonight, but first thing in the morning, he would leave.

Chapter Sixteen

Russ didn't sleep much that night. Thoughts of Lydia tortured him. Memories of the agony in her eyes when she talked about her sister. The sincerity in her face when she had claimed she really had tried to tell him about the network.

When he rode out of Whirlwind early the next morning, his temper hadn't improved. He had to stop in Abilene first to give the banker what money he had, which consisted of the first month's rent from Jericho and Josie, plus the little bit of money Russ had squirreled away.

Lydia was never out of his thoughts. The woman infuriated him. If she was willing to throw away whatever this was they had started, then it was fine by him.

He wasn't going back to Whirlwind until he had a buyer, no matter how long it took. Once he paid the loan in full, Lydia Kent would be out of his life for good, her secret network still operating.

He couldn't dismiss the significance of that to her and the women she helped. It was of life-or-death importance.

And had him asking if he'd been in Lydia's shoes, would *he* have told her about the network?

No, he admitted. At least not until he thought they were together for the long haul. And maybe not then, because it would be safer for her not to know. Safer for the women she helped, too. Russ saw her point.

Had he overreacted because of his past? Yes. He wasn't proud of it, but there it was. He grudgingly admitted that it was likely she would have told him the truth that night in his office if he hadn't had to ride out with the posse.

She'd claimed to care only about being with him after he had returned. Russ had felt the same way about her. Nothing and no one had held his attention until he'd gotten her alone. Until he'd taken her to bed. The love in her eyes before and during their time together kept torturing him. She couldn't have faked that.

Though her silence had hurt him, he also admired it. She was willing to risk everything to protect the women she aided. He loved that about her.

He loved *her.*

The realization had him reining his horse to a stop. Now that Russ knew the truth about everything, he had to think about those women, too. He couldn't sell his interest in The Fontaine. Doing so might put the network at risk and Lydia, too.

He had no idea how he was going to pay the bank, but he couldn't do it with money from the sale of his interest in the hotel.

He was two miles from Abilene when he turned his horse around and raced hell-for-leather back to Whirlwind. And Lydia. He hoped he hadn't ruined everything.

Lydia cried herself to sleep, but by morning, she was good and mad. If Russ Baldwin didn't believe her, he was not the man for her.

She had wanted to go after him last night when he stalked

out of the hotel with his things, but she hadn't. It would only have made the tension worse between them. Besides, she had apologized and pleaded all she was going to. He was hurt? Well, so was she.

He had accused her of being intimate with him to somehow seduce him into looking the other way. She had given him her virginity, for goodness' sake.

He'd said some awful things, tried to make her think that their lovemaking meant nothing to him. He owed her an apology.

Thankfully, she hadn't confessed she loved him, although how the mule-headed man couldn't see it was beyond her.

Anger kept her going for a few hours, but soon regret began to creep in. Could she have handled things differently? She didn't see how.

As lunchtime approached, Lydia went to the kitchen to help Naomi set out the buffet. The food was set out but her friend wasn't there or in the storage room. Lydia didn't find her on a quick search of the first floor, either.

It wasn't like the woman to just disappear. Lydia began asking the guests and other staff if they had seen her. Finally, one guest who was visiting from California said he had seen the maid going up to the third floor with a man.

Ef? Who else could it be? Still, it was odd that Naomi and Ef would go upstairs together at all, let alone right before one of the busiest times of the day. Was something wrong?

After thanking the man, Lydia hurried to the rooms she shared with the other woman. When she found the door unlocked, she was relieved. That meant her friend was here.

"Naomi?" Lydia called out as she stepped inside and closed the door.

The maid appeared in the doorway that separated Lydia's

office from the bedrooms. Her face was streaked with tears and fear pinched her refined features.

"What's happened?" Lydia rushed to her friend. "Is it Ef?"

"No, don't!" the black woman cried out.

Lydia realized too late that Naomi's hands were bound behind her back. Danger screamed at her at the same time she heard a masculine voice behind her. A hated voice.

"Hello, sister."

Philip! Lydia whirled to face him. Before she knew his intent, his fist shot out and slammed her jaw hard enough to make her vision blur. She stumbled back and fell, swallowed up by darkness.

As she came to, the room swam into focus. A dull ache throbbed in her jaw as her gaze moved slowly over the familiar blue chairs in the corner next to her, the large walnut wardrobe.

Rope bit into her wrists and ankles, the pain helping her to focus. She was on the floor propped against the wall between the small marble table and one of the chairs. Her hands were bound behind her, just as Naomi's were. Both women sat with bent knees, their feet tied at the ankles and a handkerchief stuffed in their mouths. Lydia's was heavy with starch, the smell and taste nearly choking her.

Bile rose in her throat. This might seem like a nightmare, but it was real. Philip DeBoard, the man who had murdered her sister, the man Naomi had gravely wounded in self-defense, was here and he had them both.

The fear and uncertainty on Naomi's face mirrored what Lydia felt.

Russ! Her stunned mind screamed his name over and over. But he was gone. Unless Ef came looking for Naomi, she and Lydia had scant hope of being rescued. They would have to help themselves, and Lydia searched frantically for a way to do that.

Philip dug through the small drawers in Lydia's wardrobe, throwing out handkerchiefs and ribbons. He stopped and held up Isabel's diamond earrings, clutched them in his hand and kept rifling.

Lydia screamed behind her gag, but the bastard didn't even look at her.

He was even more slight than before, gaunt now after suffering the life-threatening wound Naomi had given him.

A cruel smile twisting his lips, he walked over in front of the black woman and kicked her legs. "You uppity wench. You probably thought you killed me, but you didn't."

Naomi shrank away.

Lydia struggled to get free. Philip stroked his thin dark mustache and moved over in front of her. His cold dark eyes fixed on her. "Don't worry, sister. I didn't come all this way to kill that wench and forget about you."

Fear paralyzed her for an instant. What was he planning to do?

He reached one long elegant hand toward Lydia's chest. She jerked back so hard, she hit her head against the bed frame. What was he doing? Trying to grab her breast?

He reached again, this time ripping off the watch pinned to her bodice. The brown fabric of her dress tore, sending a ripple of panic through her.

Tears of fury filled her eyes. That was all she had left of Isabel!

She screamed at him, the sound muffled behind the gag. He arched a brow, holding the watch in the same hand as the diamond earrings. The hate in his eyes said he was capable of anything.

He knelt in front of Naomi and the woman flinched. Lydia's breath hitched painfully in her lungs as frustration overwhelmed her. There was nothing she could do to help her friend.

Philip had tried to rape Naomi before. Surely he wouldn't try it with Lydia here. Why not? What was to stop him?

Her mind raced to form a plan—

A knock sounded on the door, causing all three of them to jump. Lydia's gaze shot to the door.

When she didn't answer, the knock came again, louder this time, more impatient. She could feel DeBoard's gaze on her.

A heavy fist pounded on the door now, the wood quivering beneath the force. "Lydia, I know you're in there. Let me in."

Russ! Lydia's vision blurred with tears.

"Sugar, I'm not leavin' until we talk so you might as well open the door."

"I'm going to take your gag off so you can get rid of him," Philip hissed. "If you even think about screaming or making any noise that might alert him there's trouble, I'm pulling this trigger and Naomi goes first."

At the loud snap of the hammer going down, Lydia jerked her head around. Philip drilled the barrel of his gun into her friend's temple. "Understand?"

Lydia nodded, her mind racing to think of a way to let Russ know something was wrong.

"Lydia, dammit, open this door!" he boomed.

Philip brandished his weapon in her face as he jerked the gag from her mouth.

She had no idea if Russ would figure out the message she was trying to send, but she had to try. Her voice shook as she yelled, "You know what I said that day you found me on the balcony."

She choked back a sob. "Stop hurting us, both of us!"

The pounding stopped. Through the door, she heard, "Hell." Then silence.

It hadn't worked! He was gone.

She struggled not to fall apart. She glared at Philip. "You murdering, cowardly piece of filth."

He lunged at her, shoving the wadded handkerchief toward her mouth. She jerked her head away and clamped her teeth together, fighting him. He raised his hand to hit her.

Without warning, the door splintered off its hinges and fell into the room.

Everything happened in an instant.

Using the momentum from the crash, Russ barreled inside, roaring as he plowed his head into Philip's stomach.

The other man wailed in pain; his gun went off.

"Help!" Lydia screamed. "Someone help us!"

She didn't know if anyone could hear her, but she kept yelling. Naomi cringed against the wall as the men hit the floor.

Philip lost his grip on the gun, and it skittered a few feet away, close to Lydia's wardrobe. Even if she had been able to reach it, she couldn't grab it because her hands were bound behind her back.

The men struggled, grunting and landing blows, but Philip was no match for Russ's brute strength. Both men reached for the weapon. Philip grabbed it and rolled to his back, aiming at Russ.

Russ dived for him, clamping both hands on Philip's wrist and twisting. After a few terrifyingly uncertain seconds, a gunshot cracked the air.

DeBoard went limp. Sightless eyes stared at the ceiling. Blood seeped through his white shirt in an ever-widening stain.

Lydia felt her composure slip. Russ. He'd come back. He'd saved them.

He slid across the floor to her, his worried gaze running the length of her body.

"I'm okay." She wanted him to hold her, but she had to make sure her friend was all right. "Help Naomi, please."

Russ reached over and plucked the gag from the other woman's mouth.

"Thank you, Mr. Baldwin." Naomi's soft voice shook and tears streamed down her cheeks.

Heavy footsteps thundered up the stairs and a group of men crowded into the damaged doorway, guns drawn. Ef was in the front and after making sure the threat was gone, he holstered his weapon and rushed inside.

Going to his knees in front of Naomi, he asked if she was all right. The blacksmith worked to loosen the ropes binding her wrists.

Russ reached for Lydia and as he bent his head to see the rope, she drew in the reassuring scent of his spicy shaving soap. She didn't know why he'd come back to the hotel, but she was glad he had.

Tears streamed down her face. She reached down to help him untie the rope around her ankles and their hands tangled.

"Let me," Russ said hoarsely, brushing aside her help.

As soon as she felt the rope give, she scrambled to her knees and fell into him. He held her tight as she locked her arms around his neck. He was still a little unsteady from what he'd witnessed.

"You came back," she said shakily into his neck.

She seemed glad about that and not only because he had taken care of Philip. Russ wasn't wasting another minute. He moved his mouth to her ear. "I love you."

She pulled away, her lashes wet and spiky as she stared at him in awed disbelief. "I love you, too."

A cold blackness swept through him when he saw the tear above her left breast. "Did DeBoard hurt you?"

"No," she reassured. "He took Isabel's watch and earrings."

Russ wanted to get her out of here so he could look at her, touch her. He stood, helping her to her feet and thumbing away the tears on her cheeks.

Behind them, Ef spoke quietly to a shaken Naomi. She stepped away and reached for Lydia.

The women hugged. "I'm so glad you're all right," Lydia said hoarsely.

"I'm glad you are, too." The black woman looked at Russ. "Thank you again."

"You're welcome."

Ef's dark features were solemn as he shared a look with Russ. "I'm taking Naomi to my house for a bit. Until we figure out what to do about this room."

Russ nodded, still shaken at the scene he'd interrupted. When Matt and Davis Lee dashed into the room, Russ gestured for Matt to stay with Lydia while he stepped over to talk to Davis Lee.

"That the brother-in-law?" the sheriff asked.

"Yeah." Russ stared down at DeBoard, furious all over again.

Davis Lee stooped to pick up the watch and earrings then passed them to Russ. "Would you give these to Lydia?"

Russ nodded, his hand closing around the jewelry. He gestured to DeBoard's bloody body, glancing at Davis Lee. "You got this?"

"Yeah."

"I'm taking Lydia to my office. When you're ready to ask questions, that's where she'll be."

The sheriff nodded.

Russ walked back over to his brother and Lydia in time to hear Matt say, "I've never seen my brother scared until today."

Russ didn't think he had ever *been* scared like that.

"I'm glad you're all right." Matt hugged her then squeezed Russ's shoulder.

Russ looked down at her. "Davis Lee, Jericho and Matt are going to take care of everything up here. I want to get you to my office and make sure you're okay."

"All right," she said tremulously. "Thank you. For saving my life. For coming back."

He slid an arm around her waist, pressing her sister's jewelry into her hand. "Davis Lee wanted me to give you these."

Lydia held them tight. Looking at the bloodstain on her cream-and-blue rug, the splinters of wood strewn about the floor, she shuddered. "We'll have to figure out where Naomi and I are going to stay until the door is fixed."

"You're staying with me," Russ said gruffly. There was so much he had to say. "Come on."

She folded her hand into his. They only made it to the landing before Russ stopped and swept her into his arms.

"What are you doing?" she asked, still looking dazed from all that had happened. "I'm all right. I don't need you to carry me."

"I know, but I need to."

She searched his face, finally seeming to understand he needed to hold her, reassure himself she was all right. The sweet smile she gave him tightened his chest.

What if he hadn't realized he loved her and come back? What would have happened? He was glad they'd never have to find out.

He held her close, filling himself up with her soft scent. She rested her head on his chest and let him carry her without protest, even when they passed the small crowd that had gathered in the lobby because of the commotion. In answer to their questions, he told them the sheriff would be down in a while and fill them in on what had happened.

Russ reached his office. He walked in, kicked the door shut and went to his big desk chair, sinking down into the soft leather with Lydia in his lap. He wasn't ready to let her up.

He might never be.

He kissed her, long and slow. When he lifted his head, he brushed his thumb across her cheek. "When I busted into your room and saw you and Naomi with DeBoard, I nearly died."

She stroked his face. "I'm all right."

He caught her hand and pressed a kiss into her palm. "I'm sorry for the way I reacted when I found out about the network."

"I'm sorry, too. For not telling you sooner."

Russ shook his head. "You handled it as you should have. It just took me a bit to admit it."

"What made you come back?"

"You." He couldn't take his eyes from her beautiful face. "I didn't even make it to Abilene before I knew I had made a mistake. I'm sorry about the things I said."

"It's forgiven. If someone had done to me what Amy did to you, I would've reacted the same way. I want you to know you can trust me, Russ. There are no more secrets."

"I *do* trust you. I know now how difficult it must have been for you not to tell me what was going on. I ran into that same problem myself."

He explained how he had wanted to tell Matt everything, then realized he couldn't.

"So you never made it to Dallas?" she asked. "You never had a chance to look for a buyer?"

"No, but it doesn't matter. I decided I can't sell. It poses too much of a risk to the operation. To you. I'll find another way to get the money. You and what you're doing here are more important to me than anything. I love you, Lydia. I never thought I'd say that to another woman."

"I love you, too." She pulled him down for a kiss. "And I may have a solution."

"What?" He feathered kisses against her temple.

She laid something on his desk. When she moved her hand, Russ saw her sister's earrings and watch. They gleamed in the white gaslight. "I can sell these."

His gaze shot to hers. "Absolutely not. No."

"Russ." She grasped his face. "This is the answer."

"That's all you have left of your sister."

"And if you don't pay the bank, you won't have *anything* left. You're willing to give up everything for me. I'm willing to do that, too."

"But—"

She placed her fingers over his mouth. "Nothing would be more perfect than knowing my sister's things helped you. Please?"

He rested his forehead against hers, finally saying, "If I accept your offer, you have to accept mine."

"Not without hearing it first."

He grinned. "Well, Madam Businesswoman, I want to help you with the operation."

"Really?"

The pleasure warming her eyes had him pulling her closer. "I figure the only way to ensure you'll let me do that is for me to become your husband."

Lydia's jaw dropped. Had he just proposed to her?

Russ chuckled. "I'll take that as a 'yes.' You can't get out of it now."

She blinked, her heart achingly full.

He turned serious. "I've waited a long time for someone like you to come along, sugar."

She felt the same about him. She smiled, brushing a soft kiss against his lips. "So if I take your offer, you'll take mine?"

"Yes, but you have to go first, a show of good faith and all that."

"No more secrets," she vowed.

"Well, maybe a couple." He lightly grazed his fingertip near her bruised jaw then murmured against her lips, "Just between us."

"Mmm, this might be the best deal I've ever made."

"I aim to make sure it is."

* * * * *

*Rancher Ramsey Westmoreland's temporary cook
is way too attractive for his liking.
Little does he know Chloe Burton came to his ranch
with another agenda entirely....*

That man across the street had to be, without a doubt, the most handsome man she'd ever seen.

Chloe Burton's pulse beat rhythmically as he stopped to talk to another man in front of a feed store. He was tall, dark and every inch of sexy—from his Stetson to the well-worn leather boots on his feet. And from the way his jeans and Western shirt fit his broad muscular shoulders, it was quite obvious he had everything it took to separate the men from the boys. The combination was enough to corrupt any woman's mind and had her weakening even from a distance. Her body felt flushed. It was hot. Unsettled.

Over the past year the only male who had gotten her time and attention had been the e-mail. That was simply pathetic, especially since now she was practically drooling simply at the sight of a man. Even his stance—both hands in his jeans pockets, legs braced apart, was a pose she would carry to her dreams.

And he was smiling, evidently enjoying the conversation being exchanged. He had dimples, incredibly sexy dimples in not one but both cheeks.

"What are you staring at, Clo?"

Chloe nearly jumped. She'd forgotten she had a lunch date. She glanced over the table at her best friend from college, Lucia Conyers.

"Take a look at that man across the street in the blue shirt, Lucia. Will he not be perfect for Denver's first issue of *Simply*

Irresistible or what?" Chloe asked with so much excitement she almost couldn't stand it.

She was the owner of *Simply Irresistible*, a magazine for today's up-and-coming woman. Their once-a-year Irresistible Man cover, which highlighted a man the magazine felt deserved the honor, had increased sales enough for Chloe to open a Denver office.

When Lucia didn't say anything but kept staring, Chloe's smile widened. "Well?"

Lucia glanced across the booth at her. "Since you asked, I'll tell you what I see. One of the Westmorelands—Ramsey Westmoreland. And yes, he'd be perfect for the cover, but he won't do it."

Chloe raised a brow. "He'd get paid for his services, of course."

Lucia laughed and shook her head. "Getting paid won't be the issue, Clo—Ramsey is one of the wealthiest sheep ranchers in this part of Colorado. But everyone knows what a private person he is. Trust me—he won't do it."

Chloe couldn't help but smile. The man was the epitome of what she was looking for in a magazine cover and she was determined that whatever it took, he would be it.

"Umm, I don't like that look on your face, Chloe. I've seen it before and know exactly what it means."

She watched as Ramsey Westmoreland entered the store with a swagger that made her almost breathless. She *would* be seeing him again.

Look for Silhouette Desire's
HOT WESTMORELAND NIGHTS by Brenda Jackson,
available March 9 wherever books are sold.

The Horseman's Bride
ELIZABETH LANE

After taking the blame for his brother-in-law's murder,
Jace Denby is on the run. He must leave the ranch,
though the beauty and fierce courage of Clara Seavers
entice him to stay....

Clara doesn't trust this farm hand, but the rugged and
unexpectedly caring man ignites her spirit...and heart.
The more Jace fights their mounting passion, the more
she'll risk to make him hers forever.

Available March 2010
wherever you buy books.

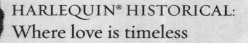

Miss Winthorpe's Elopement
CHRISTINE MERRILL

Shy heiress Miss Penelope Winthorpe never meant
to wed a noble lord over a blacksmith's anvil.

The Duke of Bellston had no intention of taking
a wife. Now the notorious rake has a new aim—
to shock and seduce his prim and proper bride.

But the gorgeous duke will be taught a lesson
of his own as scholarly Miss Winthorpe becomes
his seductive duchess!

Available March 2010
wherever you buy books.

HARLEQUIN® HISTORICAL:
Where love is timeless

The Earl's Forbidden Ward
BRONWYN SCOTT

Innocent debutante Tessa Branscombe senses that
underneath her handsome guardian's cool demeanor
there is an intensely passionate nature. The arrogant
earl infuriates her—yet makes her want to explore
those hidden depths....

The Earl of Dursley has no time for girls!
Miss Tessa Branscombe, in particular, is trouble.
She tempts this very proper earl to misbehave—and
forbidden fruit always tastes that much sweeter....

Available March 2010
wherever you buy books.

REQUEST YOUR FREE BOOKS!

HARLEQUIN® HISTORICAL:
Where love is timeless

2 FREE NOVELS PLUS 2 FREE GIFTS!

YES! Please send me 2 FREE Harlequin® Historical novels and my 2 FREE gifts (gifts are worth about $10). After receiving them, if I don't wish to receive any more books, I can return the shipping statement marked "cancel." If I don't cancel, I will receive 6 brand-new novels every month and be billed just $4.94 per book in the U.S. or $5.49 per book in Canada. That's a saving of 20% off the cover price! It's quite a bargain! Shipping and handling is just 50¢ per book in the U.S. and 75¢ per book in Canada.* I understand that accepting the 2 free books and gifts places me under no obligation to buy anything. I can always return a shipment and cancel at any time. Even if I never buy another book from Harlequin, the two free books and gifts are mine to keep forever.

246 HDN E4DN   349 HDN E4DY

Name _____ (PLEASE PRINT) _____

Address _____ Apt. #

City _____ State/Prov. _____ Zip/Postal Code

Signature (if under 18, a parent or guardian must sign)

Mail to the **Harlequin Reader Service:**
IN U.S.A.: P.O. Box 1867, Buffalo, NY 14240-1867
IN CANADA: P.O. Box 609, Fort Erie, Ontario L2A 5X3
Not valid for current subscribers to Harlequin Historical books.

Want to try two free books from another line?
Call 1-800-873-8635 or visit www.morefreebooks.com.

* Terms and prices subject to change without notice. Prices do not include applicable taxes. N.Y. residents add applicable sales tax. Canadian residents will be charged applicable provincial taxes and GST. Offer not valid in Quebec. This offer is limited to one order per household. All orders subject to approval. Credit or debit balances in a customer's account(s) may be offset by any other outstanding balance owed by or to the customer. Please allow 4 to 6 weeks for delivery. Offer available while quantities last.

Your Privacy: Harlequin Books is committed to protecting your privacy. Our Privacy Policy is available online at www.eHarlequin.com or upon request from the Reader Service. From time to time we make our lists of customers available to reputable third parties who may have a product or service of interest to you. If you would prefer we not share your name and address, please check here. ☐

Help us get it right—We strive for accurate, respectful and relevant communications. To clarify or modify your communication preferences, visit us at www.ReaderService.com/consumerchoice.

HHI0

HARLEQUIN® HISTORICAL:
Where love is timeless

The Accidental Princess
MICHELLE WILLINGHAM

FROM DUTIFUL DEBUTANTE...
TO PASSIONATE PRINCESS!

Etiquette demands Lady Hannah Chesterfield
ignore the shivers of desire provoked by
Lieutenant Michael Thorpe's wicked gaze.

Thrown together by scandal, a defiant Hannah joins
Michael on an adventure to uncover the secret of his
birth—is this common soldier really a prince? If so,
will the man who taught Hannah the meaning of
pleasure now make her his royal bride?

Available March 2010
wherever you buy books.

www.eHarlequin.com

HH29585